THE
MOONLIT
MR SPRING

Robin Campbell

Published by
Llyfrau Cambria Books, Wales, United Kingdom.
Cambria Books is an imprint of
Cambria Publishing Ltd.
Discover our other books at: www.cambriabooks.co.uk

DEDICATION

I would like to dedicate the book to my dear wife, Gill, who died in September 2021, and to my lovely kids, Nia and Siôn.

Also, the book is in memory of Thomas Haydn Miles of Pontrhydyfen.

Er cof am **Thomas Haydn Miles**, Cerrigllwydon, Pontrhydyfen (5 Mehefin 1930 – 7 Ionawr 1983)

Thanks, too, to Keith Johnson, the Mark Twain of the upper reaches of the Cleddau and no relation to Sid.

Diolch hefyd i Mark Hughes.
Artwork by Mark Hughes @theartofsok

AT LAST!

Many of you have been waiting years for this book to be published, completing a puzzling trilogy of four bizarre, yet unrelated novels. My parrot, Mr Sparky, calls it a 'twilogy', on account of his former owner being unable to pronounce her arse.

The irony is that there was no need to wait, the stories having been published within a stone's throw of each other, but don't take my word for it; having been brought up in Pembroke Dock, doubts are often voiced as to the veracity of my character. Friends brought up in the same town can vouch for these sort of things.

Those of you looking for deeper meaning should immediately reach for your Bible, for you are unlikely to find it in this book. Verily, my friends, there is no allegory of the futility of Welsh existence within these pages and there are no conspiracy theories. Some of you have taken issue with me over the meaning of the maxim, 'Curiosity killed the cat.' Well, I have ignored most of the discourteous remarks that have appeared on my Facebook account, but let me explain once again, in simple language that everyone (even Daily Mail readers) should be able to understand. It was Mr Brian Badbreff, the dentist, who killed the cat. He ran it over on the road outside my house on March 11th. For those of you that don't believe me, and believe me, there are many that don't, (see the earlier reference to Pembroke Dock) why don't you take a little trip down to his surgery where he has erected an enamel plaque in the entrance hall commemorating the 'hit and run' in less than twenty words. By the way, a word of warning! His wife, Nora Badbreff, is filling in for him while he sorts himself out looking for the tooth fairy.

In this particular work, *The Moonlit Mr Spring*, I have great pleasure in revealing that Mr Spring is a real person. Do not let anyone convince you otherwise.

The Cactus

The cactus is an ugly thing
That lives upon the plain,
And anyone who sits on it
Never sits down again.

The reason for this strange affair
May not be clear my friend,
But if you cannot see the point
You'll get it in the end.

Sid Johnson
(aged 14 and a half)

1

"You say he's from Downhill?"

"Yes, guv," replied PC. Ian Davies.

DI. Cudgel coughed a nervous laugh and exchanged a knowing glance with his partner, DI. Hammerhead. Several months previously they'd been requisitioned to that very town, where a bloke called Spring had made a monkey out of them. For the sophisticates who worked in Swansea Central Police Station, the rule was to steer clear of the community nestled in the beautiful rolling countryside some miles west of the city. It had, in fact, become an official directive written in bold red ink on the noticeboard, to which some wag had added the words, *'OBEY or REGRET FOR THE REST OF YOUR DAYS.'*

"And he says he's murdered two of his ex-teachers?" DI. Hammerhead this time.

"Yes, guv. And he's going to murder the local scrap merchant says killed his friend. Reckons three will make him a serial killer."

"Well, he's got more ambition than most of them live in that backward hole," sniggered Cudgel. "It'll certainly put our little country on the map. Anything the Yanks can do ....."

"Really should refer it back to Dyfed-Powys, but they won't be interested. Bloke sounds like a nutter," reasoned DI. Hammerhead.

"He's bright enough," said Davies, "but there's something a bit off-beam about him."

"No! Off-beam? Lives in Downhill? Wants to be a serial killer? Can't believe that," chortled the larger of the two detectives.

"Even showed me the murder weapon."

"What the hell!"

PC. Ian Davies opened his hand to reveal a lightweight dart with a red plastic flight. "Not this little beauty, but one in the same set. Reckons he stabbed his old PE teacher with it." The detectives took turns to feel its weight and assess its killing capability. Messrs Cudgel and Hammerhead were not noted for their sensitivity and could see a clear opportunity for a bit of sport. Ian Davies was a keen, intelligent police officer, too honest for his own good. He was wasted on the beat and his superiors had him lined up for promotion to sergeant, then DI.

"Why don't you take it on unofficially, Ian? Do a bit of snooping around. It'll all be grist to the mill when it comes to your exam." DI. Cudgel was famous for his generosity in dispensing sage advice to other souls living on the same planet as himself.

2

If it wasn't for that damned gas fire, Paddy Trahern would never have been a likely candidate; serial killing just wasn't in his blood. He hadn't been violent as a child – in fact he was the only boy in his class with a doll's house, and he'd built one for his favourite teddy bear, but as he'd grown older he'd become less tolerant of the fools around him. By the time he'd reached his two-score years, Paddy was looking to avenge those who had offended him in the past. He couldn't convince the police that the incident with the gas fire had sparked it all - in fact, the boys in blue never twigged who was responsible for the panic engulfing the little town. They didn't even seem to be interested.

He had been fed up with Alwyn Tucker boasting about his weekly forays into the world of scrap. Copper was fetching a good price and a length of piping had, apparently, covered last week's beer money. And Alwyn Tucker – 'A.F.' to his friends – was not averse to sinking a few. A bit like a torpedo, except he looked more like a tortoise when he gulped down his pint. He looked like a tortoise when he leant his elbow on the bar and when he waddled to the toilet. To be honest, he looked like a tortoise, full stop. Quite why he didn't munch lettuce was a mystery to all but himself, neither would he stick his neck out in any fractious debate between tedious drunkards. He was the type of reptile that always had money in his pocket, but never shelled out on a round.

Paddy had always lived in the little terraced house in Bridge Street, inheriting it from his mam and dad after they'd died. The old gas fire in the shed was a nuisance more than anything else, tripping him up every time he reached for one of the implements hanging precariously on the six-inch nails to the right. On one occasion he had disturbed the axe, which angrily embedded itself in the floor within an inch of his bare toes. Well, bragging Alwyn had given him an idea; by ridding himself of the cumbersome fire and picking up a few bob at the scrappy, he could kill two birds with one stone.

Problem was, Paddy didn't and couldn't drive. Not a car, anyway, though he had assumed ownership of his father's bike. Mr Kenneth Trahern could turn his hand to anything, be it electrics or doing the jive. He would take his bottle-green 1950s Raleigh Roadster apart each month and had won the prize for *Most Gleaming Machine Around Town* five years running. Paddy found the two-hour maintenance session a bit of an ordeal, his father's enthusiasm for putting bits of funny-shaped metal together not rubbing off on him. With one eye on what was happening, their dog, Rusty, undoubtedly picked up more than the boy ever did.

His father didn't lack patience but was tested sorely by his one male offspring. Little Paddy invariably handed Ken the wrong tools, mixing up sockets with sprockets and unable to differentiate between a flat-head and a Phillips screwdriver. He was fascinated by the Stanley knife, pincers and wire cutters, the bad boys that could slice through anything without mercy, but his father annoyingly kept these out of reach. So, too, the trusty pliers, with the strength to grip and twist any nuts and bolts that came its way. The only fun the boy had was right at the end, when he was allowed to pump the brass oil can at will. The bicycle was stood upside-down, and he whizzed the chain around, squirting the lubricant into the dog's face when his father wasn't looking. Rusty didn't seem to mind, licking it casually away, and no-one could ever remember him being constipated.

Paddy could never master the art of riding a bike, his father finally throwing in the towel after his son fell into the nettles, his right foot jammed between the spokes of the front wheel. His loving parents scratched their heads, and one Christmas a tricycle appeared under the tree, heralding a new chapter in Paddy's life. He was now able to ride with the other kids, but come his eighteenth birthday, his father could raise the saddle no further. By this time Paddy's friends had progressed to motor bikes or mopeds and he presented a sorry sight as he bumped along the pavements of town, trying to catch them up. His parents were embarrassed. One night, Ken Trahern dismantled his son's beloved tricycle and shamefacedly dumped the parts in a skip. Paddy believed the story that some lowlife had broken into the shed and stolen it.

His dad's bike was still living in the shed, fitted with a rack, which could be used to cart the gas fire to the scrappy if only he could ride the ruddy thing. He waited until nightfall before wheeling the ailing Roadster to a rough piece of ground alongside the canal, out of sight of prying townsfolk. For three weeks and in all weathers, Paddy did his best to balance on the saddle, which was gradually eroding his crotch. In a last-ditch attempt he tried to mount the machine like a cowboy, but he wobbled straight into the freezing water, narrowly avoiding old Mrs Zimmer-Jones and her yappy poodle.

He had to drag the reluctant bike through the night, relieved to reach the safety of the shed, pick up the claw hammer and smash the icicles that had formed over his body. Yes, he broke two of his fingers in the initial frenzy, but he was home safe and sound, and would soon be tucked up in bed.

The following day, Paddy was determined to make a new start. Why had he bothered with all that cloak-and-dagger stuff? No-one would be expecting him to ride a bike with a gas fire firmly tied to the rack. He could wheel it the two miles to the town's scrapyard. Most of it was uphill, granted, but it would be worth the look on Alwyn Tucker's disagreeable mush when he waved a fiver in front of him that evening. He might even offer to buy him a pint, really rub his porous nose in it.

By the next day the weather had decided to turn mild, but heavy rain was forecast. The first job of the morning was to free up the wheels of his dad's bike, which had been so clattered that the mudguards were indistinguishable from the tyres. Paddy made for the chest of drawers in the shed and flung out an assortment of screwdrivers and tyre levers. By using some elbow grease and by hammering the mudguard into a right-angle, he managed to create enough daylight to mobilise the bike.

Fastening the fire to the rack wasn't as difficult as Paddy had feared. His father had kept a tidy shed and hanging from a nasty looking nail were a set of elastic hook fasteners, used to secure the roof-rack of their mustard Austin 1100. Even someone as clumsy as Paddy could manage such a straightforward job, and three hours later he had it sussed. He leant the bike and its hefty passenger against the front gate while he went to retrieve his orange anorak and bandage his fingers.

A quarter of a mile up the first hill he overtook the bandy-legged figure of an old man, struggling with his shopping. He was a familiar figure around town, though Paddy had never talked to him. He rested the three bags in a puddle and called after Paddy.

"Whoah there, boy. Wharra' you got by there?"

"Bandages. Broke two of my fingers with an 'ammer."

"I can see that, boy. No, wha's that you got on the back of yer bike?"

"Gas fire."

"I can see that, boy. Moving house are you?"

"Taking it to the scrappy."

"Bastard's?"

"Yeah." The rain was now making its presence felt and Paddy wanted to move on.

"Family firm they are, Jeff Bastard and his three boys. Old Ronnie, their grandfather, started it off. He was the original Bastard. Think they'd have changed their name by deed poll by now, wouldn't you?" chuckled the man. Paddy was in no mood for witty conversation, merely wanting to complete his journey and pick up his wad of cash.

"I'm going that way. I can show you where it is. In fact, you can give me a hand." To Paddy's great astonishment, Mr Spring looped a carrier on to each handlebar with great sleight of hand,

6

leaving him with just the lightest. "That's better," he said, "don't you worry about this one, I'll manage it somehow."

Mr Spring lived at the far side of a small council estate, designated *Policeman's End* by the locals. He was a man who didn't always make things crystal clear, and when he implied that he, too, was on his way to the scrappy, he only meant the next fifty yards. Paddy couldn't remember volunteering to turn onto the scenic route that ended at the old man's upstairs flat in Policeman's End. By the time he got back to the main road, he'd had a four-mile detour.

The rain had been booked for the day, and Paddy arrived at the small industrial estate resembling a drunken dogfish. It didn't take long to find the family business, the sign signalling the only *Bastards* in the area. Paddy wrestled the bike up to the fence, where he found a young man slamming the gate in his face, ready to apply key and chain.

"Shuts at half-past four, mate." Paddy was most devilishly surprised, not because he'd lost track of time, but because no scrappy worth his salt would turn down the chance to make big bucks. Not wishing to be drawn into a lengthy exchange with the weird stranger, the man relented. Paddy followed him into the yard, holding back nervously as the hulk removed a huge padlock from an old, weathered wooden door. He slid it open a touch and fumbled for the switch, Paddy taking this as an invitation to enter his den. Unable to manoeuvre the handlebars through the gap, the scrappy told Paddy to turn the bike around, but the rear end proved more of a nuisance. In a huff, the metal dealer waddled over to the door and lugged it open a further smidgin to allow his unwelcome guests access.

Paddy smiled uneasily, hoping the incident had broken the ice and that genetics had given this man a sense of humour. He evidently expected Paddy to make the first move, but he was like a dogfish out of water in these strange surroundings. Another huff, then big man grunted,

"Been on my own all day, wouldn't mind getting home

sometime."

"Your father not in, then."

"My dad! Wha's he gotta do with it? He works on the buses." He glanced at his watch. "He'll be driving the Number 111 to Llanelli now."

"Oh, you're not one of the Bastards then?"

"Me, no. I'm not a Bastard. Just work for them, that's all."

Though not the quickest wit in town, Paddy felt relaxed enough to carry on the banter, bouncing off Mr Spring. "Surprised they haven't changed their name by deed poll." The other man stared blankly at him and Paddy felt obliged to bumble on. "You know, they could change it to something like 'Twat'. The sign wouldn't cost so much, neither."

"Can't see the point of that," surmised the younger man, "they'd just be known as Twats instead of Bastards, not a whole lot better if you ask me. Funnier though, I suppose."

Paddy felt on edge again, not helped by the scrappy's inaction, standing there with hands in the pockets of his overalls.

"Are you going to put it on the scales or wha'?"

Although Paddy had been brought up by his nuts-and-bolts father, he could see nothing resembling a scales. The man roughly took hold of his bike and clonked it onto what looked like a small aluminium platform.

"Right, give me a mo', I'll 'ave to open the office up, give you the weight." Paddy was confused, still in shock when the man returned.

"Ye'r lucky, mate. Just over a fiver, I can write you a cheque."

The awful truth was beginning to dawn on Paddy – his bike had been weighed along with the gas fire. It wasn't the sentimental value of his father's old Roadster, more that it was Paddy's only means of transport, even if he did have to push it around. When he explained it was just the fire that was being sacrificed, the kind young man escorted Paddy and his belongings to the door and then to the gate.

"I don't get nothing for the gas fire, then?" he asked, a final shot at salvaging something from the wreckage of a miserable day.

"Listen, mate. We only write cheques. An' we only write cheques for £5 or more. Ye'r gas fire on its own's prob'ly worth about two quid, so I can't give you nothing."

"What if I come back later in the week and ask Mr Bastard," said Paddy bravely.

"He'll tell you the same thing, mate, only not as nice as me."

"Well, I'll come back anyway."

"You do that, mate, you do that."

"Can I tell him who I was talking to?"

The man seemed thrown for a minute. "Talking to? Oh, yeah, see what you mean. My name's Klaus – Klaus Kuntz."

3

The next time Paddy encountered Mr Spring, he was ready for him. It was five days later, the rain was having a break, and the citizens of Downhill in an upbeat mood. Local poet, Sid Freeman, loved the weather forecast; the language they used was almost lyrical these days, reminding him of Wordsworth, Percy Bysshe and John Keats. *Blustery, breezy* and *bleak* were his favourite words for some reason, while *hazy rain drifting in from the west* sent him into raptures. Across town, Jack Harries saw it differently - the highlight was when the girl with the big tits teased viewers by slipping *murk, moist* and *it's not time to put your winter drawers on just yet* into the mix.

A two-day sunny spell persuaded Paddy that it was time to deal with the gas fire once and for all. He'd spent Saturday evening in the bar listening to A.F. bragging about the enormous profits he was making, and imitated slitting his own throat to show how he felt about the man. He wasn't sure if a tortoise had an arse, but that's where he'd like to stuff the copper piping. Better still, heat it up to 1700°F. first.

The bike was waiting patiently in the shed but had no way of telling Paddy the tyres needed mouth-to-mouth. He struggled down the street before realizing, leant the bike against Mrs Probert's wall and went to fetch the pump. He was back within minutes, only to find Mr Spring lurking.

"Wharra' you got by here, then boy. Another gas fire, is it?"

"Same one." He didn't feel that he owed Mr Spring any explanation.

"Shouldn't be leaning your bike on Mrs Probert's wall. Not today of all days. Disrespectful, that is."

Paddy waited. He wasn't going to play a game with bandy legs.

"She lost her husband last night. Went in his sleep, apparently."

"Oh, sorry to hear that."

"Yeah, poor old bugger. He was a handsome feller 'til he lost his arm in that accident. Operator, he was, up the water works. Din't get no condensation off the Water Board 'cause they reckoned it was his own fault. Din't turn off the machinery 'fore he tried to clean it."

Paddy lugged his bicycle into an upright position and propped it against a nearby lamppost. Despite the discomfort of two broken fingers, he was determined to show the neighbours he could still use a pump. He was beaten to it, however, by a large mongrel dog, a newcomer to town, determined to flaunt *his* pump. According to reliable witnesses, after cocking his leg, he released about two yellow pints of steaming piss onto Paddy's unsuspecting bicycle. Fair play to Mr Spring, he did his best to boot Bowser in the bollocks, but he was no Maradona, and with his bandy legs his scissors kick looked as if he was performing on a sheet of ice, and he fell arse over tit. There was no rebound off the post and to rub salt into the wound, the mongrel picked up Mr Spring's rain-sodden cap in his slobbering chops, shiggled it about, then licked the top of the old man's head.

Their attention was diverted by Mrs Probert at her front door.

"Sorry to hear about Mr Probert, Mrs Probert," offered Paddy.

"Tha's all right, Paddy, love, we was expecting something like that to 'appen sooner or later." *That's one way of putting it*, thought Paddy. Detecting Mr Spring in a bit of a pickle, it didn't take long for her motherly instinct to surface. "Good God, wha's that dull bugger doing down there?" She picked up her pint of milk from the doorstep and disappeared inside.

Paddy fetched a pail of hot water from the house, suffused with a splash of bleach, and returned to find the man struggling like a house-fly in a tin of treacle. Paddy cursed God for giving him a conscience, making him an easy target for sad-fishers. He flushed as he recalled giving ten pence to a pauper standing at the corner of St Martin's Road. Four little mouths to feed at home. He should have had more sense! The 'blind beggar' turned out to be Emlyn Tomos, first-born son of local optician, Mr Pepys, rubbing extra salt into the wound by flashing his cash at the bar that night.

Paddy knew he was playing a dirty low-down trick, but here was the chance to alight on his journey without Mr Spring nagging him. He dipped the old man's cap in the solution, squeezed it out, and put it on the wall to dry. He poured the rest of it over the spokes, pedals and other discoloured parts, taking care not to splash Mr Spring's head. After checking there was no-one on the street, he hung the bucket over the handlebar and made towards the scrapyard, parking his conscience firmly behind him. Unbeknownst to him, he'd been spotted by a passer-by at the top end of the street.

4

Without any baggage from the recumbent Mr Spring, Paddy arrived at the scrappy's in good spirit. That soon changed when he clocked the person he assumed owned the place. He was a fat ugly gentleman with eyes bigger than his head, an unnerving experience for anyone meeting him for the first time. And this morning it was Paddy's turn. He either didn't notice Paddy or he was looking at something else.

"Mr Bastard." No answer. "Sir?"

Bastard picked up a large cast iron saucepan from a stack of assorted hardware and wielded it above his head. "What did you just call me?"

Paddy started to sweat, welded to the spot with no ready answer, but he needn't have worried. This was plainly a well-worn party piece, and a wide grin spread across the big man's face – at least that's what Paddy hoped it was. The scrapyard boss launched the saucepan at a pair of magpies that were tucking into the entrails of a dead rat. "Two for joy, be buggered! Can't see no fun in feasting on rodents." He then turned his attention to the nervous-looking stranger and his old-fashioned bike.

"Got something for me, have you?"

"I called by last week. Did Klaus mention me?"

"Klaus? Who the hell's Klaus?"

"Klaus Kuntz he told me his name was."

"He's off today. Changing his name by deed poll. Not surprised with a name like that."

Paddy laughed. "Yeah, I didn't dare tell him, though."

"Thinks it sounds too German. Changed it to 'Hans'."

"You mean he's kept the 'Kuntz'?"

"No, no, you're not listening to me, son. Just told you. Sounds

13

too German. He's getting rid of the 'z' and changing the 'K' to a 'C'. Much better." Paddy couldn't argue with that; neither did he want to, it was not worth the risk.

Mr Bastard waddled into the outbuilding, leaving Paddy in the forecourt like a penguin in the desert. He'd had plenty of practice being passed over in school and in work and was now determined to channel his resentment positively. Today, he'd left his conscience in the gutter and would chart a different course. He needed to toughen up, give the world notice he existed. Um .. that was all very well, but first he'd have to find Mr Bastard.

The new, self-confident Paddy Trahern made straight for the warehouse door, but was stopped in his tracks by one of Bastard's men carrying an electric cooker. Giving away at least 90lb., he decided to become less assertive for a minute or two.

"Thank you so much," declared the man politely, belying his Welsh accent. *Got to be pulling the piss*, thought Paddy. Yet he demonstrated his good breeding further by shouting over his shoulder, "Bastard, someone to see you."

From within came a now familiar retort. "What did you just call me?" Followed by the familiar chuckle.

Paddy put his cards on the table. Klaus Kuntz or 'Hans Cunt' as he was now known, had explained no cash exchanged hands and that the smallest permissible cheque was for goods worth £5. The gas fire would only net him about two quid.

"Ah, I got you, mate, so this time you brought the bike along. Shove 'em on the scales, you got five quid's worth there, prob'ly."

"No, wanna keep the bike, I do."

"What else you got for me, then."

"Nothing. What about the fire?"

"Di'nt Klaus weigh it?"

"Not on its own, no."

Bastard groaned. Not because Klaus hadn't weighed the fire as a single item, he simply couldn't get over Joe Public's ignorance of all things metal, be it ferrous or non-ferrous. Still, better let the idiot have his way.

"Untie it, then."

"Could you hold the bike for me, please." Assertive, but courteous.

"No. Fuck off, what did your last maidservant die of?" Aggressive, slightly insensitive and possibly misogynistic.

Ten minutes later, the squat gas fire had been unravelled, but found to be only a flyweight in scrap metal terms. Jeff Bastard blew out his cheeks to leave Paddy in no doubt his cautionary advice had been well-founded. The moral of the story was 'never argue with one of the Bastards.'

"Tell you what, son, you can leave the gas fire with me if you want."

Paddy's face lit up. "What – you'd give me a couple of quid for it?"

"No, told you, we don't deal in cash, but it'll save you lugging it back home on that thing you call a bike."

It had taken just fifteen minutes to beat the newly confident Paddy into submission. He could see the tortoise necking his pint at the bar of the *Globe* and openly taking the piss. He picked up the fasteners, said good-bye to the old gas fire, stumbled backwards over the saddle of the bike, then made his way forlornly to the door.

"What if I throw in the metal bucket?"

"Tha's what they all say, son. You'd have to fill it with hex bolts to make the weight." At that moment one of his cronies barged past Paddy.

"Mr Bastard, I presume!"

"What did you just call me?"

"Bastard!" muttered Paddy as he wheeled towards the gate, leaving the cackles of merriment fade behind him. He had let another person ride roughshod over him and as he wheeled his bike back home, felt an uncontrollable anger and for the first time in his life, a desire for revenge.

5

Having calmed down a little, Paddy realised he'd left himself in a predicament. Whichever way he approached his house, he wouldn't be able to ignore Mr Spring if the old man was still floundering on the pavement. He cleverly turned right into Priory Street, then left on to one of the back streets, a circuitous route bringing him out at the top of Main Street. He called into the newsagent, where Mr Phawsgin was standing at the top of his stepladder, busy perusing the classics on the top shelf. Not someone you'd want to rub up the wrong way, Paddy carefully stepped over a pile of papers that had slid to the floor, making for the counter. Willy Phawsgin performed a neat pirouette, then jumped to earth without breaking either ankle.

"Shall he help us, Paddy?"

"Looking for cards, I am, Mr Phawsgin."

"Shouldn't be so formal, boy, call him 'Mr Phawsgin.' Cards lie in the corner, yonder," he added, taking a peek over Paddy's shoulder. He could see Paddy's bicycle outside. "Got rid of that old fire, then, did he?"

"Yes, he did, Mr Phawsgin. Got a fiver for it up the scrappy's." There appeared to be one card for each occasion, indexed alphabetically – 'A' for 'arseholes you don't like', 'B' for 'bastards you don't like', 'D' for 'delinquents you don't like', and so on. He wondered if a card of congratulation on reaching five foot six would do but decided to play safe. "Looking for a 'sympathy' card, I am."

"Sympathy for which, boy? Broken leg, car broke down, cursed by a witch…"

"It's for a death."

"Ah, he don't get much call on them sort of grounds, do he,

now? Someone are dead, should they?"

"Mr Probert – went in his sleep, apparently."

"Poor bugger, shouldn't have done that. Not with only one arm. Now then, let him have a look."

"Sympathy – should be under 'S', shouldn't it?"

Phawsgin fished out his reading glasses. "Yep, here that be, he's lucky, there are only one left. Under 'S' for 'stiffs'" It was a bit grubby around the edges, but the words of comfort more than made up for it. Phawsgin cleared his throat and read out the verse.

> *I'm sure that it is for the best*
> *That he or she is now at rest*
> *This is not the time to tarry*
> *You never know, you might remarry.*

Both gentlemen were visibly moved. "He believes those words are wrote by a local man, Sid Freeman. Wonderful ambassador for poetry in those parts."

"You're not wrong there, Mr Phawsgin. Have you got a biro or something I could use? May as well post it on my way home."

"He's from around here, then?"

"Who, Probert?"

"No, no, the other one."

"Lived here all my life. Same street as the Proberts."

"He knows that, mun. Here you were."

"Thank you." Paddy wrote his short message, paid swiftly for the card with loose change, then left the shop a happy man. There was no sign of Mr Spring on the pavement, now the day was nearly over. He slid the card through Mrs Probert's letter box, his duty done. He would have his tea before deciding whether to spend the evening watching the box or supping beer in the pub.

6

As Paddy made his way up to the Globe that evening, he felt an overwhelming pride in his community. He was one of many locals who'd lived in the area all their lives and was content to be 'a man of his square mile'.

Nobody, not even the area's first local historian, Dan the Lanwad, could shed a light on the origins of the name 'Downhill' with which the old settlement had been blessed. That there was a 'hill' to the west was beyond question, so people approaching from that direction would come 'downhill.' Perhaps they had beaten the grim-featured settlers from the east who may well have called it 'Uphill' had they arrived first.

Paddy had bought two copies of Dan's *Downhill – A Concise History*, in case he lost one of them. Although a great scholar, many of Dan the Lanwad's assertions could be dismissed outright. There was no 'sustained period of religious tyranny,' neither were there any witch trials 'that made Salem look like a banal garden party'. Adolf Hitler may have heard of Downhill, but there is no record of him ordering its total destruction or of diverting a *gruppe* of *Heinkel* bombers from a mission over London in January 1941 to do the job.

What the Lanwad had uncovered, however, was something of the truth behind whispers passed down from father to son, describing the bitter feuds and bloodshed of the past. The bone of contention was nothing more than the terminology used to describe the settlement – 'a large village' favoured by the grim-faced easterners, or 'a small town' as the rest wished to refer to it. In 1925 local builder, Isaiah Vanisarse, had erected a grand edifice and provocatively named it *The Town Hall*, only for a vociferous drunken mob to burn it to the ground, rather than paint the word

18

'*Village*' over '*Town*'. It took forty years before a smaller version rose from the ashes, after a compromise had been reached between the two factions. *The Hall*, it seemed, was an inspired epithet, acceptable to all.

Those in the 'town' camp made a clever move when in 1983 they persuaded the mayor of the old settlement to apply for 'small town' status, entitling the residents to a grant of £500, or in reality a bribe of 50p to each 'villager'. The move gathered momentum when Downhill won the Prince Philip 'small town mentality award' five years running. Youngsters now talked about the 'town' they lived in rather than the 'village' they came from, unaware or indifferent to the communal battles played out in the main street on Saturday nights. When hostilities officially ceased in 1989, the call for ready weapons diminished and the four hardware stores evolved into a quartet of impressive charity shops, reflecting a cross-section of worthy causes. Small town mentality became a badge of honour and those who chucked eggs at Mrs Edith Jones for spending most of her daylight hours fondling the one-legged Barbie Doll in *Pet's Rescue* and the cracked toby jug in *Electrical's Accepted* now had missiles directed at themselves. Some of these were free-range, others regular, but the majority were brown, according to scrambled bystanders.

Further evidence of the growth of the small town saw the opening of the *Gravel Patch Childrens Park*, sadly closed a fortnight later when it came to the attention of the authorities it was located beside the canal. Erwyn Thomas saved the day by plonking a pot of rhubarb in the centre of the gravel patch, thus creating Downhill's first municipal gardens.

After the demise of the hardware stores, the Downhill Waterworks became the town's biggest employer. The union fight for overtime payments became a bitter ongoing saga, management denying in a most unconcerned manner that they were extracting the piss.

The economy of the town was boosted by the annual visit of a coachload of dumb Americans who had been persuaded that

19

Petula Clark's smash hit 'Downtown' was based on the community of Downhill. The marketing strategy was the brainwave of 'Shorty' Reynolds who had spent a year in the USA on a small-town mentality exchange scheme. Captivated by his deep Welsh accent, the dames fawned over him, and learning that he came from Downhill asked what state it was in. When he answered, 'a hell of a state,' they fought over who would be first to bed him and it dawned on Shorty that the Welsh were well behind in the gullibility stakes and that there was money to be made. He played on Petula's Welsh roots, claiming to be her cousin, and it wasn't long before the first trip to 'England' was organised, with London, Merthyr and 'Downtown' on the itinerary. The visitors from across the pond, representing a different state every year, spent freely in the four 'antique' shops and were treated to a performance by Downhill dramatic society in the Hall.

*

The pub was quiet that night, landlord Freddie Sauce comatose on the bench by the window, not expected to wake up until Thursday at the earliest. Paddy poured his own pint and one for 'Arrows' Parry who had been waiting patiently for someone to buy him a drink and challenge him to a game of darts. Paddy would oblige this evening as there was no-one around to witness the humiliation, but he stood his ground when it came to playing for tokens, which could be used in any of Downhill's charity shops. By ten o'clock the score was 33 sets to nil, but Paddy's last throw of the night actually hit the dartboard, a significant milestone in the development of his new career. Paddy was chuffed as hell and though Arrows was too mean to buy him a drink, he skipped out of the door a happy man.

The moon was up. Paddy knew all about the moon. His father had spent a week glued to the telly in the summer of 1969 following the Apollo 11 mission and Paddy was roped into the marathon session. Because it was such an historic event, he was allowed to mitch off school, giving him an extra week's holiday. He had been grateful to the moon ever since and checked on it every night. It made him feel good and helped him sleep. Tonight it shed an eery light on the slate rooves of the main street, picking out the ragbag army of chimbley pots and steering Paddy in the direction of the flickering lamppost that would see him safely home.

Or so he thought. Paddy had been for an eye test only a month before and been declared 'perfectly visible' by Ezra Pepys. He had no problem identifying the new mongrel on the block, loping away into the shadows at the far end of the street, but there was something unfamiliar, something bright, lying on the pavement below the lamppost. Had someone dropped a set of white crockery on the way home from *Pre-Loved Pickings*? Perhaps it was a large puddle of water that had absorbed the light of his celestial friend, but that was unlikely, for there had been no rain.

As he drew near, Paddy froze. Lying on the slabs was Mr Spring, or rather a chalk outline of the old man, his arms splayed north and south, the bandy legs a dead giveaway. Paddy would have preferred a body to the sinister epitaph in red chalk,

RIP Bandy Legs

Paddy surveyed the murder scene for clues, but the thoroughfare was deserted and a-fluttering of curtains there was none. Arrows Parry had flown off in the opposite direction, Freddie Sauce was unavailable and everyone else seemed to be tucked up in bed. The longer Paddy stood over the corpse, the more guilty he felt, ironic in view of the fact that this is where he'd parted ways with his conscience.

7

Paddy didn't sleep well that night, the chalk outline of his bandy-legged friend transforming itself into a spectral belly-dancer, who performed all the moves in her repertoire. Paddy declined her invitation to cavort, but when he woke, felt as if his hips and abdomen had had the mother-grunt of a workout. He was exhausted, but before firing up for the day with a hot chocolate, decided to check on the masterpiece outside.

Leaning against the lamppost he found PC. Prys Paddler, whose morning shift had just started. Paddy approached cautiously, but needn't have worried; the pavement was clean as a whistle, apart from a dog-turd cornetto. There had been no overnight rain to wash away the chalk and Paddy assumed the mongrel's tongue had been at work. PC. Paddler was resting on account of the pain he suffered with 'policeman's heel' or *plantar fasciitis* to those that spoke Latin, such as the Pope. Paddy glanced down at the PC's legs, wondering what the fuck he was on about. Did it mean if he'd chosen to be a pharmacist, he'd have 'chemist's heel' and would be working in boots?

"Thought you were investigating a murder when I saw you there," joked Paddy.

"I'd be so lucky. There's been no unlawful killings in these parts since peace terms were agreed fifteen years ago this July. Folks have gone too soft, Paddy. I'll be out of a job soon."

His speech was interrupted by Mrs Probert picking up her milk at the front door. Paddy took the opportunity to escape the verbal clutches of his favourite policeman.

"Morning, Mrs Probert."

"Hello Paddy, love. Thanks for the card."

"Yeah, so sorry 'bout Mr Probert. When's the funeral?"

"What funeral's that, Paddy, love?"

Paddy was stumped for a minute. "Mr Spring told me he went in his sleep."

"Yes, he walks in his sleep. Found him at the back of *FK's* mini-market having a wazz." As if to corroborate his wife's version of events, the man in question appeared behind her, dressed in striped cotton pyjamas and bearing a pronounced squint that raised Paddler's suspicions. Mr Probert pushed his wife out of the way and started to trot in a northerly direction toward the village of Llandwpsyn. Paddy scampered after him and steered him home, where Mrs Probert rudely bumped him into the house and locked the door. PC. Paddler consulted his notebook in the hope that sleepwalking was an arrestable offence.

"Says here he's a somnambulist," he informed Paddy. "I'll see if Tony'll enroll him in the town band. Practice every Thursday night. I play cornet, see. You play anything, Paddy?"

Paddy didn't want to be reminded of the Christmas his parents had bought him a plastic mouth organ, and unable to get a sound out of it, he'd fed it to the dog. Fortunately, local vet Billy Barker came from a musical family, one of only five people in the world who'd mastered the *Richter* scale. Once he'd eked the harmonica out of Rusty's arse, he was able to eke out *John Brown's Body* in the key of F Sharp. The instrument was taken *in lieu* of payment, saving Paddy's parents over £6, a fortune at the time.

Paddy was again grateful for Mrs Probert's intervention, when her nose appeared through the crack of the door.

"Mind you, Paddy, next time you send us a sympathy card, write it in pencil. Easier to use again, then, see, love." Then she turned her attention to PC. Paddler. "Know of anyone I can send this to, Prys, do you? Any suspicious homicides?"

Prys Paddler consulted his notebook for the second time in less than fifteen minutes. He could sense this was going to be a busy day and stuck his chest out importantly, examining the list of misdemeanours committed in Downhill and district over the last five years. "No, I've got a Gerallt Dylan Jones here for sticking a

23

postage stamp of Her Majesty upside down on a letter to his Aunty 'Fanw."

"Oh, can I send him a sympathy card, then?"

"'Long as you stick the stamp on obsequiously," laughed the PC. Mrs Probert stared at him blankly. "I was saying to Paddy, by here, what Mr Probert needs is a hobby, something to keep him occupied."

"Don't think I 'aven't tried, Prys, but 'e do get fed up of putting the mower over the gravel at the back."

"You haven't seen Mr Spring lately, Mrs Probert?"

"Not since he bounced off that lamp post yesterday, Paddy. Probably sleeping it off at home now. Drunk, was he? Have you checked the back of FK's? Might 'of gone for a wazz. Tidy place to have a wazz, that is, love." She closed the door on the tittle-tattle and made her way to the kitchen, hoping her husband hadn't done anything in the cat's bowl. Paddy and PC. Prys Paddler went their separate ways on amiable terms, once the policeman had warned the young man against cycling through the red-light district at the top of town. 'Always wait 'til they've changed to green' was his perceptive advice on this occasion.

8

Alone for a minute, Paddy examined the pavement more closely. Not a speck of chalk dust in sight! Before deciding on a course of action, it was back to the house and the business of the day. Paddy's mam had stressed the importance of breakfast, and fried eggs and streaky bacon were no strangers to the Trahern household. As a child Paddy had always wanted to help his mother by opening the fridge, but he'd not grown as quickly as other children. One day, his mother relented and drew up a stool for him to stand on. As he pulled open the door, the smile on his face said it all; he thought he was cheese.

Old habits died hard, but these days Paddy preferred a simpler meal to start the day. The boys up the pub didn't believe he could survive on such a frugal breakfast, but that was their problem. Hot chocolate was a must, as was his tin of pilchards topped with lemon curd. It wasn't to everyone's taste, but he was a grown man and took full responsibility.

After he cleaned his teeth from left to right, Paddy checked the calendar to confirm he wasn't working. Full of both pilchards and remorse, he would make his way to Policeman's End to try and solve the mystery. The chalk outline had unnerved him and he wondered if it was the work of Downhill's own 'Chalksy'. This mysterious creature had left his calling card all over town, attracting visitors from as far away as Rhyd-y-fro in the Swansea Valley, so boosting the local economy. Was last night's gem an authentic Chalksy or merely a calcium carbon copy? But why destroy your own work? No, it wasn't Chalksy, he thought, but some neighbour laughing behind his back.

Paddy set out in a determined mood and soon reached the junction, where he scooped up a bag of onions that had fallen off the back of Percy Trick's fruit and veg van. Twenty minutes later he reached the small block of flats, where, to his relief, the top-flat buzzer was working. He wasn't expecting a pretty girl to open the door, 'specially one wrapped in a huge dressing-gown, and a hot water-bockle strapped to her waist. She yawned, rubbed her eyes and looked at Paddy for an explanation.

"I'm looking for my friend, Mr Spring."

"Who? Oh, Eddie you mean. He's in *my* flat now, downstairs. We swapped over the weekend. Fed up of 'im falling downstairs, waking me up all the time. Hang on, I'll see if he's in." Paddy followed her downstairs, where she knocked on the door. "Ed, Eddie, someone to see you." As soon as she heard sign of life within, the girl made for the stairs. "Nice to meet you, love. My name's Gwanwyn by the way."

"Pleased to meet you, Gwanwyn. Paddy, I am, Paddy Trahern."

The unmurdered Mr Spring appeared at the door and grabbed the onions from Paddy's hand. "Thank you, boy, that's very decent of you." He invited him in and told him to sit at the table.

"You can have a bit of breakfast with me. Bacon and eggs do you?" Paddy explained that he'd already eaten.

"Well, it's good of you to come all this way. Grow 'em yourself, is it?" Paddy realised he wouldn't need to tell the old man the real reason he'd come.

"Yeah." He didn't elaborate. Since the death of his father he'd neglected the vegetable patch, though he'd kept the grass down every summer with the help of a scythe. He'd studied his dad grinding and honing tools with a grey sharpening stone, something deemed too dangerous for Paddy, but the boy remembered exactly how his dad had held the blade at an angle and worked the stone in an arc, always moving away from the sharp edge. He was annoyed Alwyn Tucker doubted his sharpening skills. It was a piece of cake and one day he'd show the man he meant business.

At the breakfast table Mr Spring set to work on his two fried eggs, the bacon safely wrapped in an inch-thick slab of white bread. He was like a donkey munching strawberries. The grease

26

clogging the stove and skitting up the kitchen wall was probably a fire hazard, but it wasn't Paddy's place to tell him. Paddy took a cuppa, as Mr Spring hadn't heard of hot chocolate, and found they were kindred spirits when it came to emptying the sugar bowl into their mugs. He found that the old man had some interesting tales to tell and that he'd been to school with his mother.

"She was a good seamstress, Winnie was." Paddy found it strangely comforting hearing her first name; most people referred to her as 'your mam' and nobody talked openly about her, as if afraid of hurting his feelings. "Darned my socks for me and stitched up my trousers many a time. Wouldn't take a penny for it," he went on.

He could remember sitting on the couch every evening with his mam, watching their favourite tv programmes together, while dad popped into the Globe for a pint. She never sat idle, always knitting a pullover for some Romanian orphan or assembling a patchwork quilt for distant relatives. He'd assumed the trousers on his mother's lap were items from his dad's wardrobe, but it seemed his mam washed and pressed Mr Spring's fine garments from time to time. He was proud to be part of the family that had helped him out.

Paddy soon learnt that Mr Spring enjoyed a good gossip – 'carrying clecs' his dad had called it – and before long Paddy felt able to tell the truth about the gas fire. Mr Bastard looked to have a monopoly on metal recycling in the area, the nearest competition ten miles away in the big town.

"He done you good and proper there, boy. I used to take stuff up to him years ago, mind, copper piping and that. Then some bugger told the Social and they even took my bike off of me. Not that I could ride one these days with my legs. Always had bad legs, boy. Kids made fun of me in school, but I was determined to ride a bike, show 'em all. Arthritis now, so the doc do say. Painful at times, but you got to keep going, boy. You give up, might as well dig your own grave."

"You go shopping most days, Mr Spring?"

27

"Call me Eddie, boy. Just like getting out of the house, that's all, seeing a few faces round the place. Life can get very lonely."

"Can I use your toilet before I go, Mr Spring?"

"'course that, boy. Through the kitchen, there. Look in the drawer and you'll find the breadknife, 'case that big brown turd is still afloat. Not mine, the vicar called in yesterday."

Paddy enjoyed talking to Mr Spring that morning and had thoroughly warmed to him by the time he took his leave. His remorse for yesterday's behaviour had reached seismic proportions and he was determined to help the old man. Mr Spring did smell a bit, but it was tolerable, not like Drewi Gwyn Thomas who he'd had to sit by in primary school.

9

It wasn't just the moon that Paddy liked. He loved animals, raising doubts about his aspiration to be the local serial killer. It is true he'd squirted oil into Rusty's face as a child, but it would be difficult for even the best barrister to prove any malice aforethought. He was particularly fond of birds, especially the sparrows, bluetits and occasional robin that nested in the bird boxes with slanting rooves his father had put together. Paddy was eager to help, but found himself unable to turn the screwdriver in the right direction.

Later that afternoon, Paddy went up to his bedroom and sat by the old-fashioned wooden window, giving him a good view of the back as well as next door's garden. He could see Mr Jenkins muttering under his breath and aiming a stone at a big half-blind ginger cat Paddy had nicknamed *Cockeyed Jinge*. Paddy took time to pet the many cats roaming the neighbourhood and didn't hold it against them when they occasionally ripped his feathered friends to shreds. Not the magpies, anyway. These black and white varmints gave Paddy a splitting headache with their harsh 'wok-woks,' and he'd seen them taunt his feline friends, working in pairs and stealing their food. Sid Freeman had written an original poem called *To Kill A Dunnock-bird* in which he'd given the green light to those wanting to shoot a magpie:

> *Our garden birds are fat and thin,*
> *Black, brown and yellow, blue and red*
> *To kill a dunnock-bird's a sin*
> *But blast the magpie's thieving head.*
> By Sid Freeman

Now, you couldn't blame the cats, it was in their nature, and he hadn't been that bothered when his neighbour shot magpies out of the trees with his air-gun. Mr Jenkins Senior, father of his old P.E. teacher, ambushed them most Thursdays, before shovelling them into the bin, ready for the Friday morning collection.

Paddy's mam had taught him that a garden should be a home for all sorts of visitors, whether birds, butterflies, or scruffy-looking plants, but Mr Jenkins liked the sanitised look, anything that might disturb his precious zinnias unwelcome. He didn't realise that pellets attract slugs, as well as killing them. After they'd suffered convulsive seizures and death by dehydration, he spent as much time clearing up the gungy carnage as he did pruning his roses. If he'd left it at that, Paddy might have forgiven him. They would never be friends, for there was a stormy history between them. When Paddy was a boy, Jenkins had turned his gun on the smaller birds and wounded a baby sparrow nesting in the box. Paddy had held the little mite as it fluttered and died in his hand. The animosity between households receded for a while, Paddy wondering if his mam had had a word, perhaps even stuck a knitting needle up his arse.

Another reason Paddy hated 'Mr Grumps' was because of an incident on his twelfth birthday. His mam had bought a football from Woolies in the big town, hoping her son would do some physical exercise. Paddy's co-ordination had been the subject of cruel comments by some small-town folk and when Paddy's first touch decapitated half of his dahlias, the good Jenkins Senior burst the ball with his pitchfork. Mr Grumps 1, Paddy 0.

Watching Jenkins Senior defend himself against *Cockeyed Jinge* turned Paddy's stomach and reignited the bitterness he felt towards the sadistic bully. Perhaps it was time for him to even up the score, even take the lead. Those darts had felt good in his hand. From that time on Paddy referred to Jenkins Senior and his son, Jenkins Junior, as 'fuckers,' indicating, probably, he didn't like them very much.

10

Paddy had invited his girlfriend, Lucy, round for a candlelit supper in the evening. He doused himself with plenty of 'smellies' in the shower, after which he went to the chippie, wittily called *In Cod We Trust*, to order two large portions of fish and chips. He put them on low heat in the oven, then located the lager in the fridge.

He had met Lucy two years ago in the club and they'd gelled immediately. She was twenty years younger than Paddy, resulting in many a witty quip from the cultured small-town folk. Lucy thought her boyfriend a handsome piece of work and rode out the storm, more than happy to be his 'toy girl.' Tonight, he looked very fit in his blue jeans and black leather jacket. She had made an effort for him, wearing her favourite red dress, subtle make-up accentuating her pretty face.

Lucy worked in the library at the top of town and was well-used to the ten-minute bus journey. Most of the drivers knew her by now and she loved the gossip on offer each day from the uninhibited local passengers. If she'd carried a notebook and pencil she'd have access to everyone's phone numbers and bank accounts by now. She wondered if Welsh people really were louder and more unrestrained than other folk, but never having been outside the area, couldn't make a judgment. She remembered her grandpa saying that in Wales hedges were for talking over, in England to keep people out.

She'd had an uneventful day and Paddy hadn't been working, but she could sense something was troubling him. Lucy was the one person he could trust and eventually he told her about the latest Chalksy, though he was too ashamed to admit his part in abandoning the sprawled-out Mr Spring. Lucy laughed.

"As it happens, Mrs Watkins was on about graffiti today. Says the kids should have a wall to themselves, somewhere they can spray to their heart's content, but Chalksy's a bit different - he must know 'soon as it rains, it's all gone."

"Yeah, but last night was different. It was dry. Someone's got it in for me."

"That doesn't make sense, Paddy. He's just a joker. Remember the last one he did?"

It was Paddy's turn to laugh. Someone had puked up outside the Globe August bank holiday and by the morning it had been encircled in chalk and the words *Caution – Wet Sick* emblazoned on the pavement beside it.

"And then there was that *Strictly No Barking* sign on the wall of the vet's."

"Yeah – and *Peas In Our Time* outside FK's."

"Remember when the mayor wanted to stop them demolishing the old police station? It was *Save Our Bacon* wasn't it? Come on, Paddy, there's no harm in him."

"Or *her*, could be a she. Might even be looking at her now, swigging from her bockle of lager. Come to think of it, looked like *your* writing." Paddy chased his girlfriend around the table and they landed together out of breath on the couch. There was nothing Lucy liked better than snuggling up to Paddy, and tonight it was her turn to choose the movie. He didn't like 'soppy' films, but because he had a good singing voice she would introduce him to *The King And I* and hope for the best. Paddy was an open book, unable to lie or keep a secret for longer than ten minutes. Lucy was gratified to hear him humming along to the songs and pressed in closer to her gorgeous hunk.

Lucy had an important meeting the next day and wouldn't stay the night. Paddy walked her home to Colliers Row, where they held hands and sang *Getting To Know You* softly to each other, before she snogged him goodnight.

Tucked up in bed, Paddy re-lived the evening, knowing he was blessed to have Lucy as his girl. She looked lush in red. His thoughts inevitably turned to the early part of the day, and Mr

Spring. Someone knew he'd let the old bugger down and he was keen to make amends, do him a good turn. Go to sleep with a problem and by morning your dreams will have given you an answer. At least, that's what his mam used to reckon. Now then, how could he help Mr Spring?

11

When Lucy came off her coffee break the next day, chief librarian Mrs Watkins asked her to help 'some grumpy old codger with a misaligned eye' who was driving her up the wall.

"He's interested in his family's genealogy."

"His what?" asked Lucy.

"Genealogy. His family tree, but they're all Joneses on his mother's side and all Joneses on his father's. His eye doesn't help."

Lucy laughed. Her boss was amiable, but could be impatient at times, and was looking to Lucy to use her charm. She entered the reading room expecting to find a grouchy old whitebeard answering to the name of Jones, but peeping out from behind a book she espied her irrepressible man. Lucy wasn't banking on seeing Paddy until the weekend, but here he was, bold as brass, his broad smile lighting up the reading room. She fingered the book he was reading.

"Didn't know you was interested in trains, Paddy."

"Trying to find a particular station, I am. It was a big town and I remember seeing the sea."

Lucy put her hands on her hips. "Pa-ddy, what *are* you on about, mun?"

Paddy explained that when he was ten, his father had taken him to a large shop to get spare parts for his tricycle. He'd been excited because it was his first time on a train. "Just wish I could remember the name of the town."

"Ye-s, and....?"

"There were some big tricycles there. You know, I think they were for disabled people."

Lucy had no idea where this was leading and began wishing that there was, indeed, a bad-tempered Mr Jones here, squiffy eye or

34

not.

"You could work the pedals with your hands."

"How can you work a bike with your hands, Paddy?"

"Trike. They was for people 'couldn't use their legs. Honest to God, Luce." He could see his girlfriend was puzzled, but she, in turn, knew Paddy couldn't wind up a clock.

"And you want to go and see one of these 'hand tricycles'?"

"Think about it, Luce. Who do we know can't use his legs very well? His arms are ok."

"No idea, Paddy, this particular plot is thickening by the minute."

"Bandy legs! Mr Spring."

"Ri-ght."

"I want to help him out. See him in town every day struggling home with his shopping. An' he lives downstairs now, so parking it wouldn't be a problem." Lucy realised that in time, Paddy would tell her why he was so keen to help his new friend. They found a map of the South Wales railway and decided it was probably a choice between Llanelli, Swansea and Cardiff. Carmarthen was too small, wasn't it? Perhaps Mrs Watkins would know.

"How long was the journey, Paddy?"

"Can't really remember, Mrs Watkins. Went up and back the same day. Seemed to be ages on the train, but I was small then. Dad drove to the station in Llan and we left the car there. Had to cross over a bridge somewhere."

"Quite a time ago, Paddy. No guarantee the shop will still be there."

"We could look on the internet," said Lucy.

"Right, you keep shop Luce, and Paddy and I'll have a deck."

Paddy was a stranger to the computer and full of admiration as Mrs Mair Watkins opened window after window like it was some giant advent calendar. The initial search was fruitless, but Mrs Watkins came up trumps after typing in 'disabled tricycles' and at Paddy's suggestion, 'hand-pedals.' If Paddy was willing to travel to a little bric-a-brac enterprise in Swansea called '*Junken Orgy*', he could pick up a disability-friendly 'hand-cranked' tricycle for £199. Mrs Watkins reckoned the heavy purple machine was a 1960s model, but all Paddy could see was the crankshaft, positioned above the handlebars with two pedals operated by hand. He visualised Mr Spring whizzing through town, his baked beans neatly stacked in the wicker basket at the front.

*

Mr Spring was delighted with the news, not only because he'd once again own a set of wheels, but an all-expenses paid trip to the big town of Swansea was on the cards. He had to correct himself there – it was a 'city' and his family had supported the Swans through thick and thin. He'd only seen them play on telly and had thrown a tin of 'peel-plummed' tomatoes at the screen when Cardiff scored in the last minute at a snow-covered Vetch Field back in 1995. A tin of FK's garden peas had followed midfielder Nathan Wigg's celebrations. Landlord Freddie Sauce was not pleased.

"Fuck's sake, Eddie, what you do that for?"

"Didn't you see him? Bastard Wigg scored last minute."

"Yeah, but the game finished two hours ago. That's the highlights you was watching on the Welsh news."

"I know that, but they didn't deserve it."

"What's the matter with you, mun. The Swans won 4 – 1, you dull bastard." Freddie confiscated the tins until such time as Eddie Spring could control his temper. When he eventually gave them back, two weeks later, another argument ensued.

"Those weren't the tins, Freddie."

"Yes, they was, Eddie. Maureen put them away, special."

"You're wrong, there, Freddie. Two tins of baked beans it was. Should 'of got a receipt off of you."

"Yeah, Eddie," said Freddie, "I should 'of given you a bloody receipt. Maureen, go and get him a couple of tins of beans, will you?" Freddie's partner huffed and puffed her way to the kitchen, aware her favourite would be off the table again tonight, *egg* on toast a poor second. On the other hand, Freddie would have egg on face for at least a month.

*

Mr Spring's new friend and benefactor had ordered them a taxi to the station in Llan, having politely turned down Kerry Efearn's offer of the horse and cart at half-fare. That would have taken longer, with the danger they'd miss their connection. As it happened the train was half an hour late. *Sod's Law*, thought Paddy, but there again, money wasn't everything. And the taxi had air conditioning.

As someone who loved shopping in Swansea, Mrs Watkins had explained to Paddy that he should head for the taxi rank outside the station. Mike Scabs was the best, apparently. They were last in the queue, Mr Spring having to engage the services of two stout railwaymen to negotiate the gap between the train and the platform, but they were having a great time. On the journey up they'd ordered hot chocolate and crisps from the nice girl pushing the trolley and had had fun working out how to use the toilet door. They'd arrived in the big city and the sun was shining.

Mr Spring was soon on first name terms with cab driver, Mike, the two swapping stories as if they were old chums. Football was first up, kicking around the need to shore up the Swans' defence and buy a decent striker before the transfer window closed. Mike lived in the Penlan district of Swansea, famous for its old racecourse, and recalled that when he was in school, some of the boys would ride horses down the corridors. Mr Spring thought more headmasters should introduce such activities. He himself had learnt the art of garrotting turkeys every Christmas in the boys' changing rooms; they never received any financial remuneration from the PE teacher, who ran a smallholding. It hadn't done Mr Spring any harm, but the county council brought the practice to an end when one of the parents, a vegetarian indispensable to the school fund-raising committee, objected. Mike thought that was

37

ridiculous.

The junk shop was in Sketty, a run-down area of the city according to their driver, 'full of wretched toffs in tweed jackets, wondering where their next Range Rover was coming from.' He parked on double-yellow lines outside a row of stylish shops that included a boutique, an antique dealer, a hairdresser and a coffee shop. Paddy recognised the *Junken Orgy* logo, and with Mike's help, manoeuvred Mr Spring into an upright position on the pavement. The driver took his time, ignoring the angry blare of car horns.

Mike reluctantly accepted Paddy's generous tip, then got back in his car and drove away, giving a generous V sign to the sophisticated motorists who wanted to string him up for his brazen act of kindness. So far everything had gone like clockwork, but now the two intrepid globetrotters encountered their first snag. The junk shop was closed for dinner, and would be back in business 'about 2.30.'

"That means two and a half hours we got to wait around," said Mr Spring. "Greedy bastards!"

"Let's try the coffee shop."

"Don't like coffee. Never drunk the stuff in me life."

Paddy led the way, holding the door open for Mr Spring, who found himself face-to-face with an old gent, also with bandy legs, leaving the shop. Both men turned sideways on, trying to squeeze past one another in the doorway, but only succeeding in getting jammed, as jacket buttons went flying. Paddy tugged his partner hard and the wrestlers eventually disentangled on amicable terms, without having to call the emergency services.

The two found a little table in the corner and a young waitress brought them a menu, promising to be back shortly. They were starting to feel peckish. Paddy looked around at the strangers prattling on, taking in the fine décor that put Downhill's 'greasy spoon' to shame. He was delighted they'd heard of hot chocolate in Swansea, though Eddie couldn't understand why tea couldn't be served in a mug. He was placated when a large teapot arrived, but mortified when told beans on toast was not on the menu.

Everyone in the world did beans on toast, surely!

"Not in Sketty, apparently. You can have a sandwich, though, Mr Spring."

"Nice big cheddar one'll do me." Not as simple as that, Mr Spring. The next challenge was the bread.

"You can have seeded bread, sourdough, wholemeal, or granary and we've got rolls, baguettes, and wraps as well. Oh, and a gluten-free option if you want it."

Mr Spring's outlook on bread was very simple – quality could be evaluated in terms of thickness, not some fancy name. A sliced loaf from FK's would do just as well as some fancy bloomer from Marks and Spencers.

"Got Branston pickle, have you, love? Good." Then he sang out the old advert for the benefit of all, including the hard of hearing. "*Bring out the Branston.*" One or two of the customers fidgeted uncomfortably in their seats, but no-one had the gumption to call for a constable. Paddy didn't want to push it by asking for pilchards, settling for a ham and tomato bap with coleslaw and salad.

After squeezing a fourth cup out of his teapot, Mr Spring needed to relieve himself. The toilet area was constricted, two square yards perhaps, and as he stood at the urinal Mr Spring became aware of someone waiting behind him. He half-turned towards the tall, dapper-looking gentleman who was breathing down his neck, and felt increasingly uncomfortable. He did his best, but his bladder could only manufacture a little dribble.

"Hardly room to swing a cat in 'ere," joked Mr Spring, hinting that the newcomer should stand back a little. Instead, he was met with a sarcastic riposte delivered in a posh accent.

"Actually, I didn't think to bring the cat with me."

Clever twat, thought Mr Spring. *Well, if he won't move, I'll make him.* Eddie Spring braced himself, then let out a thunderclap of a fart which blew the man backwards and had him feeling for bullet holes. *Arrogant fucker.* The trickle became a torrent and Mr Spring sighed in sharp relief, before nudging over to the washbowl.

39

"Next time bring the cat, it's good at measuring distances." The clever arrogant twat-fucker smiled back weakly.

12

Now it was time to complete their mission. The owners of the junk shop, Felicity and Oliver, normally welcomed visitors, but the rough and ready commoners peering through the window had put them on edge. They took them for car boot merchants, looking for a job lot that would earn them a quick buck. Learning that they were from Downhill put them in a completely different light – they were probably time-wasters with little more than spare change in their pockets. Come to think of it, they did look like a couple of e-fits. Better keep an eye on their thieving hands.

The small-town boys slowly made their way around the shop, hypnotised by the magical items on offer. Paddy was careful not to touch anything, but his companion seemed comforted by the old familiar objects of bygone days and on his second lap, picked up a toby jug. The owners looked on aghast as Mr Spring appeared to be falling, first to one side, then the other, before steadying himself and reaching out for another jug. He raised it to his left ear and gave it a shake, a method his father had used to see how much beer was left in his tankard. When he accidentally ripped the arm off the lead figure of a toy chimpanzee, Flick and Olly Smurthwaite had had enough. Before he could put his hands on a pair of porcelain cats, they latched onto his arms and tried to pin him back. Mr Spring didn't appreciate their help and shook them off, causing the fragile Felicity to reverse into an antique display of plates, which fell off their shelving and shattered on the tiled flooring.

Mr Spring apologised politely and asked if they would accept a couple of quid less for the chimp, now that it was broken. Oliver helped his wife to her feet, then went to fetch a brush, Paddy offering to hold the dustpan. With order restored Paddy asked about the tricycle, explaining that it was for his friend, Mr Spring, with the aim of giving him more freedom to get around. Felicity felt that the less mobility this bandy-legged creature had, the better.

Oliver led the two gents out the front door and down the side of the shop to a back yard. He unbolted the shed and wheeled out a beauty of a machine which had been well looked after. Despite a few chips in the purple paintwork, it was clean and shiny and the brakes in good working order. Paddy had brought his own pump in case the tyres were flat and got to work straightaway; no slow puncture and solid metal caps on the valves. So far, so good. Mr Spring stood motionless with his mouth open – he'd never seen a tricycle like this. And now came the big test; was the chain working and willing to set the cogs in motion?

If the trike belied its forty-year old age tag, then the old man with bandy legs who jokingly referred to himself as 'no spring chicken' fairly swept back the years, using his sturdy arms to lift himself on to the saddle.

"Never knew these things existed," he said, ready to set off on his journey.

"Hang on!" squeaked the nervous Oliver, "make sure you know how to use the brakes. They're on the hand-holds."

"Piece of piss," laughed Mr Spring, and he raced around the yard as if he was doing a time-trial, scraping his knuckles skilfully as he buffeted the walls. He swerved just in time to avoid Felicity, who was curious to know what was going on, coming to a sudden stop before hitting the main road.

"I think he likes it," said Paddy, "I'll pay you for it now." He dipped in his jacket pocket and unfurled a roll of banknotes, adding four pound coins to the mix. "One hundred and ninety-nine pounds exactly," he beamed, slamming the money into Olly's hand. Felicity was not impressed.

"What about the plates, Olly. They were Wedgwood – limited edition."

"He's paying cash, Flick."

"Huh, it's probably counterfeit – or stolen. Look at the pair of them."

Paddy had the feeling that 'Flick' didn't like them very much. "I'll need a receipt. Mrs Watkins told me to make sure I got a receipt."

Olly thought as much. "Right, we'll go back inside." Then, to appease his precious wife, added "I'll check each one with the pen."

"That'll take ages," whined his wife. Oliver glared at her as if to say *I can't win, whatever I do*. However, he calmy led the party past Mr Spring, who was patiently waiting on the pavement, and into the shop. Felicity stomped off upstairs in a huff, leaving her husband squander the profits. Once the deal was closed to everyone's satisfaction, Paddy offered his hand and crunched Oliver's fingers. The man winced, but Paddy took it for a congenial smile. After all, they had just made Oliver's day.

Outside, Mr Spring was nowhere to be seen. Paddy decided to check the back yard before he would panic. With no signal on his mobile, he availed himself of the services of Oliver's phone. Unable to contact Lucy, he was fortunate to reach Mrs Watkins at the library. She realised the return journey hadn't been planned in any detail, but told Paddy his friend would likely be waiting for him on the platform.

"Don't you worry about Mr Spring, he's a survivor." Oliver was more than happy to give Paddy a lift to the station, though his wife wanted him to sign a binding agreement they'd never show their faces in Sketty again.

Paddy could find no-one who'd seen Mr Spring. A bandy-legged seventy-year old pedalling a big purple tricycle by hand wouldn't exactly be hard to miss, but he seemed to have disappeared off the face of the earth. Paddy checked his phone again and this time it was behaving. Lucy's voice was like finding water in the desert; she would know what to do. As it turned out, her advice was similar to that of Mrs Watkins – get the next train back to Llan where she and her dad would pick him up. Mr Spring was a resourceful old rascal and would turn up sooner or later.

Lucy was right. Several startled motorists reported an unusual vehicle bombing down the hard shoulder of the M4 between junctions 47 and 49, powered by an unbalanced madman of indeterminate age. It was considered newsworthy enough for *Wales Today* to give Mr Spring his five minutes of fame and to confirm what everyone already knew about life in Downhill. When Mr Spring arrived in town, sitting in the cab of the breakdown lorry, he looked as if dripping wouldn't melt in his mouth.

13

Paddy had worked in the local Co-op since leaving school in 1981, over twenty years ago. He had never been ambitious, content to help the delivery drivers, sweep the yard and stack the shelves. He'd had one boss in that time, Mr Eifion Thomas, who would be retiring next year. He treated his staff well and Paddy was very fond of him. On his first day, Mr Thomas had called him into his office and welcomed him to the 'coop,' as he called his enterprise. He spent time showing Paddy the ropes and introducing him to the staff, making it clear that in his 'family' no-one was better than anyone else. They all had qualities the Co-op valued and in taking Paddy on, he'd recognised an honest, considerate young man. Phil, the assistant store manager, took him under his wing for the rest of the morning, by which time Paddy felt truly at home.

Paddy revelled in the responsibility he was being given – wheeling boxes of goods around the store, helping the old folk find their packet of bacon and mopping up any spills. And Mr Thomas didn't mind you having a good old chinwag with the customers, in fact he encouraged it. Paddy knew half the town before he started working there and within six months was on first name terms with the other third. He was even asked to keep an eye on shoplifters, reporting straight to Phil, but he'd never seen the police called. One inveterate thief was the doddery Edna Flanagan who called in on a Wednesday afternoon, pushing her two 'babies' around in a pram. It took Paddy weeks to twig what was happening, the rest of the staff evidently used to her antics. She would take half an hour appraising the aisles, before picking up some baked beans and concealing them in the pram. She then made for the door hell-for-leather, where Phil would block her exit. The pantomime came to an end every time with these well-

45

rehearsed lines,

"I don't think you've paid for those, Edna."

"What's that, boy? Just taking my babies for a walk, I am."

"Babies? Can I take a look?"

"'Course you can, boy," and she lifted the knitted pink blanket to reveal the beans. "See, there's my little bairns – identical tins they are!" And that was it for another week.

The Co-op was considered to be a few notches above FK's, stocking a greater variety of goods of a better quality. The wages, too, were superior, the rumour being that the employees of the smaller shop were often paid late and sometimes not at all. Unsurprisingly, morale was low, not helped by the sign that greeted customers as they entered the store, *We Tolerate Any Abuse Towards Our Staff*, a clever ploy that attracted busloads of the obstreperous.

Paddy worked four days a week and was always willing to do more, at a loss to understand the boys in the pub who couldn't wait for the weekend. From Friday afternoon until Sunday night they'd get wrecked, pissing their wages down the pan, only to work another week to repeat the scenario. Unlike them, Paddy equated work with freedom, after he'd endured a miserable five years at the secondary school in Llan. Most of the kids had been tidy and he'd steered clear of the bullies, but there were two teachers who constantly picked on him. Maybe they'd given him grief because he was a shortarse, though Lucy reckoned that where it mattered, he was no teeny-weeny. She took enormous pleasure guiding his Great Jehovah, feeding her 'til she wanted no more.

Miss April Chatterley had been his physics mistress in school, a shifty-looking creature with long black hair, scary teeth, a hooked nose and grey, misty eyes. She claimed to be human, though an absence of any rapport with the normal world gave rise to rumours that she'd risen from the dead. Paddy had only chosen the subject because chemistry was the alternative and his father an electrician. In hindsight, the chemistry bomb-making class in the third year would have been more useful. Seeing Miss Chatterley blown sky-high in her Vauxhall Chevette would have been very therapeutic, but such acts were considered inappropriate, even criminal, at the time.

So what had made Paddy hate their very own Morticia so much? It wasn't because she continually belittled his attempts to get to grips with the laws of motion or Archimedes' principle, for there were a tribe of teachers equally proficient in the dark art of sarcasm. Some aspects of physics he enjoyed, such as magnets dancing with iron filings and the diagram of an electric circuit, so pleasing to the eye. No, it was an incident that happened one humid June day in his fourth year and could well have been an episode of *The Addams Family*.

It had been unbearably hot for some days and as the sticky pupils made their way across the yard, the Devil painted the sky jet-black and the gusts of wind suddenly stopped. There was no warning, no distant rumble of thunder, this storm was already at the front door. The children broke into a run, the girls dubbing the boys 'cissies' as a thunderclap exploded behind them. Everyone prayed that the next stab of lightning would find its way into the staffroom, Mr Seaflatt, the music teacher, an ideal conductor.

Paddy felt a sense of foreboding every time he entered the physics lab. The room was always dark, the blackout still in force, despite the ceasing of hostilities in 1945, but the gloomy atmosphere had been heightened by the storm and Paddy certain that today an episode of mystery and horror was imminent.

Paddy and his classmates shuffled their bums on to the tall lab stools, chattering excitedly about the hailstorm outside. As yet there was no sign of Miss Chatterley, and Matthew Griffiths at the front bravely announced she must be mixing her mascara. He turned around, intending to milk his audience further, but was stopped in his tracks when a figure emerged, corpselike, from the nether regions. The creepy apparition glided serenely towards her bench at the front, debating whether it would be toad or rat she'd turn the class clown into before donating him to the biology class for dissection.

It was pure coincidence that electrical conductivity was the subject of the day's lesson, but it would, no doubt, win her brownie points from the headmaster, assuming he hadn't been electrocuted. Brownie points could not be awarded posthumously. Some of the lesson was easy to follow. Paddy had seen his father re-wiring the house and knew that metals were good conductors of electricity. Other materials, such as wood, plastic and glass, don't allow the electric current to flow through them and were known as 'insulators'. After unscrewing the switches his father had wound insulation tape around the bare copper wire, to prevent getting a shock when turning the power back on. Surely that's all you needed to know to keep you safe?

Paddy had kept his eye on the clock behind the teacher and though the second hand was doing its job, the minute hand seemed to have stopped. When she wrote Ohm's Law on the blackboard, he started to doze off, wishing he was at ohm in front of the telly, but then the fireworks began. Black-clad Morticia licked her lips, lifted her arms and uttered 'kappa, sigma and gamma' over and over again, raising Patrick's blood pressure. He was certain she was casting an evil spell over him and that 'kappa' and whatever were slimy creatures destined for the bubbling cauldron.

He was brought to his senses when his name was called out and he felt Penny Price's pencil poking him in the back. Paddy was one of three 'volunteers' summoned to the front, indebted to Miss for inviting them to her party. She had rigged up a simple electrical circuit using a battery, bulb and wire that appeared well-insulated to Paddy.

Matthew Griffiths, Nicola Hughes and Paddy were instructed to hold hands, the rest of the class giggling uneasily as Miss Chatterley took charge of an electric switch behind her. With thunder and lightning as backing music, she caught hold of the class clown and dragged him towards a bare copper wire, his mouth downturned in deep regret. The teacher proffered him the wire with all the charm of Marishka, second bride of Dracula.

Pogo grimaced, closed his eyes, then bit the bullet. As he tentatively gripped the wire, Miss Chatterley pretended to turn up the current, generating a collective gasp from the misdirected mites. Mathew opened his eyes, happy not to be dead.

Miss Chatterley feigned surprise when the three guinea pigs reported feeling nothing, not even a slight tingle. She told Mathew to go to the back of the queue. It was now Nicola's turn to feel the heat.

"The current that passed through the wire last time – when our friend Mathew was holding it – was very low. Less than one milliampere. This time I'm going to turn it up to one milliampere. Are you ready, Nicola?" Nicola nodded calmly, refusing to be daunted by the creepy executioner. She felt a very faint shock and the reaction of the other two indicated it had passed to the end of the line, but it was no great shakes.

It was now Paddy's turn to take his medicine, but he realised his teacher was playing a game of mental torture, that the anticipation was the worst part. Any slight shock he felt would be transmitted to the other two, so they were all in the same boat. *Here goes*, he thought, *easy peasy*, though he didn't like the malicious grin on Miss Chatterley's chalk-white face. The shock was bearable, and when their teacher retired to her bench the three headed for their stools, assuming the experiment was over.

"Not you, Paddy. Stay where you are!" Miss Chatterley instructed the class to open their exercise books, everyone breathing a sigh of relief on reaching dry land. They'd willingly take the huge dollops of sarcasm thrown their way as they struggled for the correct answers. Class clown Mathew kept his head down, glancing over at Paddy now and again, wondering what the bonus prize entailed.

Miss Chatterley was gratified by how attentive her pupils had been and vowed to conduct more live experiments in the future. She hoped her pupils would pass the principle of conductivity on to others, though that joke passed well over their vacuous little heads.

It was time for the finale. The witch picked up her wand in her right hand, then held up three envelopes and asked her devotees if any of them had heard of 'Russian roulette'. Harold Worse said he'd seen some growing in his grandpa's allotment, unwittingly booking his place in the next round of experimentation. No-one dared laugh, though Grandpa Worse, fair play, grew all sorts of stuff. He'd once planted a 9 oz. can of beans in the spring and harvested a catering size tin weighing 6lb. 10oz. in August, so Harold may have been right.

Miss Chatterley explained that within each envelope was a number denoting an electric charge. She cleverly chalked up a traffic lights on the board, in reverse order, to indicate the effect each current would have on youthful bones.

GREEN:	*0.8 milliamperes* = *NO feeling*
YELLOW:	*8 milliamperes* = *shock NOT painful*
RED:	*8 amperes* = *certain DEATH*

Once everyone was conversant with the 'indisputable consequences' for young Paddy when he held the wire, she conducted a straw poll on the likely result, increasing the tension. Which lottery ticket would Paddy win? There was overwhelming sympathy for the poor lad, who was plastered in sweat by this time. Only Harold Worse voted for 'death,' only Ruth Evans for the 8 milliampere dose

The class clown was selected as magician's assistant, the one who'd open the envelope sealing Paddy's fate. The storm outside played its part to perfection, putting the Hammer horror films in the shade. The erstwhile jester was now a crumpled sack of contrition, unable to look Paddy in the eye. A crash of thunder provided the drum roll, the cue for Mathew's trembling fingers to pick at the flap. He lifted the scrap of paper and when he croaked 'eight,' his teacher asked him to repeat it.

"Louder, boy!"

"Eight," he shouted. Several stools creaked, the rain continued to lash the window panes, but Miss Chatterley had never seen such an attentive class.

"Not '0.8,' Mathew?"

"No, Miss."

"Then 8 'what'?"

"Doesn't say, Miss."

"Really? So, it's either eight 'milliamperes' or eight 'amperes'. Um…..," she said, turning to the board, "I wonder what's in store for our diminutive friend here." She looked at Paddy with an evil leer that left him in no doubt of her murderous intentions, then turned her attention to Mathew. "Turn it over, stupid!"

The stupid boy had a stone in his stomach, knowing his career as a clown was dead in the water. He might join the monks on Caldey Island when he grew up, or train as a stunt man. His brain did its best to direct his fingers, amid nervous laughter from those in the ringside seats. Had he deliberately let it flutter to the floor? It made no odds to Miss Chatterley if it meant prolonging the show. She looked over again at Paddy Trahern. If only she had an instrument for measuring mental distress, wouldn't life be wonderful!

Mathew Griffiths picked up the slip, wondering if the monks needed a stunt man, but his voice had gone. His teacher barked at him to show the class, the sigh of relief confirming the death sentence had been commuted, drowning the protestations of Harold Worse.

"Eight milliamperes, nothing to be worried about, Paddy. Take hold of the wire and let's see what happens." Paddy took her at her word, willing to put up with a slight shock if it meant getting back out in the storm. Miss Chatterley had graduated from Oxford University with a First Class Joint Honours Degree in Physics and Additional Malice, and knew that eight milliamperes was too risky, but she'd give the 'six' a go, calculating that Paddy's short stature would just about take it. "Here we go. Everybody – one, two, three!"

"Ah!" Paddy jumped back as the current rattled him. She quickly turned it off, elated she'd got it bang on. Just enough to be painful. With time running out, she asked her spellbound acolytes to write up the 'conclusion' of the experiment as homework. She instructed Paddy and Mathew Griffiths to tidy up, disappearing into her storeroom. The erstwhile clown was about to bin the envelopes when his thirst for knowledge got the better of him and he opened them up. He motioned Paddy over.

"What is it, mun?"

"Shush – look at this." Each piece of paper revealed the same figure, '8 milliamperes'.

"Cow!" was their joint summation of proceedings.

14

Mr Spring enjoyed his new-found freedom and soon became a fixture in small-town traffic, signalling left when he was turning right and shouting felicitations at discourteous drivers. Paddy loved his visits to the Co-op, accompanying him around the store and pointing out the bargains.

Mr Spring never bought a huge amount, a basket sufficient most of the time, but something on wheels was easier. Paddy proudly pushed the trolley for his friend and fetched the steps if they needed anything higher than the second shelf. The shopping completed, he would help Mr Spring load the trike, the old tactic of bags on handlebars brought into play when the wicker was full. Their friendship quickly blossomed, and Eddie Spring invited Paddy and his girlfriend to Christmas dinner. Paddy had already been booked by Lucy's parents, and not wanting to disappoint the old man they arranged to get together on Boxing Day. Mr Spring took his responsibilities seriously and on the Tuesday before Christmas did a big shop, including ten tins of beans, a jar of cranberry sauce and two large packets of chicken pieces. He merrily threw items into the trolley that he'd never normally consider, and on reaching the check-out it was creaking under the weight.

As was their custom, Messrs Spring and Trahern hadn't really thought this one through. Eddie dealt strictly in cash, as he explained to Phil, showing him the pound coins bursting out of the money bags in his back pocket. The assistant manager patiently pointed out that he was £40 short, not expecting Mr Spring to announce to one and all that he had money stuffed under his mattress at home. Phil cupped his hand over the old man's gob before he could tell them how much.

Outside, the only vestige of seasonal joy appeared in the form of tinsel draped around the traffic lights. The coldest day of the year had become the wettest and windiest, a veritable winter storm. Mr Spring had come prepared in his yellow sou'wester, oilskins and galoshes, but it took three return journeys to ferry the goods to his flat in Policeman's End. His face and knuckles were raw by the time he finished, but he was not one to let a sore nose or a throbbing thumb get in his way. As he often explained to astonished onlookers, 'It do keep me alive, mun.' He was so absorbed in completing his mission that he forgot to pick up the money, and Phil could find nothing in the Co-op's Mission Statement to cover such an eventuality.

The Boxing Day dinner was a resounding success, Eddie Spring surpassing himself with Beans on Toast *Au Gratin*, reheated chicken bites and lashings of cranberry sauce. Lucy told the boys to sit down, while she washed up, made a cuppa and furtively attempted to degrease the oven. She took the opportunity to throw in the bin something that had been lurking in the fridge for some time – possibly a pork chop, but now beyond identification. She'd also packed the eyebrow trimmer into her handbag, hoping he'd let her snip the sizeable hairs protruding from his ears, but didn't have the heart to ask him.

Once Mr Spring had twiddled his crackling wireless and found a channel acceptable to all three music-lovers, the scene was set for a cosy chit-chat in front of a cracking coal fire. The talk inevitably turned to the tricycle, something that supplied the boys with endless anecdotes and fuelled Eddie's self-deprecating humour. Lucy played the amused bystander, well-used to ear-wigging conversations between her boyfriend and his friends.

Lucy had heard Paddy's version of their trip to Swansea and the narrow scrapes in the hectic Downhill traffic, but Mr Spring had the knack of embellishing a story and playing to the gallery. When he related Tuesday's encounter on the Cwmglas bend, battling to pass Farmer Cack and his tractor in a gale-force wind, the soft chuckling exploded into unrestrained laughter.

Paddy reckoned the money he'd spent on the trike was an outstanding bargain. Eddie did his best to maintain it, housing it in one of the council lock-ups allocated to residents. Paddy spent Thursday afternoons washing and polishing the vehicle and giving the chain and brakes their customary dose of lubricant. Eddie helped by holding the machine firmly in place with his iron grip. Job done, Paddy would cling on tightly round his friend's neck as he taxied him back home.

Talk later turned to the family car in which Paddy had spent many a Sunday afternoon exploring the local highways, Rusty slobbering the window until some kind soul wound it down. His mother, Winnie, didn't drive, content to relax and provide a running commentary on the flora and the fauna of the countryside. Her husband was a careful driver, but once a year insisted on testing the engine immediately the mustard Austin 1100 had passed its MOT. For a hairy twenty minutes his father's maniacal stare took over, and it felt as if they were on the Welsh leg of the World Rally Championship. Paddy invariably puked over the dog as they passed the chequered flag and his mother threatened to divorce her husband and walk home.

"Your father'd see to the electrics, though?"

"Yeah, but Dai Grease done the MOT and serviced the car and that."

"His son runs the garage now."

"Gary?"

"Does the tricycle have to be MOT'd?" asked Lucy. None of them knew, but neither of the boys were worried. Lucy suggested that Mr Spring fit another basket to the back of the trike to save him on the shopping trips.

"Good idea, that is, Luce."

"I've got a couple of coupons for one of the charity shops you can use."

"Oh?"

"Pet's Rescue, I think."

"Could look for a trailer. My dad used to have one, take garden waste to the dump. Sold it in the end."

"Now, that *is* a good idea, Paddy my lad. Could throw all the shopping in."

"Get some sort of canvas to cover it up. Shame my dad got rid of his. I think Dai Grease helped him knock it up. Perhaps it's worth asking Gary."

15

Having learnt his trade from the age of eight in his father's garage, no-one doubted Gary Grease's ability as a mechanic. Dai had officially handed over the business to his son, but liked to keep his hand in, doing the odd repair job and helping out with the books. They worked well together, but when it came to communication skills, were like torque and cheese. While Dai patiently explained the job to each valued customer, his son's tongue was as rough as his ratchets.

Three weeks into the new year, Paddy was skating on thin ice. He enjoyed cold winter mornings, when he could pit his wits against the numerous patches of glass that had formed on the main street. He slipped on his arse once, much to his own amusement and that of the wandering mongrel, who was eyeing up the display of sausages in Billy Hook's shop.

Paddy turned left into the Old Conduit which housed a row of old stone cottages, built by the first solid settlers back in the day. Beyond these stood a 1950s petrol station sporting three old-fashioned *Esso* pumps, reminding folks that 'happy motoring' was still a part of their lives. Perched at the top of the lane at right-angles to the petrol station, Dai Grease's workshop commanded a view of absolutely nothing.

Paddy could hear a knocking sound from within the mighty shed and after some investigation found Gary Grease inspecting the undercarriage of a bottle-green car old enough to be his grandfather. Gary didn't notice his visitor at first, and Paddy waited patiently for a lull in proceedings to beam a friendly 'hello'.

"Who the fuck are you?" This greeting was par for the course in most parts of town and Paddy carried on in his own genial way, assuming the mechanic would help him in his quest to find a trailer.

"You can drive, then, can you?"

"No, 'snot for me, it's for Mr Spring." Unlike his father, Gary Grease had no desire to familiarise himself with the town's strange inhabitants. The creature called Spring was not on his radar.

"There's an old one round the side. Needs a bit of work to get it on the road, but if you want it, you can 'ave it for fifty quid." Paddy ran outside and located the trailer, which even the kindest soul would have said was beyond hope, but to the delighted customer was an answer to his prayers. Paddy wasn't worried about the price, his earnings topped that amount every week and he'd done a bit of overtime before Christmas. He did a quick calculation in his head, ready to tell Mr Spring; there was room for 500 tins, which worked out at ten pence a tin, if he wasn't mistaken. What a bargain, a win-win situation for everyone!

He artfully dodged the ice in his hurry to get home and fetch his bank card, before skiddling up to the hole-in-the-wall. He never got it right first time, but a tenner at a time was still fifty quid eventually. He counted the crisp notes carefully and rolled them up in a rubber band, just as his father used to do. Gary Grease wasn't expecting to see the short, squat odd-ball so soon, but was willing enough to take the readies on offer. As the man rightly told him, it was win-win all round.

Two days later, Paddy and Eddie were parked by the petrol pumps, surveying their purchase in the cold light of day. Mr Spring was delighted with it and just as eager as his young benefactor to get started. Paddy had brought along his pump, but the valves of the trailer tyres were too big for the adaptor. Mr Spring told Paddy to hold the trike firmly while he stood against the handlebars and heaved the arse-end of the trailer with all his muscle.

"'S no good, Paddy. Them tyres are like squished tins. Have to find a garage." As it happened, they were *at* a garage.

Gary Grease was in no mood for a couple of clowns, his services required by the area's impatient hot-rod community. Grease Senior, arrived to help service an Audi, bumped into the two friends as they disconsolately shut the workshop door behind them. Dai had great respect for Paddy's father, who had on many occasions assisted the mechanic when he was short-handed.

"All right, boys!" The boys were all right, but Paddy, as unselfconscious as ever, related the whole story, dobbing Gary Grease right in it. Dai knew what his son was like, having brought him up with his wife, but this was a step too far and he blew a gasket.

"Them tyres need new inner tubes and that tow-bar is just about rusted through. Give 'em their money back, Gary."

"Can't!"

"Gee-gees again, is it? Right, name a day next week and we'll work on it. You find a couple of decent bars and I'll do the welding. We'll work out a way to fit a coupler, hitch it up."

"That trailer's too heavy for a bike, mun."

"It's a trike he's got, hand pedals. And there's plenty of horsepower in them shoulders, I can tell you." Eddie Spring showed Gary his herculean arm muscles, not for him to doubt his father's words.

Paddy had landed lucky again. The two Greases grafted all day Tuesday, Gary grumpily modifying the length of the cart while his father sweated under his welding gear. It took a couple of hours on Wednesday morning to hitch it up to the trike. They'd even thrown in a tarpaulin for free, to stop any tins from rusting.

Any doubts concerning the trike's capability to lug its custom-built trailer around the streets and byways of Downhill disappeared with Mr Spring into the morning mist. He was as pumped up as the five tyres he now commanded, and the trailer treated the gaping potholes peppering the town with disdain. Paddy was no less excited, sweeping the pavement outside the shop into submission, in the hope of witnessing the race against the clock. Mr Spring had forgotten his promise to stop by, intent on running in his new toy, which extended to a twenty-mile round trip to Llan.

16

Not everyone was happy with the appearance of the charabanc. It wasn't that townsfolk objected to Mr Spring *per se*, a nutter with bandy legs wasn't the issue; no, they questioned his right to be on the road at all. The man obviously had no idea what the Highway Code was, his hand signals were bizarre, and he believed that keeping to the left-hand side was optional. Imagine meeting him on an escalator!

Scotland Yard didn't want to get involved, neither did the Swansea gendarmerie, who had been caught with their pants down whenever they'd interfered in the affairs of Downhill. PC. Prys Paddler was more than happy to take on the case and commandeered Elwyn Olwyn's 25-speed mountain bike without his knowledge. When Elwyn reported it missing, the PC told him he should be more careful and gave him a leaflet entitled, '*Home Security – 15 Ways To Keep Your Burglar At Bay.*'

But despite his clever plan, Prys was unable to catch Mr Spring red-handed. Even on Allt-y-Malwod, the steepest hill in the area, he could get nowhere near Eddie Spring and his trailer, despite his many-geared bicycle. The man with the bandy legs quickly became a legend in the recalcitrant part of the community and Eddie Spring Appreciation Societies sprang up all over Wales, including Monkton and Pembroke Dock.

But decent people had had enough, and PC. Prys Paddler was under pressure to resolve the issue. He was called to an emergency meeting of the small-town council and given two weeks to sort it out. For thirteen days and thirteen nights the normally even-tempered policeman slumped around town, the deadweight of his boots reflecting his despondency. His wife, Pamela, paraded in front of him in a sexy black negligee Mrs Probert no longer had any use for, but she'd misjudged his mood and anyway, the Fruit and Veg aisle in *FK's* mini-market was not the place to do it.

On the fourteenth day, ninety-three year-old Reggie Hopkins, one of the youngest mayors in the town's history, stood in front of a disgruntled mob at the High Street traffic lights. When they changed to amber he was escorted back to bed by his carers, leaving PC. Prys Paddler face the music, played by Tommy Hump on his trumpet. He started with *Three Blind Mice* in an unusual quintuple meter, followed twenty minutes later by the jazz version of *The Teddy Bear's Picnic* in L Sharp Minor, because everyone knew the words in that particular key. The music failed to lift the mood or the drizzle that engulfed the thoroughfare. On the opposite side of the road, a wilful crowd of twenty or so Spring supporters had gathered, taunting the policeman by baring their arses and taking any resultant frostbite on the chin.

An impassioned cheer signified that the outlying scouts had reported sightings of the man himself. Chief engineer and colour expert Rhodri Truds signalled that he'd accomplished the task of governing the lights. They were all permanently on red – red for 'stop,' red for 'danger.' Prys Paddler felt somewhat comforted by these developments, but couldn't hide his uneasiness; Spring was a veritable Houdini, evading every ambush that had been laid for him thus far, be it in a rural or urban setting.

Pamela Paddler brushed the dandruff off her husband's collar, before running home to change out of her slutty schoolgirl outfit. At the top of the road stood Elsie Brittle, known as 'the loud girl around town' and now on her fifth husband. She had contemptuously dismissed the policeman's offer of a megaphone and strode to her chosen spot carrying a bunch of daffodils. Her part in the drama would be discussed in the taverns of Downhill for years to come. With a prime view of proceedings, she opened her lungs to full effect,

"Spring's around the corner!"

The law-abiding citizens gathered at the traffic lights shuffled nervously and jostled their PC into position, before retreating a safe distance. Mr Spring and his contraption appeared out of the mist at the top of the hill and hurtled towards the policeman, the hairs in his ears like broken cobwebs flailing in the wind. The constable puffed himself up to his full height and raised his right hand in a clear indication that oncoming vehicles should stop. With the tricycle within five yards, self-preservation kicked in, and he dived to his right into the arms of Pamela, now in a lush pink sequin bikini. Mr Spring deftly clattered through the barbed-wire barricade and made his way home, much to the jubilation of his unsophisticated followers. For the exasperated authorities, it was back to the drawing-board.

17

Normally Paddy would go straight to sleep on a moonful night, but this evening it had been nobbled by inclement weather. Desperate Dan hailstones attacked his bedroom window, joined later by the thunder and lightning that had been waiting in the wings. Paddy reached over to turn on his bedside lamp and retrieve a photo album from his chest of drawers. There weren't that many pictures, but the familiarity of it all brought him great comfort. He'd stuck them in in great chronological order, him and Lucy first, himself as a baby, then his Nan and Grampa Davies, Rusty the dog, family outings in the car, his grandparents on his father's side and finally a class photo of his last year in school. Tonight, he was unable to close the book, his eyes glued to his class teacher towering over a bunch of terrified children, like the bully he was.

He hated Miss April Chatterley for the one humiliating incident he'd undergone in her physics lab, but Mr Griffith Jenkins, son of Jenkins Senior next door, was one to be feared. Not only had he been Paddy's form teacher on three occasions, but he'd had to endure years of tortuous P.E. and rugby lessons under his sadistic supervision, the scars resurfacing on stormy nights.

First year in school hadn't been so bad because he was one among many small lads dawdling along the corridors. He'd heard stories about the rugby master, but didn't encounter him until his third year, by which time he was still the shortest boy in school. In gym lessons he encouraged the rest of the class to laugh at Paddy in his feeble attempts to execute a handstand, and when he failed to mount the pommel horse Griffith Jenkins yanked him up by the shorts, with a firm grip on the boy's testicles. In a kinder mood, Jenkins gave Paddy tuition in how to catch, throwing a medicine ball at him and knocking him down like a skittle time and time again. Paddy never complained or cried, but it did nothing for his self-esteem.

On the wind-swept rugby pitch the ordeals were no better, though the giant of a teacher had less time to pick on individuals. Paddy invariably dropped the ball, but when it did come into his possession, Jenkins pulled out his stock of sarcasm.

"Come on, Paddy, run with it. Let's see the blood of the Irish in you!" Paddy could understand football, but rugby was a vicious free-for-all, with people contorting their bodies for no purpose. On one grey November afternoon he ran across the pitch after being delivered the ball, then changed direction and touched down as he'd seen the other boys do, scoring the only 'own-try' in the history of the school. For his efforts, Griffith Jenkins hoisted him in the usual way, before throwing him face down in the mud and standing on his head. When he emerged, spitting the sludge out of his mouth and looking like a parody of a black slave, the teacher handed him the ball and told him to convert his own try. Paddy didn't have a clue what this meant, and on being told he had to kick the ball from in front of the posts, succeeded in connecting at his third attempt, the ball spinning a distance of two yards into the quagmire. Great guffaws all round and another anecdote for the staffroom, no doubt.

By the time these mid-winter matches had ended, Paddy was a degree or two colder than the rest of the boys for the simple reason that he didn't take part in the heat of the battle. It was safer to stay well away from the ball, but it meant that the changing rooms became another source of mental and physical torture. With his hands frozen stiff, Jenkins's advice was to get straight into the hot shower, where Paddy's fingers turned red and he felt such a searing pain that he was ready to cry. He looked around to see if the effect was the same on the other lads, but they had long learnt to bathe their fingers in tepid water. The show wasn't quite over; on coming out of the showers, his teacher made fun of his shrivelled willy, though this was a commonplace affliction on a cold day, even for 'Big-Bull' Johnny Phelps.

If Paddy had been any good at Maths, he would have realised these incidents were having a negative cumulative effect. On the plus side, they'd all taken place in P.E. lessons or on the rugby field; he hadn't yet been humiliated in front of the girls. His tormentor would soon put that right. Each Monday morning, it was the custom for pupils to hand over their dinner money to the form teacher. On the same day that class clown Mathew Griffiths received a dead arm for delivering his payment in penny pieces, Paddy had clean forgotten to pick up his loot from the kitchen table. Griffith Jenkins fondled his steel ruler and barked at the boy to bend over and face the blackboard. The expected blow failed to materialise, Paddy paralysed in that position for an eternity, before a burst of raucous laughter alerted him to the fact that his teacher was standing at the back of the room with his arms folded. Ha, bloody, ha! Big man, aren't you, Jenkins?

18

In the library, time was ticking by. Mair Watkins had a meeting at ten o'clock with the County Librarian, but Lucy hadn't turned up to work and she was becoming anxious. The girl was the embodiment of reliability, her sparkling personality lighting up the place a full twenty minutes before the doors officially opened. She'd first met Lucy in her adult literacy classes five years ago and had been able to offer her a job two years later.

She could ring her at home, but didn't want to risk embarrassing her in front of her parents. Perhaps she'd called in to see Paddy at the Co-op, perhaps she wasn't well, perhaps... she'd have to leave it for now, Mair had a meeting to get to.

Mair liked Daniel Reeves and didn't mind him polishing off the giant packet of lemon puffs she brought in when he visited. The feelings of deep respect were reciprocated by Mr Reeves, who knew he had an outstanding colleague on his hands. She was highly intelligent and had worked hard to make the library the hub of the community. For his part, he diplomatically spent half his life praising the master plans of dull-witted power-hungry councillors, before persuading them that doing the opposite was their idea. He had saved a few old buildings and ancient oak trees in his time, and quietly argued that libraries contributed to the wellbeing of society.

With money tight, it was more difficult to argue the case for retaining a library in a semi-rural location such as Downhill, but Mair had made his job easier. In addition to the well-established maths, Welsh and English classes, she had managed to find enthusiastic tutors for embroidery, pet care and cider-making. Her most recent triumph was the darts session, having acquired the services of Arrows Parry on idle Monday evenings, the odd breakage covered by petty cash.

"What little play have you got lined up for us this year, Mair?"

"*A Penny For A Song.*" Daniel was a well-read English scholar, but she could tell that she'd stumped him. "John Whiting – English playwright, wrote it back in the 1950s."

"Oh, same bloke wrote *The Devils*. Um... got to put my hand up here, that's the only one of his I'm familiar with. Based on Aldous Huxley's book? God, Mair, it's a bit heavy for Downhill Repertory Company, isn't it? You haven't made a pact with Satan, have you?"

From her desk in the main library, Jan could hear Mair giggling; Mr Reeves was a real card.

"*A Penny For A Song* is completely different. It's set in Dorset during the Napoleonic Wars. It's a comedy, farce really, though there are lovely touches of satire."

"Oh? Doesn't sound like a comedy to me."

"Oh, yes, it's wonderfully light, delightful characters, but serious issues are touched on, you know, warfare and poverty. Whiting was a conchy, changed his mind later and joined up, but the play discusses the stupidity of war."

"Can't see our Milwaukee crew going for that. I mean, something like a free healthcare system is pretty stupid, but a fondness for warfare shows how well-adjusted America is, doesn't it?"

"They won't understand the subtleties. Maybe I could introduce a mass shooting into the script!"

"A serial killer at the very least. That would go down well."

"To be honest, there are plenty of pretty costumes and visual effects to keep them happy."

"And what about the natives?"

"They'll probably think it's a pantomime."

"Not a musical, then?"

"Yeah, I know, they all want to sing. Fortunately, it was adapted into an opera by Richard Rodney Bennett in 1967, so we can use a couple of songs. I want to stick to the original script, though I'll shorten some of the dialogue. Talking of which, the book's out of print. Don't really want to use photocopies. I've managed to scrape ten copies together through inter-library, but I need another five. Perhaps you could use your contacts. Here, take a copy with you, I'd like your take on it."

Daniel Reeves flicked through the booklet. "And what about our American friends?" Daniel asked mischievously, a big grin sweeping across his face.

Mair Watkins laughed. "As long as we include a Petula Clark number, they'll be happy."

It was Daniel's turn to laugh. "How's Lucy doing, by the way?"

"Oh, she's great, Daniel. Come a long way in three years. I want her to play *Dorcas* in the play. She'll have a song, she's got a lovely voice. Auditions next week, but she's got the part."

"Anyone else penned in?"

"We need a handsome soldier. No, not you, Daniel," she added, as he playfully raised his eyebrows. "I realise you're a very distinguished actor, but we need someone in their twenties."

"Toy boy, eh? Careful what you say, Mair. Wait 'til I tell Talfryn." Anyone else and she'd have punched him in the face, but Daniel and her husband were good friends.

Having seen him off with a big fat *cwtsh*, Mair Watkins returned to regular duties. She wondered if Lucy's ears had been burning. Damn, Lucy! During the sixty minutes she'd spent in the charming company of Mr Reeves, she'd forgotten all about her. She looked over inquiringly at Jan on the desk, who mimicked a sad face and indicated the reading room.

She found Lucy sitting in the corner, elbows folded on the table, head down and likely to stay there for a while. Mair sat next to her and put her arm gently around her shoulder, letting the silence do the work. A light tap on the door was not quite enough to stir her, but Lucy could sense that a mug of tea awaited her, courtesy of Jan. Biscuits as well, probably.

Mair had first met Jack and Alison Harries, Lucy's mam and dad, when they'd escorted her to the literacy class, and realised they were very protective of her. Parents of any vulnerable and impressionable teenage girl would be wary of the predators lurking around every corner, but their daughter was not stupid and could teach Jack and Alison a thing or two about sex. How to enjoy it, for a start! Unknown to Lucy, her father shadowed her every time she went out, making sure she was home safely.

Mr Harries was not someone Mair Watkins found attractive; in fact, he looked as if his face had been sucked through a straw. You'd have to get on the waiting list if you wanted to murder him, but it couldn't be done by slitting his throat – he didn't have one. Basically, he was safe, respectable and boring, not one to set the party alight. He had followed the antics of Mr Spring with increasing consternation, mortified that the town's law enforcement officer should suffer such humiliation at the traffic lights. That damn 'Chalksy' had resurfaced, alluding to the incident with great 'wit,' adding to the dismay spreading like wildfire amongst the upright and virtuous. The town mongrel was now loping about the streets with a board around his neck bearing the words '*Spring rolls over Plod*.' Whatever next?

The librarian's instincts were correct, though it took her a fair bit of coaxing and a box of tissues to elicit the story. At breakfast that morning Lucy's father had 'gone nuts,' waving the evening paper in her face. Based in Swansea, some hack had cobbled together a short article which linked the infamy surrounding Mr Spring to the bad blood that had existed in the past over trivialities baffling to any rational person. If he was to be believed, the 'economic backwater' of Downhill was in a state of civil war. Her father had described Mr Spring as a 'bow-legged freak' who had made their town a laughing stock. God help them if the London tabloids got hold of it.

It was what Jack Harries said next that had devastated his daughter. Reading betwixt the lines, Mair could see Lucy's mam twiddling her apron in the background, fearing that her husband was losing it.

"We'd never have this problem if he hadn't got hold of that

bloody pile of junk he drives around like a lunatic. Jesus Christ!"

"I wish you wouldn't swear, Jack."

"The man's a pest, someone should put him down."

"Now, Jack....."

"And where did he get that juggernaut? You don't see many of them to the square mile. Where did he get it, Lucy?"

"Jack!"

"I'll tell you where he got it. That boyfriend of yours takes him all the way to Swansea and pays for it out of his own savings. Not satisfied with that, he lays on a broken-down waggon as well. Can you believe it!"

"Not Paddy's fault."

"You think that old weirdo would have thought of it by himself?"

"He's not a weirdo, he's a nice man."

"Ha, sooner you finish with that half-wit of a boyfriend of yours, the better." Lucy was in tears. She'd heard other people call him similar names. She ran upstairs to her bedroom, but her father hadn't finished. "And he's too old for you, my girl, you're only half his age."

Alison Harries found Lucy's room shut tight and could only hope she hadn't been locked out of her daughter's life. Lucy emerged an hour later, freshly made-up, and made her way to the bus stop. Having lent an ear for an hour or so, Mair was determined to finish on a positive note, delighted when Lucy accepted the part of *Dorcas*. She hoped that the whole affair with the tricycle would soon blow over, but acknowledged she'd aided and abetted Paddy in acquiring the trike, a serious violation of British law.

19

Saturday evening was 'darts night' in the Globe, attracting a boisterous crowd of unmanageables, disorderly long before they became drunk. The team of six heroic warriors played in the local league once a month, January's home fixture pitting them against *The Drovers Arms* in Moch-yn-dra, famous for its outstanding slaughtermen. 'Arrows' Parry as captain was top-drawer, but led a mediocre team, their only victory coming against *The Lamb and Flag* crew, who had turned up 'cockles' before Christmas, unable to find their fingers let alone their darts. Arrows didn't take kindly to Mr Spring shaping his face into that stupid grin of his and describing the Globe boys as the 'Farts Team' to anyone who would listen.

He'd started the darts class at the library in the hope it would help sharpen the team's skills, as well as attracting new blood. Unfortunately, the boys hadn't improved over the three years they'd been playing and no amount of practice made any difference. Any new blood usually ended up splattered over library books. Paddy was the first to enrol, but his fiery enthusiasm couldn't make up for poor co-ordination. Arrows rewarded his effort by making him the seventh 'member' of the team, explaining to the opposing captain that when Paddy threw, his darts wouldn't be counted.

Lucy was a big fan of Phil 'The Power' Taylor, but her interest in the sport was confined to armchair viewing. Paddy was gutted that his girl hadn't come along to support the team, but she found the atmosphere too rowdy. That had all changed after the run-in with her father, Lucy taking every opportunity to defy the Trading Standards Officer and his petty rules. When she marched through the doors of the pub, a delighted Paddy scuttled over to give her a *cwtsh*, pushed her to the bar and ordered two cokes.

There was always room at the table for a pretty girl, and a dust-up developed amongst a scrum of dirty old men competing for Lucy. It was a choice between loathsome, repulsive, or nauseating, and in the end she squeezed herself between two of the least repugnant gents. While she enjoyed male attention, she had been sheltered from the world of coarse beer-drinkers and felt increasingly uncomfortable. She was offered enough coca cola to dissolve a vatful of Mexican drug dealers and by the end of the evening had the option of more than twenty hunks to take to bed. What more could a girl ask for?

The match kicked-off at eight after the referee blew his whistle, amid great cheering from the assembled drunkards. From then on, darts took second place, the object of the game to use each second of their valuable drinking opportunities, or 'VD' time as it was known parochially. Despite Arrows's best efforts, the result was so predictable that bookmaker Ricard Sharp would only accept each-way bets.

Lucy sought the peace of the ladies' toilets as often as she dared, her attempts to engage her boyfriend scotched by the misogynistic slaughtermen. She managed to witness one of Paddy's throws, acutely aware that the *Drovers* were pulling the piss out of him and his own team embarrassed by his ballistic malfunctioning. Lucy's first emotion was one of sadness, but she was getting angry; angry her boyfriend was oblivious to the humiliation, angry at herself for pitying him and angry that she was angry. She considered leaving halfway through the evening, easy enough to push the saloon doors open and make her way into the freeze, leaving the sour notes of the piano behind, but she returned to her throne where she had to endure half an hour of smuttiness disguised as wit and repartee. Was Paddy good in bed? Did he have a big cock? Did Lucy enjoy giving him a blow job? But what hurt her most was when Dai Peep told her he'd make a far better sugar daddy than Paddy Trahern ever could. She burnt through the icy air on the way home, angry for thinking her father might be right, after all.

20

Phil suggested that they all chip in a fiver, more if they wanted to. Eifion's retirement had been brought forward six months, the Co-op parachuting in a new boss from Swindon, the cultural capital of Wiltshire. Paddy threw £50 into the hat and nobody could persuade him it was excessive. Mr Thomas had been a good manager and he wanted to repay his generosity. Paddy was elected to present the engraved watch, Lucy willing to help him write a little speech. Mair told him not to worry, he was a good talker and could ad-lib when necessary. The party took place a week after the darts match and Paddy insisted on addressing his audience from Mr Thomas's tabletop. He had practised hard at home and wouldn't let himself down.

"Dear Mr Eifion Thomas, on my behalf and my colleagues, you have been a great boss here at the Co-op and now you can embark on a new journey. And of course, Brian, your dog, can bark on a new journey with you. (*expected laughter*) You can no longer rely on Phil, your assistant manager, to make you coffee, but your wife Beryl Thomas will be happy to do so if you ask her nicely. We thank you for your support, encouragement and opportunities, and for turning your blind eye to our many mistakes. You have our permission to put your feet up and though you will miss us sorely, we have dedicated this engraved watch to you so that you can remember us by. Congratulations, Mr Thomas, and best of luck in your future."

Eifion Thomas was visibly moved by the warmth shown by the staff he had nurtured over the last thirty or so years. His philosophy was simple – respect those working for you and they in turn would mirror that respect – and it worked. Not that he hadn't rapped people over the knuckles occasionally, but it was always for a reason. He had seen Paddy grow in confidence, reflected in his eloquent oration, and knew that Phil would have his back when he walked out the door. He would happily accept Paddy's permission to relax, intent on pursuing a few outdoor hobbies, as well as reading books that had been gathering dust for years.

Maurice Spackman was a decent enough bloke, but had the personality of contaminated tripe, having attended countless management courses which specialised in tedium. He regarded himself as the finished article, but it only took a week for Phil to conclude he was an article he'd like to finish. Whereas Eifion would seek his opinion, Maurice invariably started conversations with, 'I have decided that.….' He talked about Swindon as though it were the hub of all wisdom, not the town that voted to twin-up with Braunau Am Inn, Hitler's birthplace.

The other workers carried on in their own sweet way, until rocked by the news one of them was being made redundant. Maurice Spackman's algorithm for measuring productivity was conclusive – Paddy's presence in the store was eating into the profits. The computer didn't recognise components he brought to the job, such as comradeship, kindness and approachability. Phil tried his best to argue Paddy's case, difficult in view of the fact he'd never been offered a formal contract.

"He may not be the most 'efficient' employee we've had, but he knows most of the people in town and folk love talking to him."

"I'm trying to run a business, Phil, not a day centre for the decrepit. And on top of everything, his timekeeping is atrocious. How he was ever given a job here in the first place beats me."

"Yeah, he may turn up twenty minutes late, Maurice, but he always works over his time. Sometimes he'll stay on an extra hour."

"Stacking tins? He can't even reach the third shelf."

Phil realised Captain Spackman could probably head-butt a ram into a coma, but stood his ground until he'd secured one shift a week for Paddy, with the proviso someone buy him a clock that worked.

Paddy didn't seem overly concerned he'd been shafted, happy to come in on a Monday and satisfied with his £200 compensation. He trotted up to the library, calling in at Pat and Bill's *Blooming Good* to buy a bunch of daffs for his loved one. Mair Watkins chatted with him while Lucy finished reading the toddlers a story, asking him if he'd be interested in helping backstage again that year. When Lucy emerged, she was doubly unimpressed - how the hell had he lost his job and why did he think to celebrate with a sad bunch of grotty flowers? Mair stood open-mouthed as Lucy made her way to the staff toilet, leaving Paddy clutching at stalks.

With nothing to do all day, Paddy's visits to the library escalated and Lucy less receptive. She regarded the workplace as *her* space, not an 'add-on' to her social life. Mair had never seen her so moody, but felt she had to sort it out herself. Would she have interfered in any other couple's business? No, but seeing Paddy go home with his tail between his legs upset her, and she decided to have a word in his ear. Paddy accepted that their dates would be more exciting if he gave Lucy breathing space. There were plenty of things he could do with his time.

21

With his new toy, Mr Spring was determined to make the most of life, spending at least four hours on the road every day. To help him avoid personal injury and death, Dai Grease had wisely screwed a series of reflective triangles to the back of the trailer as well as fitting front and back lights, powered by a dynamo. The tricyclist didn't know the meaning of 'leisurely motoring' and with his yellow oilskins became a common sight on the roads, lit up like a mobile lighthouse.

He wasn't yet aware of Paddy's misfortune, using his wheels to shop at the big Tesco store in Llan rather than the local Co-op. The first time he rolled up, he parked plum outside the entrance and asked a heavily pregnant lady to help him dismount. It wasn't long before he'd explained the drill to the young trolley boy and an unofficial arrangement was reached. Just as he'd seen in the big Hollywood films, the important guest now had a valet to park his artic and retrieve it once he'd done his shop. Unlike the story on the silver screen, his personal attendant received no remuneration.

Paddy assumed he'd be spending more time with Mr Spring, but it seemed his friend had disappeared off the face of the earth. Gwanwyn reckoned their friend set off early in the morning and returned late evening, when the harsh clanking sound told her he was manoeuvring his five-wheeler into the lock-up.

"God knows how he de-saddles, Paddy, but I hears him cussing and laughing at the same time. I think he jus' falls off the trike and the wall keeps him upright. Wouldn't be surprised if he got some nasty abrasions running up his arms," she added, impressing Paddy with her medical knowledge.

Paddy was not one to sit around moaning all day. As a boy he'd been an avid fan of *Blue Peter* and had taken part in the Garden

Birdwatch with his mam a couple of times. He still had the *Ladybird* book of garden birds she'd secured from Electrical's Accepted against fierce competition from Mrs Tarling, who was researching her family tree. The RSPB survey at the end of January had become more popular over the years and Paddy was determined to take part. He would utilise the pair of old binoculars Mr Spring had bought him as a thankyou present from the only shop catering specifically for dogs, the *Salivation Army*, but first he needed to tidy up the garden.

He had given the grass a good scything in May, but it had collected a colourful following of wildflowers by August and was now an untidy mess. The autumn leaves which had come tumbling down were heaped up all over the garden, courtesy of the four winds. And the vegetable patch, which his neighbour tut-tutted about, had gone to seed years ago, a ragged army of drunken waifs and strays in which the cats prowled and piddled. Paddy knew that it was an ideal environment for attracting wildlife, but the whiskered fraternity had seen off too many sparrows and robins for his liking. He had hung feeders on the two trees, mixed-seed on the dead cherry tree in the centre, peanuts for any little birds that wanted to visit the wych-elm shading the bottom of the garden.

Talking of tits, Miss Humidity had given them a few dull, grey days, cold enough, but ideal to work in. And when he set his mind to something there was no stopping him, willing to slog through the dark early mornings as long as he'd hoovered up his mug of hot chocolate. His father's compost bin was still there, waiting to be complimented on its condition after all this time. Paddy would need to replace the bottom slat, and if he couldn't get the hang of the screwdriver, would hammer it home. The tip on his dad's Phillips screwdriver had eroded and Mr Spring advised him to go to the surgery, ask specifically for Dr Eurig Lake, and tell him his right hand was sprained repairing the compost bin. As an avid DIY enthusiast, he would be sure to prescribe Paddy a new screwdriver. Dr Lake was hard of hearing, so he'd have to speak up – on one occasion, Brian Griffiths, the local plumber, had asked for his prescription and been told 'you're a short, ugly bastard, Brian.'

He raked up the leaves first, using them as a base for the compost, then jumped off the stepladder into the bin, stamping up and down on them. Over the next two days he hacked away at the grass, weeds, wildflower corpses and blackberry brambles like a manic golfer, before meticulously lopping it all into tiny pieces. He did the same with twigs and fallen branches, until he had a wonderful stack of chippings to add to the mulch.

Friday January 29th was his chosen day and he rose early to make a list of garden birds, optimistically adding golden eagle, flamingo and parakeet to his inventory. He went downstairs to unlock the shed, hauling out the bags of seeds and peanuts to get at the stepladder. He remembered his mam's warning to wipe the steps dry, before mounting them and retrieving the two feeders. He felt a thrill of anticipation as he topped them up, not worried about an ounce or two of spillage. Grumps next door had told him they would attract rats, but Paddy thought rodents were smart creatures. He'd never seen one carry a gun, let alone shoot a human. And he certainly didn't want a sanitized backyard in which nature was frowned upon.

Paddy settled himself at the back bedroom window, binoculars, can of coke and jumbo packet of cheese and onion to hand. He was so excited when the first sparrow landed that he absentmindedly took a bite out of his new alarm clock. The RSPB directions were to count the birds that landed in a particular spot over a one-hour period, but Paddy thought a shift of four hours would be of more help. It was the first time he'd spent time studying the garden visitors with the glasses and was amazed by the detail they picked up. He'd assumed it was the blue tits that took charge of the peanut tower, but was now able to recognise coal tits as well. It was mainly sparrows that descended on the seed feast, a crew of about twenty, relieved by a different family shortly afterwards. A couple of ravens bust a gut trying to peck at the seeds, but the bird-feeder was designed for small players, and they soon tired of flapping their wings. They wisely joined the collared doves, wood pigeons and one cheeky robin that fed on the scraps falling from above. The magpies were keeping an eye on proceedings, as usual.

One bird Paddy hadn't seen before turned out to be a bit of loose bark flapping in the wind, bigger than a thrush, but smaller than a crow. This he designated to the column headed 'unknown species,' going some way to redress the huge decline in bird numbers. Paddy added a red woodpecker and seagull to his list just in case, visitors the RSPB would be cock-a-hoop about.

With his stomach telling him it was dinner time, Paddy closed the book and put the pencil to bed. Out of the corner of his eye he saw a couple of birds making for the compost bin. At first, he thought the one in the lead was a raven, but this was a smaller chap with a striking orange beak, Mrs Blackbird close by. His mam had taught him that blackbirds mate for life, but he'd never seen a pair together. Paddy followed the male through his binoculars as it foraged around, before popping next door. And then came the crack! Paddy froze as the bird keeled over, its wings beating for a moment, then lay still, his beautiful beak unable to save him.

Out of his bunker came the brave assassin, smoking gun in one hand, shovel in the other. He unceremoniously scooped up the still warm corpse and deposited it in the shiny aluminium dustbin, unaware of the grieving widow at the top of the elm tree. He'd had two kills that week, proving he had the upper hand over anything Mother Earth could throw at him.

A horrified Paddy screamed 'fucker' at Jenkins Senior, but he'd retreated to his living room and his rugby, opening his six-pack and hurling abuse at the opposing team. Paddy threw on his coat and ran to the library, wanting to share the sickening spectacle with someone who'd understand. He found Lucy at the desk, chatting to a tall, fair-haired young man, and Paddy fidgeted in an attempt to get her attention. They were getting on well, joking about Mrs Watkins's play. Rehearsals were about to start, and from what Paddy could make out, the bloke his girlfriend was talking to was

79

taking one of the main roles.

He felt a hand on his shoulder and Mrs Watkins guided Paddy over to a vacant table, aware he wasn't helping his cause by hanging around like a lost puppy. She felt slightly guilty that Lucy was lapping up the attention of handsome Gwilym James, the mercenary, *Edward Sterne*, with whom *Dorcas* falls in love. Paddy brought her back to earth by relating the execution of the beautiful songbird by Jenkins Senior next door, but refrained from calling him a 'fucker' in front of Mrs Watkins. She knew Paddy well and concurred with Lucy that he was incapable of concocting a story and was someone who naively took everyone at their word.

"You know who he is, Paddy?"

"Yeah, he's Griffith Jenkins's father." Paddy's old P.E. teacher and tormentor often visited his dad, sharing a beer in the garden if the sun was out.

"Jenkins Senior was P.E. teacher when *I* was in school. For the boys, anyway, we girls didn't have much to do with him, but he had a bit of a reputation as a hard man, played second row for Llan for years. Captain in the end. And Griffith followed in his footsteps."

Paddy wondered if Mrs Watkins was now giving him permission to use the word 'fucker,' but again held back, knowing that you were supposed to talk quietly in the library, and whispering it wouldn't have the same impact.

"Lucy's talking about the play with that man."

"Yeah. We'll be starting on it properly next week. You're going to help paint the scenery and put the props together like last year, aren't you, Paddy? We need all the help we can get."

"Of course, that. Have you got a screwdriver class at the library, Mrs Watkins?"

Mair laughed. "No, but Mr Parry tells me you're improving at darts every week. In the pub team, now, aren't you?"

"Yeah. My dad's darts were too heavy, so Mr Parry told me to buy a small set with plastic flights he'd seen in *Electrical's*. Easy to use. Now I want to learn how to turn a screwdriver the right way.

Help Mr Watkins with the props, then."

Mair's husband was a kind, patient man and invited Paddy to the house on a Wednesday evening for a 'screwdriver class'. Paddy was surprised his first lesson comprised colouring pictures, cutting paper with a scissors and catching a ball in both hands, but he went along with it.

Paddy spent the first twenty minutes of the second week patiently extracting assorted nails Mr Watkins had driven into a wooden batten. Neatly returning the pincers to the tool box, it was time to tackle the screws. He followed carefully as Mair's husband drilled some holes in the wood, before he deftly drove a screw into place.

"Your turn, now, Paddy. Start with this Phillips, it'll be easier." Unlike his father's battered tool, Mr Watkins's screwdriver had a magnetic tip and placing the screw was painless, but when he tried to turn it, old clumsy childhood memories came flooding back. Mr Watkins went to fetch an old clock, a bit like one of the antiques Paddy had seen in *Junken Orgy*. They had a bit of fun differentiating between 'clockwise' and 'anti-clockwise,' Mr Watkins encouraging him to turn the hand faster and faster, first in one direction, then the other. Mr Watkins took over duties on the clock, handing the screwdriver to Paddy and telling him to copy the movements, as if he was doing the job for real. It took a while, but, at last, success! In the next ten minutes, Paddy screwed and unscrewed six of the little cross-heads and Mr Watkins gave him the screwdriver to practise at home. Next week they'd have a go with the flat-head.

"What props are we doing for the play, Mr Watkins?"

"Oh, it'll be more fun this year, Paddy. Apart from the usual, we need a tree, a well, and believe it or not, a fire engine and a hot air balloon!"

"Hot air balloon?"

"Yeah, and we've got to get it to appear above the stage and descend into the well. Think we need scaffolding to build a small bridge. Bloke who runs the scrapyard does scaffolding on the side."

81

"Bastard, you mean."

"Yeah, funny old name. Do you know him, then, Paddy?"

Paddy knew him all right.

22

"Whoa there boy, steady up!" Mr Spring enjoyed all the cowboy films and talked to his trike as if it were a horse. He had seen Paddy on the pavement and squeezed the brakes hard, causing his vehicle to jack-knife, bringing him at a convenient right-angle to his friend. Ben Davies, who had been following him in his milk float, had to swerve, losing a crate or two, but he didn't mind. He liked Mr Spring and the trouble he was causing in his home town.

"Where you been hiding, boy?"

"We got a new manager. Only working one day a week, now."

"I've been shopping up in Llan, now I've got wheels. Got my own parking spot."

"Is that where you're off, now?"

"No, mun, just going for a ride, that's all. Tell you what, jump in the back and we'll go home, have a cup of tea. You can tell me what's been happening."

Ben had swept up the last of the glass and was more than happy to give Paddy a leg up into the trailer.

"You'll have to keep a step-ladder in the back, Paddy."

"Couldn't spare us a pint, Ben, could you. We're going home to have a cuppa. Not one of them broken bottles, mind."

"Here, take two in case you breaks one of them," joked Ben.

A modicum of cussing and grunting later, and Mr Spring and his passenger were on their way. Paddy had never felt so exhilarated, the cold wind quaffing his hair like Tintin, and lighting up his nose. Mr Spring turned right off the main road without indicating, causing a white van driver to scream a string of recommendations at him in alphabetical order, beginning with the letter 'F.' The trees on the left-hand side became a blur and once on the common the ditch may as well have been a precipice, but they survived, news that would have been greeted with much chagrin by all upright folk had they known the situation.

Paddy soon put the kettle to work and Mr Spring brought out the chocolate biscuits. The nattering went on until early evening, to the accompaniment of a plague of Richard Clayderman CDs, including *A Little Night Music* and his *Thousand Greatest Hits*.

"I was watching a good film last night, Paddy."

"DVD?"

"No, on the telly, mun. Old film, *5.40 from Paddington*. 'Bout a woman gets strangled on a train. You never been murdered on a train, Paddy?" he joked.

"Not as far as I know." It was worth thinking about, though.

"I was murdered once, just getting into Port Talbot. Reported it to the police, but they didn't want to know."

Paddy laughed.

"I love any film with a train in it, mind. Best one was Burt Lancashire – *The Train* - set in France in the war. I could watch that every day of the week, never get tired of it."

"*Sound of Music*'s my favourite," replied Paddy.

"Yeah, I've heard you and Lucy sing some of your favourite things."

The conversation turned to all aspects of music. Eddie Spring wanted Paddy to listen to some opera, on which he was an authority, but darkness had fallen and Verdi could wait another day. That didn't stop him belting out the Anvil Chorus, or as much of it as he could remember.

He had a voice similar to Pavarotti's, but out by a semitone or two. He intended to join the local choir, having seen a notice in Mr Phawsgin's shop urging the sons of the town to attend rehearsals on a Friday night. They were particularly looking for top tenors, but everyone was welcome.

"You should come along, as well, Paddy, you can keep a tune. And Lucy, if she wasn't a girl. How is she, anyway, haven't seen her since the darts match."

"Ah, she's ok." Paddy didn't want to reveal she'd missed their last two dates, once because she was unwell and last night because she'd been washing her hair.

23

Mr Spring and his young benefactor went from strength to strength, with cultural visits to the cinema, circus, fair, the races, the hairdresser and religious churches. Eddie drove straight through the nettles in the old graveyard of Twpsant to find the headstone of his father, Andy, the famous pole-vaulter who had represented the colony of Wales in the 1938 British Empire Games in Munich. He had been beaten into last place by the famous Thelma Moorcroft of Southern Rhodesia, his disappointment quickly fading on being introduced to the even more famous Herr Hitler, who spoke perfect German.

Mr Spring told Paddy to unroll the wrapping paper he'd cadged off Billy Hook and tie it top and bottom to the gravestone.

"Make sure it's flush, Paddy."

"Eh?"

"Right up against the surface of the stone. Use the step-ladder, tie the top." With no wind to battle against, Paddy eventually managed to wrap the chord twice round the stone and secure it by weaving the end tightly enough through the double thickness. He wasn't yet able to tie a knot, but realised that the screwdriver classes were paying off, and was dead chuffed when Mr Spring heaped praise on him.

"Catch!" Eddie chucked a bag of charcoal sticks over and Paddy achieved another first by catching it first time. "Now, what you got to do is rub the charcoal gently over the paper. The inscription – the words – on the tombstone will show through. Stand on the step-ladder, start at the top and work your way down, I would. Not too gently, mind." Paddy concentrated so hard his tongue seemed to have grown into a snake.

"Right, we'll roll her up carefully an' take her home." Back at the flat, Paddy used a wadge of blue-tac to secure the gravestone rubbing above the headboard of Mr Spring's bed. The step-ladder was becoming an invaluable friend.

"Bloody marvellous, mun. Every time I go to bed, I'll be with my dad. Thank you, Paddy, boy!"

Two days later, with snow in the air, the two friends braved the elements and set off for Llan, where the ragged circus big top stood proudly beside the fairground. Mr Spring persuaded the ringmaster that there was plenty of room inside for his trike and trailer and that the audience would think he was part of the act. Although he did run the clown over on the way in, raising hoots of laughter, he and Paddy were excused the entrance fee. The highlight of the show were the two pigs that balanced on the see-saw held up by a beer barrel, exotic animals long since banned by law.

On to the fair. Helped by the hefty bouncers and trusty ladder, Messrs Spring and Trahern were able to have one go on the dodgems before light flakes of snow caught their attention. Probably best get home. With the wind behind them they made good time, but Paddy had to face the southerly wind blowing from Mr Spring's arse. Despite the draught, it was still pungent.

"Oh, Eddie, mun!"

Today Mr Spring wouldn't blame the beans as he usually did. He turned his head round best he could. "Sorry, Paddy, peas and swedes colluding with evil intent."

"Colliding, more like!" laughed Paddy.

About a mile from Downhill the flurries turned into a blizzard and even Eddie Spring's muscle was impotent in the face of such violence, the road a toboggan run. Fortunately, they'd become marooned outside a gate and they managed to pull and push the trike into the driveway, off the road. Using the step-ladder as a sled, Paddy dragged the prostrate Mr Spring towards the large, grey house. With no-one at home, Paddy managed to break one of the windows of the back door, thank God, and gain access.

The living room was colder than the storm outside, but once

again fortune favoured them. Stacked neatly to one side of the fireplace, a pile of logs and branches were waiting patiently. With doors and curtains closed and kitchen located, Eddie and Paddy dragged the sofa in front of the fire and spent a comfortable night listening to *Oasis*, *Blur* and *Pulp* CDs, in the absence of Richard Clayderman. Not very considerate hosts.

They woke to the unique silence that heavy snowfall brings. By mid-morning Mr Spring judged the road to be passable, though lesser mortals would have shivered and gone back to bed.

"Do you think we should leave them a note?" asked Paddy, "tell 'em we'll pay for the back door."

"Say nothing's best," answered his partner. "What we will do, though, is stack the fire right up for them so that the house is warm when they get home."

"Ah, good idea." Paddy was already hurling more logs on to the blazing hearth.

"Couple of branches as well, Paddy. Chuck 'em on, boy."

Mr Spring shuffled out to the kitchen and shouted for Paddy to open the cupboard under the sink. Wonderful, a small bottle of paraffin to add to the mix. Sad to say, Paddy tripped over the sofa, spilling the liquid onto the carpet. Eddie was annoyed at such a waste, but didn't want to draw attention to the young man's clumsiness, going out to check on the state of his vehicle. Wiping the layer of snow off the trailer would only take five minutes, then they'd be on their way. Paddy yanked the front door shut, the wood happily crackling away in the fireplace, liberally spewing a cascade of sparks onto the carpet.

The journey back was slow, the sky a clear winter blue, a gritting lorry doing its best to turn the pristine white blanket into mush. Mr Spring worked up a sweat ploughing through the snowdrifts, blasting the crystal glazing into busy little showers, left, right and centre. It was Paddy who saw the legs of some animal sticking out of the snowbank as they rounded the corner by the old red telephone box.

"Whoa, Eddie, stop!"

The two men trudged back to the upturned corpse and found that it was dead.

"It's a fox," said Mr Spring.

"You ain't seen his face yet."

"Can tell by its legs. It's a fox all right. Poor bugger, frozen solid. Can't do nothing, Paddy, come on."

But Paddy carried on shovelling the snow away with his hands, curious to see Reynard's face. He was greeted by a wretched sight, the animal looking as if its last act was to laugh at a very droll joke.

"Hang on, look at that Paddy." Eddie Spring was referring to a bullet-hole which had split the fox's forehead.

"Bloody hell! Someone shot him."

"Not necessarily, Paddy," said his partner, taking in the landscape around him. "We wouldn't be able to see it in all this snow, but there might be a suicide note somewhere." Paddy wasn't sure if Mr Spring was having him on, but their conversation was rudely halted by the deafening sirens of two fire engines racing in the direction of Llan.

24

Mr Spring and Paddy were unaware it was they who had set 'Sunnyside' alight, a holiday home owned by a couple from Wiltshire, though they didn't hold back in condemning the arsonists. After an absence of over ten years, it appeared that *Meibion Glyndŵr* had been resurrected, sending the London press into hysterical mode and the British establishment into a cold sweat. MI5 agents were dispatched to the area to bug, burgle and bust anyone over the age of seven who had bought a box of matches or were overheard using the word 'paraffin.'

The trip to the circus had been a red-letter day, but the following Friday passed all expectations. Paddy lacked the confidence to join Downhill Male Choir, but Mr Spring rode up to the primary school entrance in good time and waited for someone to help him dismount. Huw Prys, the conductor, was first on the scene, a little nervous on seeing the man in yellow oilskins with his sights set on joining the choir.

"Heard you wanted top tenors. Well, that's what I am, see." Prys located the step-ladder in the trailer and helped Mr Spring on to dry land. With the cyclist's permission he wheeled the trike and trailer round the side of the building, so that they weren't blocking the entrance. When he entered the hall to run over the notation of one or two pieces with Sioned, the accompanist, he saw that the newcomer had sat down in the front row of the tenor section. The conductor was mindful of how possessive the boys were about their seats, especially those at the front who regarded themselves as the elite singers. Prys accepted the configuration, unwilling to upset the apple cart by moving people about and causing an unremitting period of sulking. He hurried over for a word with Eddie Spring.

"Evening! I haven't introduced myself. Huw Prys, conductor of our little choir."

"Pleased to meet you, Huw. Eddie Spring I am, saw your advert for top tenors in Willy Phawsgin's shop."

"Ah! Well, Eddie, what we do normally is give everyone a voice test before they join the choir."

"No need for that, mun. I know all the songs. Big fan of opera, I am. You sing the Pilgrim's Chorus from Tannhäuses, don't you?"

"Yes, we do, but….." Before he could finish his sentence, Mr Spring was on his way, chest out, head vibrating.

"*Once more with Joy, in my home I made meat….*" Sioned, on her way back from the toilet, stopped in her tracks and started to gurgle. "*….. the cheese I made before is mine…*"

"Mr Spring, Mr Spring!" It was no good, he'd started so he'd finish. Huw Prys would have to be patient. The man had a sweet, delicate voice, but changed key at the start of each line, coughed when he ran out of breath and his eyebrows twitched with every syllable. He'd have to put him off, somehow. "Uh, Mr Spring, Eddie…. We actually sing that one in Welsh. We're doing it at the National this year."

"Tha's all right, mun. Do you want me to sing you a couple of verses of *Myfanwy*? *Paham my dick for you M'fanny….*"

"Oh, shit!" Huw Prys turned to Sioned with a look of desperation on his face. A sensible, sensitive soul, she stepped into the breach, using her charm to persuade the man in oilskins to sit at the side of the hall during rehearsal and that they'd speak to him during the break.

Within the next five minutes the hall filled up, first and second tenors, baritones and basses fired up to set the world alight with their mellifluous tones. They settled into their seats, most of them unaware of the human blaze of yellow on the right-hand side of the room. Those tenors in his vicinity assumed he was one of the visitors that turned up occasionally, often from abroad, eager to witness the magic of a Welsh male voice choir. Jack Harries, an accomplished second bass, had been held up at work and slipped

91

into his place two minutes after practice began. They started with *Crossing The Plain*, followed by *Nidaros* and *Blaenwern*, all numbers designed to clear the vocal cords and test the diaphragm. Like his fellow-choristers, Jack didn't immediately twig that the four-part harmony they loved so well was being challenged that night by a third tenor an octave higher than anything they'd heard before. The opening pieces were so loud that Mr Spring and his unrefined *fortissimo* technique made little impact. It was when Huw Prys asked the boys to fish out their copies of the traditional melody, *Suo Gân*, that the practice went into reverse.

The quieter numbers required subtlety and control, the lullaby proudly regarded as a *tour de force* in the choir's repertoire. Mr Spring wasn't to know this, but even if he had, wouldn't have changed tack; he was a devotee of 'Can Belto', power more important than refinement. The shockwaves rattled all those with false teeth, the whole choir under attack from a strange, discordant clown. The conductor wisely brought the half-time interval forward, Lucy's father and other members of the committee ushering Huw and Sioned into the kitchenette for a pow-wow.

They'd already been rocked at six o'clock that evening by the stern face of BBC's Huw Edwards conveying the news that Sir Wynne Turd-full had had to withdraw from their concert, having 'cleverly' fallen off the podium at the Royal Garden Party and 'accidentally' sniffed the Queen's arse, giving Her Majesty a horrible sense of déjà pooh. Fixing his brown nose could take up to three months. Jack Harries was in no mood for any further disruption.

"What the hell's going on, Huw?" asked the irate treasurer. "You know who he is, don't you?" The conductor lived in Llan, though the antics of Mr Spring *had* come to his attention, and he wanted to skip the bit about him helping the miscreant into the hall.

"He says he saw the advert we put out for top tenors. Wants to join us."

"Well, that is *not* going to happen. You'll have to get rid of him."

"I'm not sure it's down to me, Jack. Perhaps the membership secretary should have a word," said Huw, turning to Philip Main.

"Only way to get that idiot out of here is to carry him out," replied Phil.

"May I make a suggestion?" Sioned's advice was always worth listening to. "How about letting him stay for the rest of the evening? Let him join in with one or two of the songs, but we'll tell him to refrain from singing items we're practising for the concert."

"And how exactly do we do that?"

"I'll talk to him. When you want him to shut up, just say, 'Only those singing in the concert to sing the next number, please.'"

"That doesn't solve the problem."

"Don't worry, Jack, Huw's already mentioned a voice test. I'll tell him we'll do it after practice tonight."

"Well, make sure you tell him he can't sing, Huw. I know you, you're too soft, mun."

Sioned's plan worked to the extent that it gave the conductor a chance to correct bum notes or tweak the tempo, though he had to stop Mr Spring in his tracks on a couple of occasions.

"Only those singing in the concert in St. Martin's, PLEASE!" One or two of the tenors sitting next to the strange man laughed to see such fun, but were pulled up by Huw Prys. "Gentlemen, if you think that your voices are perfect, then you can refrain from singing as well." They'd been told, and shamefacedly diverted their eyes to concentrate on their copies. Jack Harries was well-impressed with his conductor, but would stay behind after rehearsal to make sure he stuck to his guns.

Sioned invited Eddie Spring to sit in the centre of the front row, but he insisted on standing, inching his way forward, before leaning on the piano itself. Huw explained that he could choose any song he liked and sing it without accompaniment.

"Any song? Will *Ave Maria* do you?" Huw looked at Sioned, who tapped her wrist to suggest a time limit.

"Ah, yes, but just the first few bars will do…" Mr Spring had already started, belting out his unique interpretation of the Latin prayer, while Mr Harries at the back, grimaced.

"Right, Sioned will give you a 'Middle C' and I want you to sing *Happy Birthday*."

"Whose birthday is it?"

"No, no, it's no-one's birthday, I'd just like to hear you sing it."

"But I can't sing it if I don't know whose birthday it is, can I? Doesn't make sense." Huw looked baffled, but Sioned could see the man's point.

"Dafydd – sing 'Happy Birthday to Dafydd'.

Having repeated the ditty in the keys of G and D, it was time to give him the bad news. It was the first time that Huw Prys had refused a potential chorister and Sioned could see he was embarrassed.

"You've got a very strong voice, Eddie, and you're obviously a top tenor who's very knowledgeable about music…."

"Yes, you modulate extensively, but unfortunately your voice is a little bit high for our choir," added Sioned.

"You mean I can't join?"

"Why don't you just tell him," came the voice by the door, "you sing too loud and you sing out of tune. No, the choir doesn't want you."

"Oh, oh!" Crestfallen, the old man shimmied towards the exit. "Can someone help me get on my trike?"

"Yes, of course," offered Huw, making for the vehicle and bringing it round to the entrance. Once Mr Spring was in his saddle, he thanked the conductor.

"All right if I come to practice next week?" Huw's face fell. "Just to listen, I mean."

25

Mr Spring's pride had been hurt, but he didn't tell Paddy or Lucy about the voice test, not wanting to bad-mouth her unpleasant father. He had enjoyed listening to the choir and planned to attend a few more rehearsals. He wasn't one to sit around inspecting his fingernails and before long had a business proposition for Paddy, now that he was only working one day a week. Mr Spring hadn't forgotten the underhand way in which Downhill's scrap merchant, Mr Bastard, had cheated his mate over the gas fire.

"We could go into scrap ourselves, see, Paddy. Put it in the trailer, up to the scrappy, bundle of readies in our hands."

"Bastard said they only pay out in cheques these days."

"Um, you're right there, boy, but you got an account, haven't you? All the money can go into your bank and we'll split the profits." And that was the business plan – no need for documentation, marketing tools, analysis of the competition or financial projections, and the company name, *Zap the Scrap*, could be painted on the side of the trailer in five minutes.

"Don't fancy going back to Bastard, mind."

"No, no, boy, we'll take it up Wustraff's in Llan."

The business was launched promptly at eight the next morning, irrepressible enthusiasm making up for the absence of market research. The first port of call was Paddy's shed, which surrendered Mr Trahern's rusty old hand drill and a bag of auger drill bits. They would do a more thorough search another day, it was time to hit the street. Mr Spring waited patiently while Paddy went from door to door, often stopping to catch up on the *clecs*. He was longer than usual in one house in Morgan Terrace, probably feeding someone's cat or helping with the washing up. The early stream of passers-by had dried up and Eddie Spring was glad to see Dai Morgan approaching.

"*Shwmae*, Dai!"

"Hello, Eddie boy."

"Cold, but dry."

"Thank God. Can't stop now, got a doctor's appointment. Apparently, I was born in Tonna, near Neath." Eddie could swear Dai had a local accent, but that meant nothing. Perhaps his family had moved to the area when he was a baby.

Where the hell was Paddy? He was becoming restless with nothing to do, hankering after a good workout in the country lanes, see if he could get those tyres smoking. Paddy, too, had become addicted to the wind crumpling his face and freezing his ears, and after putting out Mrs Budr's bins was willing to settle in the back of the trailer. Two hours' work had only added a few nuts and bolts to their collection, but the word was out – there was a new business in town.

Driving into the harsh February sunlight, both gentlemen sported their sunglasses, bought at a snip in Willy Phawsgin's, a 'two for the price of three' bargain. Willy's 'giveaway week' took place every new year in recognition of his loyal customers, but you had to get there early to catch the worm, in this case the pair of sunglasses.

"Shall he want them in a box? Only, that's a hextra pound, probably."

"No, the cases will do. Good Christmas?"

"They were quiet, as usual. What about us?"

"Yeah, on my own. Boxing Day was great, though, had Paddy and his girl come over."

"Lucy, Jack Harries's little children?"

"That's right, pretty little thing. Lovely voice, too."

"They've had the police in, snooping about."

"Oh?"

"Asking 'bout boxes of matches and paraffin. We didn't want to buy nothing, mind. Wasting his wife's time."

"How much do I owe you?"

"Seeing as it's him, girl, he can have the two for the price of four. How's that?"

"Are you sure?"

"Course he is. Old finger bandage thrown in. He'll tell the wife, now."

*

Looking like a couple of rock stars, the boys decided to explore a few new roads, past the odd farm, an old airfield unbeknownst to them, and an abandoned petrol station. Here they did a bit of scavenging, turning up a rusty exhaust pipe, an assortment of carriage bolts and a bonus in the shape of some garden furniture round the back. The weight was not, as yet, enough to slow down Mr Spring, and he had to suppress Paddy's eagerness to go straight to the scrappy. The following week was a barren affair, a short scaffolding pole the only thing of value to be unearthed. Neither of them would admit it, but they were beginning to feel danted, all the hard work bringing little return.

Changing tactics, Paddy procured the services of a stiff brush and spent a full shift sweeping the rain-sodden streets of Llan, filling twenty potato sacks to the brim. They emptied them out in the municipal park, running them through a garden sieve, only to find that the dog turds greatly outweighed any morsels of scrap. Relations between themselves and the ungrateful residents of the town had soured a little and Mr Spring felt it was time to call it a day; waiting around getting wet was not his idea of fun. They felt better after treating themselves to a hot meal in *Riccardo's Olive Garden*, Riccardo happy to open the beans they had brought with them, and only charging for the toast. The tea was free with the meal. The sun had slyly made an appearance while they were scoffing and the return journey past the gutted holiday home a pleasant experience.

As they came into Downhill Paddy noticed a microwave on the pavement and called for his friend to brake. Further along they found an old iron bucket filled with lead flashing, a car battery wrapped in electrical cable outside another house, and then a real cracker – two pieces of copper piping that had been bent into a U-shape. They weren't to know these were items left out for Mr Bastard on his own pick-up run.

Having secured the tarpaulin tightly, Paddy spent the night at Eddie's flat, before they set off for Wustraff's in the thickest morning fog the area had seen. Mr Spring knew the roads like the back of his hairy hands, but the weight of the scrap slowed them down, resulting in the lights front and back dimming, especially when scaling the hills. The boys had wisely tied a red fluorescent rag to the scaffolding pole and placed it at the rear of the cart as an extra precaution, the traffic happy to follow in convoy. To get to Wustraff's scrapyard Mr Spring had to navigate Llan's busy town centre, then take the road to Colley Industrial Estate. At the traffic lights, motorists peeling off the cavalcade in different directions parped their appreciation. Startled pedestrians began to applaud, unsure for what reason, but certain in their own minds that they had witnessed something momentous. The Mayor of Llan, Idris Nyfe, described Mr Spring and his young friend as lifeboatmen of the highway, who had averted a disaster comparable to the great flood of '92. He wiped away a tear as he asked the crowd to remember Evan Floe, the brave coxswain who had gone down with the inshore lifeboat that day.

'Ropey' Wustraff's scrapyard was well out of town and it needed to be. Approaching it reminded Paddy of old film he'd seen of valleys' slagheaps up around Merthyr and Aberdare. The sun was trying to break through, eager to show the two heroes the harsh civilisation that lay hidden beneath the fog, a jumble of metallic settlements competing with each other in terms of bulk and physique. They parked outside a cabin to the right of a huge iron gate, but could find no human life form on their newly-discovered planet.

Mr Spring was not one to hang around, Paddy off balance as he careered down a rough track and spun to a sudden stop, narrowly avoiding a pallet of car batteries. The son of Wustraff, a veritable giant, appeared from the confines of a storehouse only marginally taller than himself.

"Got some scrap for you," said a delighted Eddie Spring.

"Graded it, have you?"

"Eh?"

"Sorted it into different metals."

"Aye, we done all that bollocks, haven't we Paddy?" but he wasn't listening. It was payback time for Alwyn Tucker and all Paddy could see was the man's sour *wep*.

Danny Wustraff took a peek in the back of the cart. "See you got a bit of copper piping and lead, I'll have to check the cans and them saucepans, see if they're aluminium. What's in them sacks?"

"Loads of different nuts and bolts and screws of all sizes. You name it, we got it."

"Osama Bin Laden in there?"

"Bin and gone. He was in town last Tuesday, but had to get back to work. Number 11 bus to Karachi."

"Islamabad, you mean."

"Yeah – goes from outside the Co-op. Sends his regards, mind."

"Ha, ha! We go back a long time, him and me. Can you reverse that thing – into the shed?"

"Paddy could help you pull it back."

"No, you're all right." Danny unloaded the non-ferrous metal and told Mr Spring to turn in a circle and drive onto the weighbridge. "Stay there 'til Delme in the cabin gives you the nod. Then drive off the other side and he'll tell you where to unload. Once you've done that, drive back onto the weighbridge from the opposite direction. He'll give you the weight and you can collect your big bucks. It'll be a cheque, mind."

"Yeah, we know that. Come on, Paddy, hold tight." It was the first time for either of them on a weighbridge, and Mr Spring delayed the descent for as long as he dared. He could have stayed there for hours, admiring the view. Delme made out the cheque to Paddy, all £32, eighty-nine pence of it, and scribbled the receipt which they would later flash around in the pub, whooping like a couple of forty-niners who'd struck gold.

Danny Wustraff Metal Recycling
Colley Industrial Park, Llan

24 Kg. mixed metal

5 Kg. copper

2 Kg. lead

1 Kg. aluminium

£32.89

26

Daniel Reeves slid into a seat at the back of the hall, having arranged to go for a drink with Mair after the Thursday night rehearsal. He'd spent two days contacting libraries and drama companies, making good his promise to dig around for copies of the play. His diligence had paid off – not only were there two for the prompter, Mrs Watkins could give one each to the cleaning lady and caretaker if she wanted.

Mair always finished dead on time, the only way to make sure the lads arrived promptly, cutting short their early visit to the Globe, but enabling them to have a sesh afterwards. The two hours passed quickly and though the grand performance wasn't until August, she knew they'd need every possible minute. And the actors were the least of her worries. Her husband, Tal, would supervise the set, an easier job than last year with no change of locale during the course of the play, but there were several crucial theatrical effects to straighten out. And, of course, the musical element; there were only two numbers, but getting the choir and town band to co-operate was like pointing your chimney with cheese sauce.

There was no way Mair would entertain the Globe, to be cornered by half the cast eager to earn her approval. Daniel suggested the *Drovers* in Moch-yn-dra which boasted a tidy lounge without competition from a juke box, karaoke or singing slaughtermen. He would drive his car and drop her back at the hall later. She was so delighted with the books that she gave him a peck on the cheek and insisted on buying the first drink. Mr Reeves would have a pint of the 'black stuff,' Mrs Watkins a large lemon and lime.

"I insisted they pour yours into a pint glass this time," said Mair.

101

"Thank God for that," answered Daniel, "trying to swig out of that plastic potty was a nightmare. I see you've got yourself a pint, as well."

"Thirsty work."

"The rehearsal? How's it going?"

"Yeah, not too bad."

"The characters are very posh. Set in Dorset, isn't it? Will our lot go for it?"

"'Course they will. We've got as much right as anyone to laugh at the English."

"How's the set going?"

"Talfryn's cracking on with that, though we're having to think out the props."

"Yeah, I thought the balloon and the well would be a challenge."

"Not so much the well, I don't think. Tal says there's plenty of room below the stage. Trap door and ladder will do the trick, but the air balloon, that takes a bit of ingenuity."

"Don't see it 'til the second act – Timothy Bellboys?"

"*Sir* Timothy Bellboys, if you don't mind, young man. Yeah, he descends the well in the first act, into the tunnel that leads to the cliffs. Remember now, Daniel, his plan is to appear behind the French army, which he is convinced has landed."

"Dressed as Napoleon Bonaparte. They recognise him as their Emperor and he persuades them all is lost and that they have to retreat. Using a French phrasebook - ingenious."

"Ha, ha. Of course, there is no French Army, but he comes across one of Selincourt's Local Defence Volunteers...."

"Fencibles, a sort of 'Dad's Army'."

"Yeah. Bellboys assumes the poor lad is a French soldier and speaks to him in French. He takes fright, assuming him to be Napoleon and tells Selincourt that the invasion has begun. Timothy Bellboys jumps into the air balloon and releases the anchor. Somehow, he steers it back to the garden of his house."

"Brilliant. And he lands in the garden?"

"Well, no, he hovers like a buffoon for a while, telling everyone he's made contact with the enemy and there's nothing to be worried about. He tries to ascend to continue his mission, but only succeeds in descending the well in the gondola of the balloon. Then we see the balloon rising from the well, empty, and it floats away."

"The audience will love it. The Yanks will go wild!"

"You can see why we've got to get it exactly right."

"Health and safety?"

"I hadn't thought of that, Daniel, but yeah, we'd need to do a risk assessment. I'll contact the council to check the scaffolding."

"So, what's Tal's plan?"

"System of ropes and pulleys. Tal calls it a multi-line system – two ropes and four pulleys and something called a counterweight to help the rigger operate the whole thing from the back of the stage. I was afraid we'd need someone on top of the scaffolding to let the rope down, but Tal laughed at me. Said he'd use a joist and make two big wooden brackets, attach the pulleys to them. Safe as houses he said."

"The ropes will be secured either side of the basket of the balloon?"

"Yeah, the gondola. The envelope of the balloon can be painted on a light piece of hardboard and affixed to the ropes. The most important thing is the positioning of the balloon above the well."

"Who's going to build the rigging?"

"Hoping Bastard will do it."

"The scrappy?"

"Yeah, he's got a scaffolding business as well."

"Good advertising for him."

"Yeah, he'll probably want his logo at the top of the balloon."

"Ha, ha. 'Bastard's Hot Air Balloons.' Have you got a good backstage crew?"

"I'm leaving that to Tal. He just wants a couple of blokes he can trust to do the lighting, electrics and stuff. Otherwise he'd have fifty volunteers tripping over one another."

"Electrocuting themselves."

"Now, that wouldn't be such a bad idea, Daniel. Paddy will help, mind, he's strong as an ox and Tal's been giving him a few woodwork lessons. Says his co-ordination has really improved."

As the evening wore on, talk turned to Lucy and Paddy, Mair still feeling a little guilty about introducing the girl to Gwilym James. If they *had* dated, Paddy didn't know about it and she wasn't sure how he'd react if Lucy did finish with him.

"I should never have helped Paddy find that trike for Eddie Spring, either. Jack Harries detests that man."

"Yeah, I've seen him once or twice shooting through town. Funny, isn't it, people call him 'mad,' but if he was posh, like our Timothy Bellboys, he'd be 'eccentric.'

"Lucy's father gave her a big row 'cause Paddy bought the bloody thing in the first place. And found the trailer for him."

"Oh well, we don't want to tarnish the town's glowing reputation, do we?"

"No, but if you got rid of all the madmen, the population would be in single figures!"

27

Jack Harries had had a good week - a formal warning to Roger Bruise, manager of *FK's*, for selling coleslaw two years out-of-date, and a ticket for the Wales v Scotland game from 'Psycho' Rees, who was flogging dud batteries at Llan market again. His only worry was which petty criminal he'd be sitting next to in the stadium. On top of that, he'd made good progress in investigating a couple of rogue traders – 'roofers' and 'maintenance experts' - who'd been scamming old people after the recent storms, confident of bringing them to court.

Alison had prepared his favourite steak pie, courtesy of Billy Hook, and he was back on speaking terms with Lucy, who was spouting on about the summer extravaganza. He knew the choir would be helping out with the chorus, but their immediate priority was the St David's Day concert in St Martin's church in three weeks' time. His wife had picked up on the fact that their daughter seemed sweet on Gwilym James, but hadn't yet discussed it with her husband. Jack, of course, would love to see the end of Paddy, though a new boyfriend would require resolute inspection.

Having had a shit, shower and shave, Mr Harries contentedly steered his black Astra Mk 5 onto the main road. The drizzle had become a torrent by the time he arrived at the school, but each committee member had been allotted a parking space, whereas the conductor had to fight it out with the rest of the boys. Jack Harries hung his coat up at the back and settled into his seat, next to Albert Snout, officially the deepest bass in the area, who could make the entire row vibrate during the *Roman War Song*, a guilty pleasure they kept to themselves.

Huw Prys ran through some of the Welsh hymns their audience would expect at the concert, items the choir knew inside-out. If there were mistakes, they would be forgiven by the *hwyl* engendered. He then turned to Wagner, warning his men that by next week no copies would be allowed. Albert steadied himself and

Jack gripped his seat firmly with both hands, having already checked that his dentures were in place. No wonder Hitler loved the composer, he had probably used his music to kick-start the Stormtroopers on cold mornings.

As the legionaries convulsed themselves into a turbulent crescendo, led by Senator Albert Snout, Huw was startled by a loud bang behind him, the rumbling rising above the *Sancte Spiritus* and anything the *Cavalieri* had to offer. The tenors noticed first, then the baritones became aware of their distracted conductor moving towards the fire-door, where it seemed someone was knocking frantically from the outside. Gossip-monger and second tenor Stanley Clegg beat him to it, releasing the push bar and flinging the door outwards. The rest of the boys gathered round to witness Eddie Spring clinging on to his handlebars for dear life.

"Sorry I'm late, boys. Had to get Paddy to blow up the tyres. Give us a hand in, will you?"

To be fair to the old man, he listened to the conductor's instructions, only offering his version during the last song of the evening, much to everyone's relief. Jack Harries was livid and spent most of his weekend on the phone to other committee members. Several suggestions were put forward, some more practical than others. Chairman Norman Rock wanted to poison him with boiled sweets, while secretary Alun Thomas proposed the sneakier solution of messing with his brakes, but in the end they decided to confront Eddie Spring at the next practice and read him the riot act. This would be done outside the building before rehearsal started, without the need to involve the conductor or any other bleeding heart.

Lucy's father ordered an early dinner the following Friday evening, before suitably preening himself and setting off on his mission. He joined Messrs Rock and Thomas, and the three of them stood conspiratorially as puzzled choir stalwarts filed past them into the hall.

"If you're sharing a spliff there, boys, I'll have a puff," joked Emrys Bevan, who had been brought up in the fifties, a witty first tenor who always wore check trousers. No-one had thought to bring an umbrella and by quarter past seven the committee looked as if they'd just emerged from the swamp, their testicles clinging to their soggy underpants. When they entered the hall, Sioned noticed the submariners first, stopped playing the accompaniment and struck up the chords to a new song. The boys gradually twigged what was happening and repeated the first two lines of the song time and time again, until the howling drowned out the words:

I'm singin in the rain, just singin' in the rain,
What a glorious feeling, I'm happy again......

There had been no Mr Spring that evening, but the posse turned up with big umbrellas the following week, despite it being a starlit night. The interval turned into a twenty-minute committee meeting, the consensus that Eddie Spring had lost interest in the choir not enough to stop Jack Harries spitting his feathers. There would be practice as usual in a week's time, the concert in St Martin's the following day at 7pm.

"If he don't turn up next Friday, that'll be three weeks," said Norman Rock.

"Yeah," agreed Alun Thomas, whose underpants were still drying on the radiator at home, "he've lost interest, no doubt about it. Probably danting someone else by now."

"We'll see next week," said his treasurer, "we'll get here early again, lock him up if we have to!" Nervous laughter greeted the suggestion, but everyone was quietly confident that the dark days were behind them. This belief was confirmed amid scenes of great joy when only those singing in the concert turned up at the next rehearsal. No sign of the tricycle or its bizarre owner. With a big performance on the horizon in front of important guests, the atmosphere was electric and Huw Prys in a positive mood.

*

The ladies of the choir had excelled themselves, St Martin's church a feast of golden daffodils, though a Welsh flag on St David's Day not yet something everyone felt comfortable about. The fifty strong choir filed into the church from the schoolroom behind the pulpit, magnificently turned out in their purple blazers, striped ties, grey trousers and bald heads. Royston Brace directed them onto the stage, row at a time. As the tallest chorister in the area, he used his height to his advantage, taking no nonsense from anyone under five foot seven.

Norman Rock and his wife Norma, a hard-looking bitch, led the First Minister and his fawning entourage to the front, where they parked their venerable arses. An army of local residents craned their necks in admiration and the flat drone of chitter-chatter became a riotous commotion. Norman joined his comrades in the front row, the coughing ceased, and a burst of applause greeted accompanist and conductor when they appeared from the rear.

Huw Prys couldn't have been prouder of his men had they won first prize in the National Eisteddfod. The opening lines of *Llanfair* hit the gathered spectators like a harpoon and from that moment they were hooked. Mezzo-soprano Elin Lloyd Evans-Jones and her ample cleavage didn't disappoint, either, swaying the audience first one way, then the other. At half time the First Minister of Wales rose to his feet, explaining that he felt more comfortable speaking English, despite Welsh being the only language he'd known up to the age of ten. However, his *shwmae* showed his commitment to the language, echoed in the nervous tittering that rebounded around the hallowed building. His next pronouncement brought a standing ovation. Much as the white dove of peace had landed on the shoulder of our patron saint, so the First Minister would welcome the siting of Britain's nuclear submarines in the deep waters of Milford Haven.

Unbeknownst to the 300 souls packed into the pews, the leader of the country had requested the choir sing *Lily of the Valley*, a negro spiritual his father had sung to him as a boy. Huw buttonholed ancient baritone Walter Garlick, who at five foot five, was familiar with every song that had ever been written. Besides, he often sang the song with the 'wet section' of the choir in unofficial concerts fuelled by alcohol, so most of the boys knew when to come in with the refrain. The spiritual would be the last item of the evening, followed by the national anthems of first, the British Empire, and then the Principality.

An entertaining second half flew by and Walter stepped forward to the front of the stage. The conductor unveiled the extra item, but kept quiet about the baritone's onion-breath. Sioned played the simple introduction and everything fell into place, Walter mesmerising each one-jack present with his enchanting lilt.

He's the lily of the valley
Oh my Lord !
He's the lily of the valley
Oh my Lord !

King Jesus in the chariot rides
Oh my Lord !
With four white horses side by side
Oh my Lord !

He's the lily of the valley
Oh my Lord !
He's the lily of the valley
Oh my Lord !

What kind of shoes are those you wear?
Oh my Lord !
That you can ride upon the air?
Oh my Lord !

He's the lily of the valley
Oh my Lord !
He's the lily of the valley
Oh my Lord !

Huw Prys didn't at first notice the panic on Walter's face as everyone looked forward to the finale with eager anticipation. He'd unaccountably forgotten the words to the last verse, his mind completely blank. Huw mouthed the next line to Walter, while Sioned kept the show going with a few light chords, but the soloist had lost the plot. From the back row of the audience a voice boomed out, a couple of semitones too high, but supplying the missing words, '*These shoes I wear are Gospel shoes*,' and the choir responded instinctively with, *Oh my Lord !* Walter had recovered and was able to join his off-key warbling compatriot in an unusual rendering of the last line,

And you can wear them if you choose
Oh my Lord !
With everyone singing from the same page, the final refrain brought the programme to an end,
He's the lily of the valley
Oh my Lord !
He's the lily of the valley
Oh my Lord !

Walter Garlick acknowledged the applause and accepted the pats on the back from his fellow-choristers as he wobbled to his position in the front row. He looked as if he'd been wired up to electrodes and patriotically wiped the sweat from his face during the national anthems. Eddie Spring's first appearance as soloist with a Welsh male voice choir put him in euphoric mood, the words of *Lily of the Valley* ringing in his ears and powering his dynamo on the homeward journey.

28

The shop fronts were ablaze with pots of bright, crisp daffodils, refusing to be bullied by the cold March wind. They had taken over from the snowdrops, their winter-sisters, which had faded during the past fortnight. Paddy walked up and down the main street with no particular place to go, his eyes scouring the gutter, unable to break the habit of picking up any pieces of metal lurking there. His career as a scrap dealer had been brief, but it had taught him to identify some of the nuts populating the area. He'd marvelled at the bits of spiral coil springs littering the roads, his friend of the same name explaining their function in ensuring a smooth drive. Just as numerous were the delightful little lead wheel weights which apparently balanced the tyres of a car, whatever that meant. Paddy enjoyed sorting them by size. The wheel nuts and lug nuts he'd netted on the industrial estate were heavier and felt cool in his clasped hands, while they'd picked up T-nuts, collar nuts, jam nuts and hex bolts after breaching the security fence at a small building site outside Llan. Paddy had felt guilty about this course of action until Mr Spring pointed out the sign, *Inconsiderate Constructors – We Are Part Of The Inconsiderate Constructors Scheme*.

Paddy dropped his haul of screws, washers and hex keys into the plastic bag he always carried with him, then decided to scavenge in Back Terrace. Outside a scruffy house with a grey blanket as a curtain, he espied a scattered stash of mini torpedoes, their silver coating shimmering in the early spring sunlight. It was as if they'd been dumped, the same as when piggy drivers emptied their car ashtrays at the side of the road, but these things were metal, twenty-three in all, and he thought they might be aluminium, which was counted as 'non-ferrous' material and worth a few bob. With his bag now full, Paddy reckoned he'd done a tidy shift.

When he turned back into Main Street, Mrs Probert waved to him from the opposite side of the road, having sprinted up *Tyle Bach* from FK's mini-market.

"'Aven't seen my Gareth, 'ave you, Paddy love?"

"Who?"

"My husband. Turned my back for a minute and 'e was gone. Normally goes down the *tyle* to 'ave a wazz, but there's no sign of 'im." At that very moment PC. Prys Paddler emerged from the doorway of Electrical's Accepted carrying a plastic truncheon, something he'd always promised himself.

Mrs Probert quickly familiarised him with the facts of the case and he wasn't long in whipping out his notebook. Gareth Probert hadn't been seen for thirty minutes, only had one arm on his left-hand side, was attired in a pair of striped mauve pyjamas, and sported a tattoo of Margaret Thatcher on the right cheek of his arse. With that description, the policeman didn't think it would be very long before someone detected him, especially if his trousers had fallen around his ankles.

"You run home, now, Mrs Probert. Put the kettle on an' make yourself a cuppa. I'll radio the information into HQ and we'll have a search party out in no time at all." Mrs Probert was glad to have some respite and made for her house, unaware that their sneaky constable had no radio.

"You can help us look, can't you, Paddy?"

"Yeah, don't mind, but I've got to call in the newsagent's. I'll catch you up later."

"What are you doing with all that laughing gas you got there, you know they're illegal, do you?" Paddy was clearly stumped, so PC. Paddler approached him and shiggled the bag he was carrying, causing the torpedoes to rattle.

"Laughing gas, Paddy. Drugs! Some people think they're a giggle, but no, they go on to become addicted to hard drugs and stimulants and most of them hallucinate and die."

This informative spiel was well over Paddy's head and not

merely because he was on the short side. The PC was all ears when Paddy told him where he'd found them, and made a bee-line for Back Terrace, talking importantly into his non-existent radio.

Willy Phawsgin had mislaid his spectacles and was glad to hear the door-bell jingling and someone enter the shop.

"Morning, Mr Phawsgin!"

"Ah, Paddy it was. Wish it will be, wish it will be, but he's lost his glasses. Shall he help look for those sort of things, boy?"

"Can you remember where you were wearing them last?"

"On his head, boy, on his head. Needs them things to read the small print."

"Not the only thing that's missing," said Paddy, with no hint of irony.

"To what end?"

"Mrs Probert's mislaid her husband again. No sign of him at the back of FK's. He usually goes there for a wazz."

"Frequently, so he's heard, Ah, here they were, here they were." He folded his glasses and parked them in the breast pocket of his blazer. "Now then, how shall he help him?"

"I'll have a packet of Love Hearts, please, Mr Phawsgin."

"Go well with them laughing gas. Does he want three for the price of four?"

"No, just the one, thanks. Keep the change."

"He will, under the circumstances."

"I'll be off, now, then, help in the police search."

"Remember, he's looking for a one-armed man."

"Like in *The Fugitive*."

"As likely as not, girl, as likely as not. Well, good-night Paddy, sleep tight!"

Paddy took a peek into Back Terrace, where the town constable was casting a trained eye over the *Skid Row* that had laid under the radar for the past forty years. He 'radioed' in, requesting a team of SOCOs secure the area, then attempted to stop the Bonkiff brothers leaving their house. When that didn't work, he stood at the bottom of the terrace to prevent their car turning into Main

Street. They merely drove around him, wound down their windows and told him to 'fuck off,' leaving him with no option but to transmit another SOS message to HQ. Paddy realised the search for poor old Mr Probert wouldn't start any time soon and decided the incident was important enough to inform Lucy up at the library. That was his excuse, anyway. They hadn't been on a date for over a month and when he'd called at her house, had been told by her mother she was out with a friend. He assumed Mrs Harries was referring to bosom pal Betty Bowen, a good laugh of a girl who was taking the part of *Hester Bellboys*, Lucy's mother, in the play. Quite how they were going to make her look old enough, Paddy didn't have a clue, but he'd leave that little worry to make-up artist Prudence Syce, who had perfected the trick on her own face.

29

After the concert, Jack Harries started making inquiries. Walter hadn't caught up with Eddie Spring to thank him for his intervention, and all he did at rehearsal was talk about his hero. Even Huw Prys, with more letters after his name than the Russian alphabet, had taken it all in his stride. He should have known better – Garlick had botched it, allowing the choir to be humiliated by the fastest idiot in the west. And in front of the First Minister of Wales! It had taken intense negotiation to net such an important guest and his attendants. It wasn't like asking Maurice Spackman to open the summer fete, though some clever buggers believed the Co-op manager did more work than the grinning politician ever did. He was slightly placated by the fact his daughter was no longer in cahoots with that other idiot, but something had to be done.

Jack Harries's work as Trading Standards Officer brought him into contact with dozens of organisations, as well as the top knobs in the local council. His first port-of-call was Lance P. Nine-Cocks, director of Llan and District Social Services, arranging to buy him dinner in the fine Italian eating house, *Zits Ristorante*, in the town's Chinese quarter. Both spouses were more than happy to drop them off, an evening without male tedium an unexpected bonus. Even better, the hubbies would avail themselves of taxis home. Empty a bottle and fuck the ironing.

Lucy's father was not a big drinker, but a few glasses of wine would lubricate the conversation and it soon became obvious the director's gullet was not an alcohol-free zone. They were on first-name terms before the first bottle had given up its contents and by the third were considering getting matching tattoos. They would share a taxi, Lance booking it for eleven o'clock and insisting on paying the fare. That was fine as far as Jack was concerned, providing he, Jack, paid for the meal.

"That just leaves the wine," joked Lance. *My word*, thought Jack, *I could only dream we'd have got on so well!*

Jack Harries felt he should strike while the iron was hot and pushed on to the business end of their little appointment. Lance didn't know Eddie Spring personally, but had heard of his exploits through the grapevine. It seemed the police were happy enough for him to stamp the local highways, but would interfere if he ever set foot on the motorway again.

"Perhaps you could arrange for him to take a wrong turning onto the M4, have the cops waiting for him."

"He's too canny for that," Jack explained. "No, what I'm hoping to do is take him out of the equation altogether."

"You mean bump him off?" laughed Lance, "that's a bit extreme, isn't it?"

Jack wasn't impressed, finding the air of jollity irritating. This was no joke. "The man is not only an embarrassment, he's a risk to all of us."

"Um, so what exactly have you got in mind?"

"I don't know, can't he be sectioned under the Mental Health Act?"

"Is he mentally ill? You'd have more luck if you could argue he poses a risk to himself."

"Could he be put in a home. I mean he's in his seventies."

"Don't know if an old people's home is the best place for him. There's a Home for the Ridiculous just outside Twpsant. I think they've got a few vacancies. Matter of finding a reason to admit him."

"Can it be done?"

"Has he got any relatives?"

"No idea, he's probably sent them all to an early grave."

"Ha, ha! Know where he lives?"

"Yeah, up in Policeman's End."

"Ah, council house?"

"Flat, I think."

116

"Well, there may be a way in there. If he's got family, it'll be on his file. Could send a social worker there, see if he's coping. Do a risk assessment – could be a danger to himself, you know, not eating enough, leaving the stove on, overloading the electric sockets. Safer in a home."

"It can be done, then?"

"We'll see what we can do." The two men clinked glasses and downed the rest of the bottle in a token of brotherly conspiracy. The door of the restaurant was flung open by an unhealthy lard of fat come to take the gents home.

"Taxi for Nine-Cocks!" A noisy group of five accountants and four estate agents at the far end of the restaurant stood up instinctively, before sitting down again to resume their meal.

Lance lived in a pretty village the other side of Llan and would be dropped off first, but made sure the cabbie was remunerated for the whole journey. Before Jack fell asleep next to him, he ventured a question he'd been itching to ask.

"Hope you don't mind me asking, Lance, but where the hell did you get a name like that? Not Welsh, is it?"

"How'd you find out?"

"Eh?"

"Who told you? You've been talking to my wife!"

"No, I didn't mean anything by it."

Only my wife knows my middle name is 'Prick'."

30

Paddy left Prys Paddler on his hands and knees in the gutter of Back Terrace, using a magnifying glass in his hunt for the Nitrous Oxide Outfit. He was breathless by the time he entered the library, Lucy diving into the computer corner to 'help' old Mr Twist do his family tree. The only ancestor he'd found so far was a man called 'Oliver', after he'd read about him in an old novel set in London. Lucy had already been very accommodating, but didn't mind him asking for more.

Mair clocked Paddy's body language as he made for the desk; a man on a mission, dying to impart an important piece of news to those he knew best.

"Have you seen Lucy, Mrs Watkins?" Mair instinctively glanced over to where old Mr Twist was crumpled up. Paddy spotted his girlfriend and Mair thought it best follow him over. When he greeted Lucy, she made no attempt to acknowledge his presence.

"Lucy!" Mair watched as Lucy continued to look at the screen, then half-turned and coldly rebuked her erstwhile boyfriend.

"Can't you see I'm working?" A downcast Paddy looked up at Mair, who pointed to the reading room and mimed a cuppa, a diversionary tactic that never failed. This time she was determined Lucy grasp the nettle – it wasn't fair to leave Paddy hanging in the air. Supplying Paddy with the biggest mug she could find, Mair took Lucy into the staffroom, out of range of any ear-wiggers. Lucy agreed to bite the bullet, once Mair had assured her she'd be by her side. The two ladies prepared themselves with a mug of their own and sat down opposite Paddy.

"Mr Probert's missing again," he informed them, "I'll go and join the search in a minute, once Constable Paddler's sorted out the laughing gas. Perhaps Eddie'll help."

"How's Mr Spring doing, Paddy?"

"We've more or less given up on the scrap business, Mrs Watkins. Made a good profit, mind, over thirty quid. Haven't seen him for a few days, but he's been busy with the choir." Yes, Mair had heard something to that effect.

"I'll bring the map up for you and Lucy to look at – when I've finished it," continued Paddy.

"Oh, what map's that? Didn't know you were a cartographer," joked Mair.

"It's for Lucy, really. I've marked down every spot where we've found bits of scrap, green for nuts and bolts, scaffolding poles in red. You'll love it, Luce."

Lucy rolled her eyes and dug her fingernails into the palm of her left hand. The conversation did the usual rounds, before returning to the woes of the Probert family. Mair gave Lucy a little nudge, indicating that now was the time, but her young co-worker had no intention of exercising her vocal cords. She loved the girl, but was losing patience, feeling Lucy sometimes used those big eyes to tease her admirers. When her phone buzzed, she excused herself, but pointedly informed Paddy that Lucy had something to tell him, leaving the ball firmly in her court.

"What 'you want to tell me, Luce?"

"Nothing."

"Oh! When are you going to come over to mine? Or we could go to the cinema in Llan." Lucy couldn't look at him, staring up at the window as though some new species of bird was pecking the putty out. Paddy tried to hold her hand, but was quickly rebuffed, and when Mair returned she could feel the tension.

"Well, have you told him?"

"Tell me what, Mrs Watkins?"

"Lucy!" Lucy averted her eyes to the table in front of her. Paddy looked at Mair and Mair sat down and held Lucy's hand. A triangle of human beings whose lines of communication had broken down. Mair would need to take the initiative.

"Listen, Paddy, what Lucy's about to say isn't easy for her. She doesn't want to hurt you, but….."

"I'm seeing someone else, Paddy," Lucy told the table.

"What 'you mean? You got a new boyfriend?" Paddy searched Mrs Watkins's face for an answer and realised he'd hit the nail bang on the head. The tears welled up in his eyes and he folded his arms on the table and buried his head. Mair stood up and put her arms round his shoulders, while Lucy burst into tears, mirroring sad Paddy Trahern opposite.

Jan and her tray came to the rescue again, a mug of hot tea and a big fat plate of chockie biscuits the best remedy. An impromptu counselling session followed, the two glum chums holding hands and promising to stay 'friends.' Mair pointed out that Paddy might find it difficult working on the set, seeing Lucy and Gwilym James acting closely together, but he enjoyed working with Mr Watkins and had no intention of letting the side down. Mair had no idea how it would play out, but was relieved that Lucy no longer had to dodge the issue.

*

Paddy couldn't understand why he'd been ditched by Lucy, but was glad they were still friends. He turned his attention to Mrs Probert and was hit by the idea that if he found her husband, he would be a hero and win Lucy back. He found PC. Paddler knocking at the Proberts' door, dismayed to see his helmet tucked under one arm, as if about to impart some bad news. Within a few seconds every door on the neat terraced street was open, Paddy thankful to see the familiar form of Eddie Spring slamming on the brakes and stopping outside the house.

PC. Paddler was about to knock again when Elsie Probert appeared, her face turning a ghastly white, giving her the look of a ghost emerging from a dark passage. The PC checked that his radio was still working.

"I'm afraid we've found a body in the canal, Mrs Probert. I'm so sorry." The timorous residents puffed out a solid gasp that scuppered the prevailing wind and sent it homeward to think again.

"Oh, oh!" Elsie looked to the doorpost for support, ripping the underarm of her cardigan. "Oh, I suppose you'll want me to come and identify him."

"No need to trouble yourself now, Mrs Probert, Mrs Zimmer-Jones has already identified the body. It's her poodle, Crawshay, must have fell in with his cataracts. We'll carry on looking for your husband in the morning, it'll be dark soon."

"Dark, be buggered," shouted Mr Spring, "it's only two o'clock, mun. What's wrong with you? Climb in, Paddy, he's as much use as a drunken tightrope artist. Elsie, me and Paddy'll turn round and head towards Llandwpsyn, that's the direction he headed last time, wasn't it? Perhaps the police could comb the town again."

"Better than that, I'll get on to the Welsh Air Ambulance straight away."

"What 'you on about? They don't go looking for missing persons. Police helicopter you want, mun."

"On to it!" said the constable, imitating the static interference that would not prevent him calling in. Mrs Probert handed Paddy a blanket, just in case.

31

Mr Spring upped his game, reaching a reckless 35mph as he hurtled down Bryn-y-Bradwr towards Llandwpsyn. In the back Paddy wrapped the blanket around himself and sat facing forward, the rag dancing wildly at the end of their scaffolding pole, but secure enough. They had dipped it in bright gloss paint, the tricycle now the most highly visible vehicle in the county.

The countryside levelled out for a while before they hit a series of up and downers, the hedges bordered by dark woodland. Then the sun appeared again, lighting up a few acres of farmland on their right. On a track leading to *Fferm Pen-yr-enfys*, Paddy noticed an open gate, and instinctively felt they should investigate, shouting to his good friend to slam on the brakes. Eddie Spring obliged with the greatest of pleasure, Paddy hanging on for dear life.

Paddy needed all his strength to steer the wagon into the bottom of the field, Mr Spring turning the trike at right-angles so that he had a partial view. Tumps and thistles littered the incline, but there was nothing exciting to report. Then Paddy noticed the top hedge swaying and a large cow came into view.

"Never seen a cow that big."

"Where, boy?"

"Top of the field."

"Fuck me, that ain't no cow, mun. Farmer Rosser's bull, that is. This gate should *not* be open. Shut it tight and we'll be off."

If only it was that easy. The two gents caught sight of a different creature, trousers around his ankles, ambling unwisely towards the beast with a ring in its nose, about seventy yards away.

"Mr Probert!" shouted Paddy. The bull looked up and realised there was more fun to be had that afternoon than the chewing of the cud. He started a slow heavy trot in the direction of the one-armed man, who was unaware of the impending danger.

The level-headed Eddie Spring issued clear instructions to his mate. Paddy slid down the stepladder into the boggy marshland, then fought to extract it from the mud and throw it back on the cart.

"Right, quick, Paddy, pick up the pole and wave the flag around. Pretend you're in Merthyr! Wave it like hell, got to get Bully's attention."

Paddy didn't ask questions; Eddie Spring was always right. He picked up the pole as if it was a bamboo stick and shook it at the big slab of black muscle now scraping the ground, its hooves sending the dirt flying behind him. A moment later and it had begun its charge. Mr Spring turned the trike, ready to continue the journey to Llandwpsyn.

"Now, Paddy, put the pole back on the cart and hide down behind the hedge. Oh, fuck!" The wheels had become stuck in the mud and the bull, now within earshot, was looking to milk the situation. Paddy heaved on the handlebars and freed the jalopy with seconds to spare, chucked the pole into the cart and dived out of the way. Drivers travelling in the direction of Downhill were treated to a scene of good cheer as an unusual vehicle pedalled by a madman in yellow oilskins powered towards them, followed by an angry bull doing its utmost to hook a bright, red flag, fluttering at the back. Paddy could only stare after them. Eddie Spring raced through the sleepy village of Llandwpsyn, ignoring the speed limit and swerving to avoid the funeral cortege outside the church. Bully weighed up his options, but preferred Mr Spring's red rag to the vicar's black scarf.

With the smell of bovine halitosis breathing down his neck, Eddie was glad to find a straight expanse of road stretching out before him. For the next quarter of a mile he zig-zagged from one lane to the other in an attempt to outwit his four-legged friend. He amber-gambled on a roadworks traffic signal, Bully coming through on red, and negotiated the hair-pin bend that signalled the otherwise sensible outskirts of Moch-yn-dra. Past the *Drovers*

Arms, which was hosting the funeral wake, Eddie Spring took a sharp right on to a country road leading to Skinners Row. Sensing he was being overtaken on the outside, the adrenalin kicked in, allowing him to kick on, the series of small lakes known as *Llynnoedd Tawel* to his left no more than a grey blur. By this time he realised Bully had given up, but used his parochial knowledge to take a circuitous route home, rather than do a U-turn and risk the bull taking him by the horns.

He caught up with Paddy an hour later, Gareth Probert's one arm wrapped around his neck, catching up on his sleep. Paddy laid him carefully in the cart and snuck in beside him, pulling up the stepladder as if it was an emergency ramp on an aeroplane. Mrs Probert put her husband straight to bed, then made everyone a cup of tea, while PC. Paddler responded over the crackle to a strange call that had come in on his radio – a bull had dropped dead of a heart attack outside the slaughterhouse in Moch-yn-dra.

32

Like any good council boss Lance P. Nine-Cocks was a qualified bullshitter. He earned over £80,000 a year, almost £10,000 for each cock in his name, not bad for a plumber's son from the Penhill area of Swindon. He didn't realise that shaking hands with another pisshead in the back of a taxi amounted to a social contract, but barely a week after the dinner with Jack Harries, he realised the man was on his case. He'd ignored the first few phone calls, but his secretary, Freda Thomas, only got paid for so much abuse and decided that her boss, on five times her salary, should pull the finger out of his rectum. He wasn't called Picasso for nothing.

And like any good council boss, Lance P. Nine-Cocks knew how to delegate. He called team leader Sarah Pilkington into his office and explained that a certain Edwin Spring had come to his attention. Yes, he was a council tenant, but until recently was not known to Elderly Services. The director had it on good authority that the man, in his seventies, lived on his own in a flat and was unable to cope. He'd like Sarah to arrange for an assessment to be made with a view to admitting Mr Spring to residential care, specifically the Home for the Ridiculous in Twpsant. There would be no need to section the man under the Mental Health Act, merely show that his behaviour demonstrated he was a danger to himself. Even better if he scored highly on the socially absurd or preposterous spectrum. Lance would leave the evaluation in the capable hands of Sarah and her team, in whom he and the Cabinet Member responsible for Social Services had the utmost confidence.

Mrs Pilkington knew the perfect person for the job, a fussy little man who dressed 'peccably and was always first on the dance floor

125

for the Chicken Song at staff parties. His tinted glasses, shoulder-length hair and thick sideburns did nothing to detract from his cool image, and he had no problem pulling the girls. Putting them back in the right place was more of a problem.

Steve Charmer had moved to Downhill three years ago, despite living in the Redbourne area of Swindon for most of his life. He knew every inch of the Steam Museum and could relate its history to anyone who'd taken enough stimulants to keep awake for two hours. With no ties, his social work salary enabled him to impress the girls with his black Ford Mustang 4.6 V8. He hadn't yet found a girlfriend to share the upholstery, either front or rear, but it was early days. Over a thousand days to be exact, but who was counting? Well, to be honest, he was, secretly chalking it up on the wall of his garage.

He couldn't find Policeman's End in his A to Z, but was informed by a reliable youth in the centre of town that its official name was *Prince Andrew Caught*, and yeah, that's how 'court' was spelled; a mistake originally, but the locals had voted to keep it that way because it gave the place status. His car caused a stir when he drew into the cul-de-sac, people drawing their curtains back when it crashed into an old pram and its sitting tenant, a Guy Fawkes halfway through his lengthy furlough.

The social worker spent a minute or two admiring himself in the mirror, reached over for his briefcase, then strode purposefully towards the flat in question. He was surprised that a fragile, elderly gentleman had been housed in an *upstairs* flat, even more when the door was answered by an attractive young girl who immediately appreciated his good looks. He swept his hair back, a ploy he often used to attract the opposite sex.

"Hi, my name is Steve Charmer, social worker. I'm looking for a Mr Edwin Spring." His dog-breath hit Gwanwyn full in the face and she retreated an imperial yard, fanning the air with a tea-towel.

"Eddie? Bloody hell, 'ave he won the lottery or something, everyone's after 'im these days!"

"Are you his carer, um, sorry, don't know your name. Pity we weren't introduced years ago." He smiled seductively.

"Carer? Ha, Eddie don't need no carer. Since he got that trike of his he goes more places than I'll ever go."

"Is he here now? Can I speak to him?"

"Ah, another one that don't know. Me and 'im swapped flats. Ain't easy for 'im to climb the stairs with them weird legs 'e've got. Lives downstairs now." She held the door wide open for him.

"Right, right, I see." Charmer was loathe to leave this lady without giving her the opportunity to get to know him better. "I'll give him a knock, er, you didn't give me your name."

"No, you're right, I didn't," said Gwanwyn pleasantly, then shut the door on the stink-hound.

Eddie Spring always welcomed a knock on the door.

"Bring the dog in if you like, we're not fussy in this house," he laughed, leaving the social worker slightly puzzled. With the electric kettle boiling nicely on the gas ring, he told his visitor to choose a CD, indicating his illustrious storage rack clinging to the wall by a few rusty screws. Steve Charmer picked out a few of them and turned them over in his hand. "You can lend that Richard Clayderman one if you want to, boy, 'long as you look after it."

Charmer soon realised that the entire collection consisted of songs by the baby-faced pianist. He feigned interest while Mr Spring sorted out the tea, but his eyes were taking in the whole living-room, complete with overloaded sockets, patched-up extension cords and holes in the rug guarding the two-bar electric fire. He'd already glimpsed the gas stove in the kitchen, fearing it could detonate at any moment.

"Or you could lend that Pink Floyd CD, *Dark Side Of The Moon*. I've got the original LP somewhere, must be worth something. Oh, man, that Dave Gilmour – plays a mean riff." Eddie Spring imitated his favourite guitarist, gyrating ominously near the stove, but ending his solo by smashing his Fender over the social worker's head and saving his arse from being scorched.

With a mug of tea in each hand, the bandy-legged man waddled over to the table, spilling a good bit onto a carpet ingrained with enough protein to prevent a famine.

"I hope you like sugar, Steve, put three spoons in, just in case. Saves me going back to the kitchen, see."

'Steve' couldn't abide sugar in any hot drink, but now was not the time to quibble with the old man. He'd subtly transfer the contents of the filthy mug to the carpet when he got the chance, thereby increasing its calorific value.

The social worker unlocked his briefcase and took out the form he hoped would decide the fate of the strange man slurping his tea.

"You must be an important bloke, Steve, combination lock like that. What else 'you got in there? No, don't tell me, 'top secret' is it? Or is it a bottle of Glenfiddich? Don't worry, boy, I won't tell no-one. We'll have a glass when you're ready." Steve Charmer's sense of humour had been restricted by his upbringing in Swindon and he didn't know how to take Mr Spring. Like any good social worker, he took out his pen, feeling more relaxed with a form to complete.

"Got some questions for me, 'ave you, Steve? Well, I'll answer them all if you can get me more dosh off the Social."

Typical of the Welsh, thought the pen-pusher, *happy to live off handouts from the English*. "No, this isn't about money, I'm afraid, this is an assessment for the Social Services."

"Assessment, eh? For what? I assess myself every day, Steve. I got two bandy legs, half-a-pound of arthritis, and cataracts Hugh Grant'd die for. And I got mobility thanks to my friend Paddy. Bought me a trike, see, powered by hand-pedals, bit like that car you got. You can 'ave a ride in the back if you like."

Steve Charmer was completely out of his comfort zone, but was saved by a nasty rapping on the old man's door. He made to get up from his seat, but Spring was on his way. A burly male, a variety of oak, barged past him, leaving him pinned against the wall in a state of breathless mystification. He was followed by his assistant, a few branches shorter, but a stout fellow, nevertheless. They could have been brothers, but were not even half-brothers or step-brothers. Both had thick sideburns and a suspicious moustache, but that didn't mean they were brothers.

Eddie Spring recovered his equilibrium and huffed his way back to the living room, where the unexpected visitors were setting about the official guest. One had the startled social worker in a mild choke hold, doing his utmost not to strangle him outright. The bigger monster was perusing the form he'd snatched from Charmer's hand, put it to his ears and shook it to see if anything would fall out. Eddie Spring offered them a cup of tea, but they declined politely with two words that almost caused him to flinch. He'd heard worst, but only when his parrot, Graham Cockorthree, was alive.

Mr Spring resumed his seat to finish his cuppa, Steve Charmer's tea having spilled voluntarily onto the carpet.

"You haven't got time for that," snarled the bigger of the two giants, trying to snatch the mug out of his hand, but not counting on Eddie's iron grip. Eddie let go with perfect timing, hot tea splashing his assailant's crotch area, notching up a victory for the little people of the world. Big man pretended not to wince. "You two are coming to the station with us."

"Oh, policemen are you? Nice of you to introduce yourselves at last."

"Don't try and get funny with us, old man, you're in serious trouble – and your mate, here."

"What!" squeaked Charmer, "I'm a social worker with the elderly. You can see that." He pointed to the lanyard that had been pulled like a noose around his neck.

"Yeah, very clever, we've been waiting your arrival for some time. Let's see what the court has to say," grunted the strongman, bouncing the sobbing support worker through the front door and into the waiting car.

"Now, you," said the detective with stained trousers, much to Mr Spring's amusement; variety was the spice of life and an interview with the police high up on his bucket list. He tried to think of something witty Graham would have come up with, but decided that asking the cop for a blow job would have inflamed the situation.

However, much against his better judgment, when he was told to get in the back of the car, he politely told the two of them to 'fuck off.' Gwanwyn watched from her upstairs window as the two brutes tried to configure a way of stuffing the odd-shaped criminal into their unmarked paddy-wagon, even turning him on his head in a last-ditch effort. She picked up a brush, ran downstairs, and with great presence of mind, boldly struck the two aggressors on the head.

"Leave him alone, you bastards, or I'll call the police on you!" The two detectives were thankful for a rest, turning Mr Spring the right way up and propping him against the car. They showed their identity cards to Gwanwyn, who stood back in horror.

"It's all right, love, they just want to ask me a few questions down the station. You know, like a quiz night. Told 'em I couldn't get in the car, think they realise now." Eddie Spring nodded towards the two sweating pigs. "Now then, boys, I'll meet you down at the cop shop in twenty minutes, or you can follow me if you like. Do us a favour, Gwanwyn, love, help us on to the trike."

33

Eddie Spring swung across the road into Llan police station and braked just in time to avoid hitting the iron security gate. Clearance was eventually granted to the car behind, but it was the trike that bagged the best parking space, arresting the policemen's progress. Mr Spring watched as the two muscle men dragged the bewildered Charmer through the side door and into a world that was unbefitting for one of his ilk. Didn't they understand he was a social worker, someone that was on the right side of the law as a matter of course?

"Let me phone my boss, she can clear this up in two minutes. I can see why you'd suspect someone like Edwin Spring, but believe me, I have never committed a crime in my life and don't intend to do so. I mean, I thought us social workers and the police were on the same side." Mr Spring laughed quietly to himself, certain he wouldn't need a three-page form to assess the man from the council. The words 'righteous prick' could be scribbled on a small scrap of bog roll.

Steve Charmer was pushed into one interview room, shouting that he was entitled to a solicitor, while the smaller of the two giants accompanied Mr Spring into another. It turned out that he had a name, DI. Hammerhead.

"Pleased to meet you, sergeant. Can I call you by your first name? What does the 'D' stand for? My name's Mr Spring, but you can call me 'Eddie'."

"I know who *you* are," sneered the detective, sitting in the chair opposite, "we've been keeping an eye on your flat for some time."

"Very good of you, Mr Hammerhead, I'm out a lot, you see. On my trike. Though I don't think anybody'd break in, to be honest. Nothing worth stealing, apart from my Richard

Clayderman CDs. Do you like music, sergeant?"

Hammerhead drew himself up in an effort to project his superior status, leaving Mr Spring staring across at his sizeable mid-rift and the tea-stain on his shirt. His osteoporosis prevented him raising his neck to make eye contact, irritating the DI further.

"First of all, my rank is Detective Inspector, not 'Sergeant,' and secondly, we are not here to discuss your taste in music, Mr Spring."

"How about football, then. Big Swans supporter, me."

"Huh! Game for nancy boys. Played rugby, I used to, now that's a real man's game."

"Yeah, a real man's game in the showers afterwards, so I heard."

Hammerhead bristled. "Welsh football team's a joke. When was the last time they reached the World Cup?"

"Five years after Wales beat the All Blacks last. You a Welshman, then, are you?"

"Not really, no, I mean we're all British, aren't we?"

"That's your problem, see, Mr Hammerhead. All them rugby fans up at the Cardiff Stadium, they love being Welsh, but only for one day. Next day they're back to their Union Jacks. *Cymry am ddiwrnod.*"

"Did you just swear, Mr Spring?" laughed DI. Hammerhead.

"*Dim ond am ddiwrnod....*" sang Mr Spring.

"You don't know what you're talking about."

"So I've been told. Could I borrow your pen for a minute, sir?"

"What?"

"Your pen. Just wanted to write down the name of your barber. Sir Jimmy Savile, is it, defective inspector?"

"Beg pardon?" spat out the inspector, catching hold of Eddie Spring's left arm. Mistake. Mr Spring brought his right hand over and within five seconds removed the offending wrist and put it back where it belonged, bending the thumb into the dislocated position for luck. He thought he heard the word 'bastard' wincing out of Hammerhead's chest, but couldn't be sure; the community nurse would be syringing his ears next Friday. He loved the sensation of the warm water being squirted into his lugholes. The appointment was at nine o'clock if he remembered right.

The elderly suspect was making Hammerhead's head swim and the detective left the room in an effort to bag a second wind. Damn it all! He couldn't let this bandy-legged codger make a fool of him. He made for the little boys' room, splashed some cold water on his face, then re-joined the fray in determined mood.

"Right, Mr Spring, what is your name?"

"Mr Spring."

"That's not good enough."

"What do you want me to say?"

"*Edwin* Spring."

"Well, there you are, you know my name, don't you? It's pretty obvious."

"Please state your name for the benefit of the tape."

"What tape?"

The two detectives had not planned on doing formal interviews that day. The idea was to soften them up, then discuss what tactics to use during official interrogation, but DI. Anthony Hammerhead had been rattled by Eddie Spring, and felt that only a formal interview could restore his authority. He'd explain to his colleague later and ride out the inevitable flak. He placed the cassette machine on the table and loaded a new tape into the recorder. Good. He was back in charge.

"Name?"

The suspect sighed. "Edwin Spring."

"There, that wasn't difficult, was it? And your address, Mr Spring?"

"You know where I live, mun, you and your ugly mate pushed your way into my flat this afternoon."

"For the benefit of the tape, Mr Spring – your address."

"That tape isn't picking up nothing, sergeant."

"Fuck!" The machine usually hissed like an angry snake, but now sounded like a demented bird cornered by a wilful tom-cat.

Hammerhead pressed the eject button and surveyed the carnage of chewed-up tape.

"Must 'of been starving," joked Edwin Spring.

"Eh? Fuck it, fuck it!" The detective held the offending object up to his face, then threw it to the floor, no effort spared to conceal his umbrage. He slammed the door behind him and stomped into the corridor. Eddie Spring spent five minutes patiently retrieving the cassette, then used the sergeant's best judicial pencil to re-wind the tape. It was the least he could do under the circumstances.

*

An hour later, the door opened and the towering figure of number two policeman cast his gloomy shadow over the room. He gruffly introduced himself as DI. Cudgel and Mr Spring could see he would get no thanks for fixing the tape.

"Pleased to meet you," said the prospective prisoner, proffering his hand, "and I'm Edwin Spring."

"Let's get down to brass tacks, Edwin, I understand my colleague, DI. Hammerhead, has had a very interesting discussion with you, *very* interesting."

"Well, I'm not sure how interesting it was. He told me what colour nail varnish he uses – it's all on that tape by there if you want to listen to it."

"And I've also cleared up a few things that were puzzling us – with your boss in there." He gestured behind him.

"My boss? What 'you on about?"

"Your 'social worker.' Yes, very clever. We've been watching your flat for a while now, waiting for someone to call."

Eddie realised he was in for a long afternoon and wondered if Steve Charmer had managed to locate a solicitor.

"I ain't following you, sergeant."

"Detective Inspector. We know you arsonists operate in secret cells, only known to the commander."

Commander? thought Eddie Spring, *the plot is definitely thickening.*

"How long have you been a member of Meibion Glyndŵr?"

"Meibion Glyndŵr?" laughed Eddie, "they packed up their matchsticks years ago, didn't they?"

"Where were you on the morning of February the fourth?"

"How the hell should I know? On my trike, probably."

"Ah, ha, now we're getting somewhere. Let me refresh your memory, Edwin, the morning after the big snow. A Wednesday. You were on the Llan road coming into Downhill."

"Was I?" Eddie remembered the day clearly, but wasn't going to admit he'd broken into a house to shelter and knew that any tyre tracks would have been blanketed by the snow. And crucially, nobody had mentioned Paddy.

"Not many people ride a hand-pedalled tricycle 'round here, Edwin. Driver of the gritting lorry swears it was you. Ha, ha!"

"Dai Gethin? Give him a fiver, he'll grit your teeth for you."

"What's your take on all these second homes in Wales, Edwin? Not fair really, is it? Pricing out all the locals."

"Got to agree with you, there, Mr Cudgel."

"You know you're going to spend a long time behind bars, Edwin. Of course, if you co-operate, we'd consider a reduced sentence."

"Prison? Extension of working-class accommodation that is. Suit me fine, probably bigger than the flat I got now."

"Oh, one of those, are you?"

"Eh?"

"Communist."

"Am I? Can't help being working-class."

"I'm just as working-class as you are. Sometimes only had one meal a day as a kid."

Eddie Spring thought he must have made up for it since, with up to ten feeds a day, between snacks and lashings of fizzy drinks. "Well, let me tell you, Inspector, when I was a boy, we were so poor, I had to roll the cheese off my younger brother's foreskin if I wanted to eat. I had four brothers and we had to do it in strict

135

chronological order. Got to say, my older brother's thumb was rough as hell." Cudgel wasn't listening.

"Working class hero, are you?"

"As I see it, Inspector, they pit worker against worker. After all, you do the State's dirty work, don't you?"

"Ah, thought it. You're a Marxist, aren't you?"

"Suppose I was, when I was younger."

"The proletariat against the ruling class, eh?"

"No, haven't heard that one. I can sing *All God's Chillun Got Guns* for you, if you like, but there's only one quote I recall, 'I wonder whatever became of me? I should have been back here a long time ago.'"

"Das Kapital?"

"No, Rufus T. Firefly, *Duck Soup.*"

*

All the hard work put in by the two DIs over the last month had come to naught. Charmer's team leader, Sarah Pilkington, turned up at five-thirty, having got half a story from Gwanwyn out at Prince Andrew Caught. She berated the two detectives for a solid fifteen minutes, fully igniting their pants. How would a twenty-year old social worker from the Redbourne district of Swindon know anything about Meibion Glyndŵr and the arson campaign? He was more interested in being first up for the Chicken Song at staff parties. Despite claiming to have extracted a confession from both suspects, DI. Cudgel knew he was on to a loser and invited his partner to buy him a pint at the *Bush*. Mr Spring spent a comfortable night in the interview room, before being released at ten o'clock the following morning, with no complaints at his treatment.

34

Paddy loved his Wednesday evenings helping Mrs Watkins's husband design the set for the play. He was delighted when Talfryn gave him the job of 'building' the brick-lined well down which *Sir Timothy Bellboys* would disappear, the two of them making detailed sketches of each stage of construction. Mr Watkins had fashioned three light metal 'hula-hoops' of slightly different sizes, into which he had drilled five congruent holes. Paddy had to make the skeleton by threading bamboo canes through the holes, using the largest hoop as the base and securing everything with duct tape. Assiduously following the plan, he wrapped a large piece of card around the frame, before calling for Talfryn and his staple gun. That was enough for one evening. The following week Paddy cut long strips of cardboard – he was now a dab hand with the scissors - and stuck them with copious amounts of paste to the existing card. By the third session, everything was dry and it was time to do the brick by splashing on the poster paint in red and black. Paddy, in his artist's apron, stood back and called on Talfryn to admire his creation.

"That's a cracking job you've done by there, Paddy boy!" The maestro beamed back at him, gratified that his contribution counted as much as that offered by any of the actors. Yes, Lucy and the others had to learn their lines, but what was the good of that unless surrounded by first-class scenery that would captivate the audience? Gwilym James might be good-looking, but could he build a well? He didn't think so. On top of that, Mr Watkins as stage manager had appointed Paddy 'props master.'

Tal Watkins used his abundant charm to rope in Jeff Bastard and sons to rig up a tower either side of the stage, spanned by a runway from which the 'air balloon' would be suspended, and Dai

Grease, mechanic, to help with the ropes and pulleys. The basket of the balloon needed to be solid to take the weight of 'Jumbo' Phillips, taking the part of *Sir Timothy*, but the only laundry basket they could find was too wide for the well and too shallow for the corpulent artiste. The ever-inventive Talfryn took an old beer barrel to pieces and patiently shaped a perfect drum for the aeronaut, even fussy Health and Safety Officer, Bliss Fuller, unable to find fault.

Paddy was more than happy to carry on his project in the hall, while the others busied themselves on the stage. He was a little wary of the scaffolders, but if the scrappy did remember him, it was of no consequence to the man. Paddy watched in awe as the four talkative Bastards – Jeff, John, Jud and Jurevicius - skilfully erected the platform, which could be wheeled into position when the time came. They would be back to fit the safety rail once the balloon and well were completed and help Talfryn and Dai Grease arrange the pulleys.

Mair Watkins had doubts she'd chosen the wrong play, that two acts would be too challenging, but it soon became obvious the cast were on board and in no danger of losing the plot. While the arguments about Romanticism and revolutionary philosophy might not grip the audience, there was plenty of comedy and stunning visuals to ensure a memorable evening.

Most of Lucy's part consisted of one-liners, but there were two chunks of dialogue in the first act that Mair considered tongue-twisters. She drew the girl aside in the first rehearsal, not wanting to embarrass her in front of her fellow-actors, and explained that she'd adapted *Dorcas*'s script a little.

"Why?"

"Well, I thought some bits were too long."

"Too difficult for me, you mean?" That's exactly what she meant, and now found herself in a pickle.

"No, not really, but…."

"Have you cut back the other parts, Mrs Watkins? *Sir Timothy Bellboys, Hallam Matthews, Edward Sterne*? All them characters got a lot to spout. Hope they can learn their lines."

"No, I haven't, but that's my intention."

Lucy could see through her. "Give me a test."

"What 'you mean?"

"Test me – any of the lines you like." Lucy opened the book. "There, page 38, go on, from the top, you take the part of Edward."

Mair had been thrown off balance and found herself under Lucy's spell. "Right, here we are: *That's what social reform is, nothing more-*"

"*But it's so simple! Why doesn't everybody do it at once?*" Lucy had a point to prove and didn't let Mair put her book down until they'd done two pages of dialogue. Not only was she word-perfect, she was as good as any professional actress, and she smiled broadly at Mair to show there were no hard feelings. As rehearsals went on, Mair laughed quietly to herself as Lucy berated the rest of the cast if they turned up late or hadn't put in the required effort.

Paddy was content to work on the set and be a general dogsbody, though Mair had offered him a small part. Everyone became increasingly curious as the props took shape, and Paddy was pleased when Lucy came over to look at the well. He proudly showed her the sketches and promised she and her new boyfriend would be amazed once the hot-air balloon was up and flying.

Paddy and Lucy had been an item for over a year and Mair was unsure if Paddy was showing bravado in the face of her dumping him. She could see him keeping an eye on the two lovebirds, the situation all the more painful because of their easy intimacy during the play. When they part on good terms, *Dorcas* asks *Edward Sterne* for a kiss, and Lucy insisted going completely over the top, almost swallowing Gwilym whole, much to Paddy's discomfort. Mair banned Lucy from 'practising' the kiss from then on, backed vociferously by the rest of the crew.

The Downhill players looked to Mair for direction, and she was willing to accommodate any suggestions that didn't ruin the plot. With everyone within farting distance, she could deal with minor disagreements immediately, preventing any serious fistfights. And she knew that Tal would come up with the goods. What she couldn't control, however, was the dynamics between the town band and the male voice choir, teamwork crucial to the success of the performance. Conductors Huw Prys and Tony Needle were old friends, but acknowledged that co-operation depended on the committee members who controlled the organisations, more specifically, one or two of the most pig-headed.

That year the choir would compete in the National Eisteddfod and the band had a series of concerts in Berlin, the scene of many of Hitler's speeches. Sandwiched between the two engagements, in the middle of August, was Mair Watkins's play, which the disgruntled pig-headed ones viewed as an irritating distraction. In truth, the two choruses were easily learnt, but time would be wasted on a period of monotonous repetition until the soloists, choir and band gelled as one big, happy team.

The other great controversy concerned location and the clock. The choir met on a Friday night between seven and nine in Downhill Primary School, the band the previous evening at six o'clock in the Gospel Hall, otherwise known as the leaning shed of Gendros.

Band members didn't see why they had to cart their euphoniums, trombones, tubas and horns all the way over to the school, the choristers unwilling to eat their evening spuds half an hour earlier than usual. Such vulgar squabbling was more deep-rooted than most people realised. The brass-blowers followed the football, while the purple-blazered vocalists preferred supping at the rugby club.

On top of this, the families that held the band together traditionally supported the 'small town' theory, while the rugby crowd enjoyed living in a 'large village.'

But more bad blood had surfaced recently, when the choir chairman's grand-daughter, Nellie Rock, admitted she was 'up the duff.' At seventeen years of age, she had taken precautions with most of the village boys, but her luck had run out with sixteen-year old Peter Jones, who was a dab hand with his flugel horn. The story doing the rounds was that they'd used the same condom half-a-dozen times, but most folk thought that was stretching it a bit.

35

Alison Harries watched her husband tucking into his evening meal, little knowing he had a lot more to chew on than his steak pie. That afternoon in Llan market, his phone had vibrated rather nicely in his trousers pocket, but the ensuing conversation with Elderly Services Team Leader Sarah Pilkington was less pleasurable. Lance P. Nine-Cocks was too much of a shit-dog to convey the message himself, but there again, what was the point of being paid all that money if he didn't delegate? Plans to accommodate Edwin Spring in the Home for the Ridiculous in Twpsant had fallen through in the most farcical manner and were now unfeasible. It appeared that the mad trike man had burnt too many fingers of the powers that be and was considered 'off-limits.' Jack Harries whistled through his teeth and stumbled around the market stalls in a daze, unexpectedly finding refuge in 'Psycho' Rees's dud-battery emporium, where he was offered a cup of tea.

Lucy noticed him glancing at his watch, but didn't want to set cat among pigeons, even though, with a decent boyfriend, she and her father were now on talking terms. He was nervous, there was no doubt about it – she hadn't seen him squeezing his right ear lobe like that since the story about Monica Lewinsky broke.

As soon as the clock on the mantelpiece struck seven, Jack Harries excused himself and made for the garden, swearing at the cat who had deliberately tried to trip him up in the dark. By the time he'd reached the back gate, he was as fully charged as his mobile phone and he waited tensely for an answer to the number he'd punched in. A number 'Psycho' Rees had very kindly given him.

"Yes?"

"Alan?" Nothing. "Alan Minium?"

142

"Is that Jack the Ratcatcher?"

"Yes. Mr Rees gave me…."

"No real names, Jack."

"But 'Jack' *is* my real name."

"And is 'Ratcatcher' your surname?"

"No, of course not."

"Hope it's not your occupation, neither," laughed Alan. Jack Harries hesitated. He was sure he'd heard that laugh before, somewhere on his rounds not that long ago.

"I was told you could help me, Alan."

"For a price, Jack."

"Yes, for a price. How much are we talking about?"

"Depends on the building."

"Building? I'm not with you."

"The size. Location. That sort of thing." Jack Harries groaned, suspecting Psycho Rees had wound him up by giving him the name of a builder pal.

His thoughts were interrupted by Mr Minium. "Listen, Jack, I know how to light a match, if you get my meaning." Jack was about to hang up when Alan became more specific about what he offered. "I can arrange for any building you like to be torched."

"Arson! No, no, no, I'm talking about a particular person."

"Person? No, Jack, I'm not a hit man. You'd have to go to one of the big city gangs to procure those sort of services. Know anyone in Chicago?"

"Ha, ha! Don't want him taken out. Someone to put the frighteners on him I was looking for."

"Ah, suppose I could arrange that, yeah. Who are we talking about?" Having agreed a fee of £500, Alan Minium smiled wryly to himself, for the victim was someone with whom he, also, had a bone to pick. A very big bone.

36

"Argh!" Poor old Paddy. A sudden pain made him withdraw his fingers from the letter-box and he could see blood dripping onto his shoes. He wondered what Lyndon Nostrils would make of the blood-spattered leaflet he'd find on his mat when he arrived home at five o'clock.

"What's up, boy?" Mr Spring saw his mate wringing his right hand in distress. "Bloody hell, boy, his dog got you, did he?" Paddy nodded. "Right, get in the back and we'll go up the surgery. Nurse'll stitch you up. Might need a tetanis, mind."

Eddie Spring mimicked an ambulance siren as he hurtled towards Cwm Medical Centre, where bountiful Nurse, Gwen Jones, was waiting in her blue latex gloves. She showed the casualty into her room or 'station' as she liked to call it, Eddie Spring bursting in five minutes later after old Mr Spit had helped him dismount.

Nurse Jones had been trained for this sort of thing. She carefully bathed thumb, index and middle fingers of the ravaged right hand, asking Paddy if he'd got the dog's name.

"No, I know his address, though. Priory Street."

"Lyndon's house. You know why he's called 'Nostrils,' don't you? Seen the size of his snout – if I had to pack them cavities, I'd need two bags of Polyfilla," she laughed.

"Will he need a tetanis, nurse?" asked Eddie.

"Um, I don't think so. I know the skin's broken, but it's nice and clean now. Tell you what though, we'll get Dr Lake's advice." That made Paddy feel happier – he wasn't sure if he could afford a 'tetanis.'

Before Nurse Jones could reach the door handle, Dr Eurig Lake burst in, having got wind of the incident. He took off his

144

glasses and wiped the lenses with sandpaper he'd illegally prescribed himself over many years.

"How much do you weigh, Paddy?" Paddy didn't know and Nurse Jones made for the scales in the corner, booting them in the direction of Dr Lake.

"He've lost weight since last week, doctor," advised Mr Spring.

"Oh?"

"Yeah, he had half a scaffolding pole in his coat pocket. Most people don't realise how heavy they are."

"We can rule out iron deficiency, then," said the old doctor wisely. No need for the scales, Nurse." Nurse Jones booted the scales back into the corner, where they would wait patiently for the next emergency in a town which took 'healthy eating' very seriously. "Now then, let's have a look!" He took hold of Paddy's hand very gently.

"Nothing much wrong here, boy."

"It's the other hand, Dr Lake," said Nurse Jones knowledgably.

"Yes, I know," coughed the doctor, eventually locating the bleeding fingers. "Ah, this is what we call a 'dog bite,' Paddy."

"Will he need a tetanis, doctor?"

"No, I don't think so. Hang on a minute, I'll go and see what I've got in my cupboard."

While Dr Lake trotted off to his office, Nurse Jones caught up on the 'goss.' The two buddies let her in on the news they were setting up as window cleaners, advertising door-to-door with their flyers. They'd wittily dubbed the company *Pane Relief* and were in the process of painting it on the side of their cart.

Eurig Lake returned five minutes later, closely guarding some sort of instrument.

"Look at this, Eddie."

Eddie Spring weighed it in his hand, turned it over, then felt the edges of the odd-shaped device. "It's an ice-scraper," he declared, "It's not car windows we'll be doing, doctor, people's houses more like."

The doctor passed it to Eddie's friend. "See anything unusual,

Paddy?"

"There's a small hole in it, doctor."

"Yes, a small hole. Any ideas, boys?" They looked at Nurse Jones, but she was as mystified as they were.

"Last time Postie Glew was in here, I prescribed him one of these."

"An ice scraper?"

"Yes, he regularly delivers to Lyndon Nostrils' house. His hand got stuck, just like you, and the dog got him good and proper. Dog's name is 'Rip,' by the way." Nurse Jones made a mental note. 'Rip' would be easy to write later on, especially if she used her green biro.

Dr Lake picked up a form and folded it down the middle. "Right, Paddy, this is your flyer. Wrap it round the handle of the scraper. Good. Now, pretend you're pushing it through someone's letterbox. Go on, mun."

Paddy did as he was instructed. "See, it's the handle goes through the letterbox, your fingers are safe gripping the blade. I prescribed this one for Postie Glew and that hole was done by the incisors of an Alsatian up Allt-y-Malwod way. Clean through two millimetres of toughened plastic."

The other three gasped.

"Can't remember the dog's name, now. Point is, once your fingers entered that house today, Paddy, they became the householder's property, or in your case, Rip's property, to do as he thought fit. Years ago you could take a dog to court, well, any animal for that matter, under a special bye-law. 'Member Farmer Grundy prosecuting his daughter's goat, Sebastian Grundy, for chomping a hole in his best Sunday trousers. Anyway, I'll prescribe you a deluxe scraper, soon as Nurse Jones has patched you up. Come through to my office."

As the doctor opened the door, he turned to face the nurse and her patients. "Mind you, that Hitler bloke…." The three of them looked up in anticipation of some insightful observation. "Saw a documentary last night. He was a right twat, wasn't he? Don't think he was Welsh, though."

"Thank you, doctor."

"What for, Paddy boy?"

"For looking at my bite."

"No problem. I'll put the scraper on repeat for you."

Once the patient had left the building with his good pal, Eddie Spring, Dr Lake slumped into his chair, a forlorn look on his face. Nurse Jones entered the room quietly, aware that this was no time for telling jokes.

"Poor old Paddy," he croaked, "Not long lost his mam and dad – and now this. A scraper is only a temporary measure," a declaration that confirmed the nurse's worst fears and sent a chill running down her spine.

"Is it serious, doctor?"

"Could be, Gwen, *does dim dal.*" He heaved himself up and made his way towards the impressive bookcase housing more than a thousand medical treatises, but he was not tall enough to reach the tome that had served him well over the years, the 1852 edition of *Hooper's Medical Dictionary* which he'd picked up at a snip from *Electrical's Accepted.* The detailed anatomical plates always did it for him.

"Don't you go up that step-ladder, doctor, let me do it," cried Nurse Jones authoritatively. Being a gentlemen, Eurig Lake did as he was told and took the opportunity to examine his colleague's impressive varicose veins.

Gwen lugged the book to the desk with palpable sweat on her forehead. The doctor studied it intensely for five minutes, expertly thumbing the fragile pages, before settling on a paragraph that had not seen the light of day in thirty years.

"Here it was, staring me in the face!"

"Shall I write him up for a colonoscopy, doctor?"

Eurig Lake closed his bible with a sigh and pondered his decision. He knew that one mistake could cost him his career. "No, not this time, Nurse. Let me think ….. either a chisel or a pair of pliers will do it."

Damn it all! She'd been outwitted again. Local chemist Islwyn 'Tacitus' Evans only accepted prescriptions in Latin and Dr Lake knew that Gwen would have difficulty translating either remedy.

37

Paddy had eyed the ladder clamped to the platform above the stage for some time. He hadn't explicitly been banned from climbing it, but knew Talfryn Watkins would be angry if he went anywhere near it without permission, 'props master' or not. Paddy couldn't see what could go wrong; after all, safety officer Bliss Fuller had given the scaffolding the thumbs-up and even if he did fall, it surely wouldn't be fatal.

His opportunity came when Mr Watkins popped home to pick up a piece of two by one, leaving Paddy in charge for ten minutes. He put down his paint brush, wiped his hands on the rag, then made for the stage, ignoring the buttons filling his pants like winnings from a slot machine. Paddy wiped his sweaty hands on the lower rungs of the impressive wooden ladder, which was five metres in length according to Jurevicius Bastard. He craned his neck back, taking in the enormous task before him; it was now or never! If he had a tail he could have been mistaken for a lizard as he glided adhesively up the steps, but within grasp of the platform he inexplicably froze. He could neither move up nor down and there were no more tricks up his reptilian sleeve.

On his return, Talfryn Watkins set about his work, and when he at last took a break assumed Paddy was 'sitting on,' as was his custom post-evening meal. Some way above him, Paddy stubbornly held on, not wishing to blot his copybook now that Mr Watkins had sung his praises to all and sundry. But he'd had extra mushy peas with his pie and potatoes before coming out and though he farted as softly as he could, he was powerless to stop the stink wafting north, south, east and west, or eventually finding a human target.

"Paddy!" No answer. "Paddy!"

"I'm up here, Mr Watkins."

"What the hell…"

"I'm stuck, Mr Watkins. Sorry!" Tal Watkins laughed, guessing that Paddy had been drawn to the ladder like a moth to a flame. And why not? But the first priority was to get the moth into the toilet. With the strong, reassuring arms of Mr Watkins behind him, Paddy's composure returned and after descending the steps, made his way to the shitter. Tal Watkins had no intention of discussing the rights and rungs of the situation, but Paddy wanted another go. And another. And another. Fifteen minutes later he had scaled the ladder ten times, Mr Watkins's presence at the bottom no longer necessary. Paddy was elated at overcoming another hurdle, proving people wrong yet again.

*

Paddy could now tackle windows at first-floor height. The partners paid a fiver for a twenty-foot extension ladder in *Buy 'Ere* charity shop and sensibly limited themselves to the rows of terraced houses that comprised the best part of Downhill. Paddy threw a bucket of water at any window that was positioned preposterously high.

Spring was well under way, the days lengthening and the frost but an occasional visitor. The advertising campaign had borne fruit, many residents happy to have clean windows for the first time in two years. The two negotiated a flat rate of five pound, double for pensioners they didn't like, and dogs had to be securely chained up. They would call every month, put a note through the door if no-one was in, collecting the cash later in the week. Lyndon Nostrils complained that his leaflet was blood-stained and illegible and that he was therefore entitled to a reduction, so Paddy only washed one of his windows, a reduction of sorts.

The new enterprise was like a breath of fresh air, bringing the residents of Downhill out onto the streets and old Mr Flick parading his body again. Paddy was eager to show his fireman's skills, putting the doubting Thomases, Len and Phyllis Thomas, firmly in their place. Their bucket became a star attraction, not only for its bright red colour, but for its 70 litre capacity, twenty more than the previous record. This enabled them to offer a one-off service to Mrs Florence Clutterbuck, 33 Ennis Terrace, whose cat, Willince, was given a much-needed bath in mild detergent. The children next door laughed when they saw how 'thin' Willince had become after his wash and how he fluffed out after a blast from the hair dryer.

The boys' beneficence didn't end with animal welfare; during their second week they were called to the same house, where Mr Laurence Clutterbuck had set fire to his living room door, using a heat gun to remove the old paint. Seventy litres of cold water extinguished the inferno in seconds, leaving Laurence and Florence extremely wet and grateful, but not in the least electrocuted.

Mr Spring was thrilled at the improvement in his mate's motor skills, Paddy unrecognisable from the awkward character he'd met on the road a few months earlier. Despite the chilling incident with the dog, Paddy was keener than ever to drum up business. It came as a surprise one Thursday afternoon to see him flinch and almost fall off the doorstep after knocking on a house in Dust Street, clearly in shock. Once the job was done and they were out of earshot, Paddy brought his friend up to date. The white-haired old stick who'd answered the door was the witch who bullied Paddy in the physics class, the 'cow' who'd tried to electrocute him. Miss Chatterley, aka 'Morticia' Addams, had risen from the dead and returned to live in Downhill. The rumour was that she'd lost a load of money investing in an American communications company and had had to downsize. There was still no Gomez around that anyone knew of.

As time went on, Paddy noticed that security wasn't high on the agenda for many of their clients, drawing it to Eddie Spring's attention as they were packing up for the week in early April.

"How do you mean, Paddy?"

"Well, them upper windows are open half the time. And a lot of people don't lock their front doors."

"Perhaps we should go into the burglary business, then, Paddy."

"You are joking, Eddie, aren't you?"

Eddie Spring laughed at his earnest young friend. "See you bright and early Tuesday morning, Paddy. Where we going to start?"

"Told Mrs Rees we'd do her house first. Then on to Bugger Row."

"Sounds good to me, boy. 'Ave a good weekend – might see you in the Globe?" And off he raced into the dark of the evening. He was delighted that a good week's work would finance his Saturday night beer and even a couple of extra tins of beans. He turned right on to the common, only a mile or so from his beloved flat; he'd heave himself in and out of the bath, have a good scoff, then listen to Richard Clayderman and Pink Floyd.

Mr Spring loved *Clawdd-y-mawn*, a straight stretch of road on which he could set his own land-speed record. As he sailed along at a rate of knots, he could see a pair of flashing sidelights in the distance, too dim to be of any concern. Twenty seconds later he was faced with large headlamps on full beam, obviously a lorry, which totally disorientated him. Two fog lights joined the party, the beams so intense that they blinded the man on the trike, forcing him to let go of the pedals and shield his eyes. From behind him came the roar of another truck, which finished the job, forcing him into the steep ditch full of dirty water. The offending vehicle stopped fifty yards down the highway, a couple of doors slammed and a snippet of conversation, interspersed with healthy chuckles, cut through the night air. Eddie Spring heard the sound of boots approaching and when he looked up, his eyes were burnt by the intense light of a heavy-duty torch sweeping the ditch. Then he passed out.

38

Come Tuesday morning, Paddy was waiting at the front door for Mr Spring to arrive. He'd enjoyed his weekend and still valued his Monday shift at the Co-op, but the new venture washing windows was making a man of him. Everyone could see that Paddy Trahern, bucket in hand, was holding down a proper workman's job, and he loved being out in the open air. Mr Spring hadn't called in the pub on Saturday and he was looking forward to catching up on three days' worth of gossip.

Paddy had never known his partner to sleep late and assumed he'd been held up by a flat tyre or puncture. Eddie liked to spend time giving a lick of oil to his moving parts, but the man was normally bang on time for their half-past eight start. What if his friend had slipped and banged his head? Or worst? He had no phone, so there was no way to reach him. The clock on the mantelpiece outstared Paddy, the loud tick-tock mocking his anxiety as it sped towards the hour of nine. There was only one thing for it! As he set out for Policeman's End, he felt better for taking decisive action, but the sense of dread increased as the little flats came into sight.

With no answer at the door, Paddy rushed upstairs, thankful to see Gwanwyn's friendly face.

"No, Paddy, love, I ain't seen him all weekend. Sometimes I don't, mind. 'Specially if I'm working."

"It's not like him not to turn up, see, Gwanwyn."

"And there's no way you could have missed him on the road?" Silly question, but people ask silly questions. "Have you checked to see if his trike's there, Paddy? Hang on, I'll come with you."

Paddy felt stupid. Why hadn't he thought of that? Gwanwyn peered through the small pane of glass in the lock-up. "No, definitely not there, Paddy. He must be out on it somewhere." She could see he wasn't convinced. "I'm sure he's all right, Paddy, but I ain't working today so I'll keep an eye out for him. Give me your number 'case I hear anything, but don't worry, darling, you know what he's like. Shall I call you a taxi?" Paddy appreciated the offer, but wanted to walk back, half-hoping he'd see a beaming Mr Spring effortlessly pedalling the highway.

Paddy kept to the right-hand side verge, something his father, an avid reader of the Highway Code, had drummed into him. When he reached the common, a gust of wind strafed the road from left to right and a single black cloud maliciously spat a bucket of hailstones at him. Something wasn't right. Paddy was instinctively drawn to the ditch, and there he was – his mate, slumped over the handlebars, up to his boots in water, but fortunately still in the saddle. If he'd fallen off, there's no doubt he would have drowned. Paddy called out to his friend and unable to climb down into the ditch, started to panic. In the next five minutes, only one car appeared from either direction, but as he tried to wave it down the driver cleverly honked his horn and gave the inevitable V-sign. Who said a neanderthal couldn't do two things at the same time!

Rather than take the quicker option of going on to town, Paddy preferred to put his trust in Gwanwyn, arriving back exhausted and bedraggled. She could see how distressed he was and took on board the situation; within the hour, the unconscious Edwin Spring had been admitted to the A and E Department at Morriston Hospital.

*

His one true friend, his business partner and back seat confidante, Paddy Trahern, was completely crushed. His first instinct was to find solace in the company of Lucy, but short of calling him a serial nuisance, she made it clear his tittle-tattle was of no interest. He looked around for Mrs Watkins, knocking every door in the library, but she was busy in a meeting and not to be disturbed. Her husband, Talfryn, would have helped, but he was at work in Llanelli. Paddy was on his own; nobody seemed to realise the seriousness of the situation.

Paddy set out for Policeman's End for the second time that day, again seeking out the only other person who valued the man lying in hospital. She'd said she had the day off and right enough, Paddy found her at home.

"Hi, Paddy, love, you're back quick. How's Eddie?"

"Eh?"

"Assumed you'd gone up the hospital, see how he is."

"Oh, no! Got no idea how he is, Gwan, I'm really worried 'bout him."

"'Course you are, boy. So am I. Can't nobody give you a lift up there?"

"Mrs Watkins 's the only one might help, but she's busy. Can you take me up, Gwan?"

"Ain't got no car, Paddy. My wages, I can hardly afford a bus!"

"Oh. And the trike's still in the ditch."

"Sit down a minute, Paddy. I'll make a cuppa and then we'll phone Morriston."

"Have you got any hot chocolate, Gwan?"

"As it happens, Paddy, ….." Gwanwyn strode into her kitchen and reappeared flashing a large jar of the stuff from behind her back. The normally carefree Paddy cracked a smile for the first time that day.

It didn't take long for the two cocoa hounds to shoot up, supplemented by an ample supply of custard creams. When Paddy asked her if she got the hot chocolate on prescription from Dr Lake, she laughed, not realising he was deadly serious. With mood restored, it was time to phone the hospital. Paddy ear-wigged anxiously as she spoke to the sister in Ward A, but as a 'friend' rather than a 'family member' was only entitled to basic information, even though it was she who'd phoned the emergency services. Mr Spring was awake, but in a confused state, not yet able to receive visitors. Did Gwanwyn know if he had any relatives. No? Would Gwanwyn be willing to be a point of contact for the hospital? Not really, but she relented on seeing the sorrow in Paddy's eyes.

"Perhaps he'll be able to have visitors soon, Paddy." She was trying to raise his spirits, but realised it presented another problem. No car. From what she could make out, Lucy's father had been willing to drive them around when they were an item, but the man hated Mr Spring and his trike with a vengeance.

"That's where me and Eddie got the trike in the first place, Gwan – Swansea."

"How'd you get there?"

"On the train. Mr Harries gave us a lift to the station."

"Well then, Paddy, when he's feeling a bit better, you and me'll go up by train." There, she'd said it. It wasn't that much of a commitment. One train fare. It was worth it just to see the grin on his face and the bounce in his legs as he went out the door - and she was sure the bedridden fox would be back on his feet before long.

By the next day the news had seeped into every nook and cranny in town, and because he was regarded as a clown on three wheels, most folk thought the whole incident was hilarious. The accepted theory was that he'd had a few pints too many and lost control on a notoriously fast stretch of road, much loved by boy racers. There was little sympathy for the idiot albatross that loomed over their highways, and even those who liked him breathed a sigh of relief. He'd had his fun, now it was time to give his arse a rest. The rough and rap scullion brigade missed him for a while, having delighted in seeing Eddie Spring embarrass the authorities, but he was merely a diversion. Entertainment could be hatched up any day of the week.

The generosity the man had shown the town was conveniently forgotten. When Hubert Llywellyn's hearse broke down with a flat battery, Eddie Spring got the corpse to the church on time. On another occasion he'd transported Dai John's stag party to Llan in

156

two shifts, after best man, Stewie Spud, had booked the mini-bus for the following night. Mr Spring had also organised a one-off trip to the races, where they'd put all their money on a complete outsider, a six year-old chestnut gelding called *Twm Siôn Cati*. The odds were 500-1, conditions on the day favouring the horse, his tenth-place finish a disappointment to all. At other times he'd delivered a boiler for the plumber, curlers for the barber and all sorts of condoms for the chemist., but he was not to be honoured in his own community.

39

Paddy's world had been turned upside down. He'd been badly shaken when Lucy finished with him, but bounced back within days, throwing himself into the theatre project and happy to spend the daylight hours with his business partner. Eddie Spring had accepted Paddy as a mate and encouraged him to push himself, much as Tal Watkins had done. He only saw Mr Watkins once a week, but he'd spent more and more time in Eddie's company and regarded him as a brother. A brother-with-arms. Strong arms, though he had bandy legs.

Generally, however, Paddy felt people didn't take him seriously, expecting the pleasant, docile character they'd always seen. When his mother died suddenly ten years ago, he didn't blame his father for lack of support. He'd have been overwhelmed by his own grief, unable to see his son was in pain. Friends did their best to help him, but he was a broken shell of a man, following his wife to the grave within six months. The talk had been of Ken Trahern dying of a broken heart, not Paddy's emotional state after losing both parents. The assumption had always been that the little feller was in a world of his own, bless him, and that nothing bothered him. And, of course, that wasn't true. Those sad thoughts brought him back to Eddie Spring, his bad legs, and the fact he'd been lying in a ditch for three days, but the good news was that he was awake and a week later the sister told Gwan that they could visit.

Gwanwyn had made jokes about the pittance she made as a care assistant with the old folk, but Paddy remembered the cost of the train to Swansea and was determined to buy the tickets. He would have asked Mrs Watkins to take them to the station in Llan, but had steered clear of the library because of rude Lucy. He insisted on paying for the taxi, then hurried to the ticket office to beat Gwanwyn to it. She ran after him and grabbed his arm, showing him the little orange tickets she'd already bought.

"You are naughty, Gwan," said Paddy, repeating a phrase his mother had often used when neighbours had done her a good turn. Gwanwyn laughed, then lost the wrestling match with her new friend, who stuffed the exact amount into her handbag.

"Right, Paddy Trahern, I'm paying for the taxi the other side, *and* the meal in the caff."

Paddy knew exactly where to get a cab and was delighted to see Mike Scabs again and tickled pink that the driver remembered him.

"But it's not your mate you got with you this time, I see, Paddy. Aren't you going to introduce your gorgeous girlfriend?"

"She's not my gorgeous girlfriend, Mike. This is Gwanwyn, my *friend*."

"Pleased to meet you, darling. Right, where 'we off this time?" Mike seemed genuinely sorry to hear about the old biker whose infamous jaunt along the motorway had been front page news and wouldn't hear of taking anything for the fare. He'd pick them up in ninety minutes and chauffer them back to town, free of charge. "And give him my best, folks. Tell him I'm thinking about him."

"Will do," smiled Gwanwyn, "and thank you, Mike."

Paddy had been born in hospital, but his only other visit was the day his mam died. It didn't take long to find Ward A, but the walk down the soulless corridor was unnerving. Paddy followed Gwanwyn's example by putting his hands under a sanitizing machine, fascinated as she did a thorough job of rubbing her palms and fingers.

"Do this at work, sometimes, Paddy, but it's much more important in a hospital. Stops germs spreading, see. Got to do it for at least twenty seconds. Count with me. Ready? One, two, three...."

Disquiet turned to shock when they spied the man in the bed. He'd always been thin, but now resembled something out of Belsen, sick and vulnerable, his chalky white hair hanging on for dear life. On the journey up they'd laughed about Mr Spring and his unpredictable lifestyle, both viewing him as something of a hero. They were looking forward to reacquainting themselves with his quick wit and optimistic outlook on life. They had to mentally adjust in the few short steps to his bed, the boot now on the other foot. As they neared Mr Spring they realised that there were no boots on either foot; they'd been replaced by an impressive pair of therapeutic woollen socks, his feet elevated on a pair of pillows. Filled with memory foam according to Eddie Spring, 'if I remember rightly,' he joked weakly.

Paddy drew up a couple of chairs, while Gwanwyn busied herself replenishing the water jug and putting the table *twt*, keeping the small talk going as she often did at work. Paddy was quiet, upset at seeing his friend in such a fragile state, and Gwanwyn roped him into supplying the latest *clecs*. Eddie did his best to respond, grunting and chuckling occasionally, but the effort was too much and he turned away, craving a bit of shut-eye.

Paddy looked at Gwanwyn, who put her arms around him in a *cwtsh* fit for a big brown bear.

"Can I have a word with you, love?" Staff nurse Bethan Hughes introduced herself to Gwanwyn, assuming she was Mr Spring's grand-daughter.

"No, I'm not family, nor Paddy, here."

"Oh, you're the only visitors he's had, so…"

"He's got no family, far as I know."

"His father's buried in Twpsant churchyard," Paddy informed them. "Told me, when he dies he don't want to go like Eleanor Rigby." Bethan Hughes laughed uneasily and indicated the office to Gwanwyn.

Paddy fiddled in his chair, dragging it back and fore like a blunt saw. Eddie Spring snuffled like a boxer dog, then turned and smiled at his friend.

"'Right, Paddy?"

"I'm all right, but you've had a right outing, Eddie."

"Aye, suppose I have."

"Sorry 'bout the accident."

"Accident? It wa'nt no accident, Paddy. Last thing I 'member was the name on the side of the lorry forced me off the road." Paddy was all ears. "J. Bastard and Sons, Metal Recycling."

"Bastard!"

"Don't you worry, Paddy, I got a little plan up my sleeve. When I'm out of this place, you and me'll pay him a visit. Not a word to Gwanwyn, mind, this is our little secret."

Paddy was in his elephant. Mr Spring was coming home and he was looking forward to them giving Mr Bastard a courtesy call.

Gwanwyn and 'staff' returned five minutes later, no doubt having had a good old chin-wag. Mike would be waiting outside, so it was time to love and leave Mr Spring, a smacker on the cheek from Gwanwyn, a *cwtsh* of sorts from Mr Trahern.

Mike dropped them off at *Kath's Kitchen*, top of the list of 'greasy spoons' he'd compiled over the last twenty years. It was conveniently located a stone's throw away from the station, though no-one had thrown that stone, according to Mike. It was just a saying people used.

"Well, hope I see you two again, especially you, Gwanwyn. No offence, Paddy," he laughed, "but she's a bit prettier than you."

"No offence taken, Mike. You're no oil painting yourself."

"Give my love to Kath, will you?"

"Who's Kath?"

Mike chuckled again and pointed to the sign. "She runs the caff. Ta-ra!"

Kath turned out to be as friendly as Mike and on hearing that the pair were 'ravenous,' wondered whether the word had Greek or Latin roots. She went through the declensions in her mind, including the ablative and accusative, but nothing was forthcoming.

The eggs, beans and chips were served up on the biggest plates Gwanwyn had seen, and working in an old people's home, she had seen a few in her time. Gwan and Paddy tucked in with relish, or rather, with lashings of tomato sauce. No conversation was forthcoming until the plates had been wiped squeaky clean with the complimentary pile of bread and butter. The mugs of hot chocolate were still steaming. Kath talked with every Tom, Dick and Harry that called in for their daily spread – notably, Tom Thomas from Townhill, Dick Dicky from Waun Wen and Harry Harries from Cwmbwrla.

During their scoff, the sky decided to change colour and turn on the waterworks. Kath's Kitchen lit up like a toy shop at Christmas, a welcome beacon in the dingy murk of late afternoon. Kath looked at her watch, Paddy made his way to the toilet and Gwan settled up at the till. Kath saw them to the door like life-long friends and Tom, Dick and Harry waved goodbye with their metal forks. Then it was an exhilarating rush through the deluge and a parking of bums on Great Western seats.

Nestling his head into the corner, Paddy decided he loved the train. It was much more comfortable than a car or a bus, and gave you a great view of the countryside. Even in the dark, there were the little lights of the farmsteads to look at, then the bigger pockets of civilisation, before the iconic stations came into sight. Looking around, he was certain that everyone felt the same way. There was only one superior mode of transport, Eddie Spring's bespoke bendy-wagon. That reminded him – now that his friend was coming home, what better welcome than to have his tricycle waiting for him! As he looked at Gwanwyn's sleeping reflection in the glass, Paddy turned his mind to how he could retrieve the vehicle. Probably Dai Grease would give him a hand, not so sure about his son, Gary. Poor old Gwanwyn, she looked shattered! It had been a long day, and seeing Eddie in such a state had taken it out of them. He'd seen her wipe away a tear earlier that afternoon. Perhaps for her, too, the hospital had brought back sad memories

40

Dai Grease was as good as his word, pressing Gary and his recovery truck into service. He didn't know Mr Spring that well, but had heard of his heroic deed the day he led the traffic through the great fog, averting a disaster comparable to the great flood of '92. The day coxswain Evan Floe had gone down with the inshore lifeboat. When Paddy brought him up to speed on Eddie Spring's condition, he was keen to help, though the story he'd been forced off the road was hard to believe.

Paddy was impatient to get the job done, but had to tear his hair out for a few days, for when Gary finally declared himself available, the rain tamped down all day. In the end, Dai Grease threatened to cut his son out of his will unless he got cracking. They picked up Paddy along the way, Grease senior realising how much the operation meant to him.

Surprisingly, neither trike nor cart had sustained any serious damage, a tribute to the craftsmanship of bygone years according to Dai. The handlebars and front wheel needed straightening, the tyres some fresh air and of course, everything needed a good clean. Paddy spent several days with Dai, passing him a variety of tools and using his vice-like grip on the handlebars to keep the trike stable. Dai let Paddy loose with the hose in the courtyard, after which he examined the brakes and oiled the chain. They then hitched up the two vehicles to check balance and mobility. Dai had noticed a couple of chips on the chain stays and small patches of rust on the head tube and chrome mudguards. He wondered if Paddy would like to sand them down, after which they could repaint the bike. Repaint the bike! What a surprise that would be for Mr Spring when he came out of hospital.

"Yes, yes, yes! Thank you, Mr Grease."

*

Jack Harries was a changed man since news of Mr Spring's unfortunate accident had surfaced. If his face hadn't been so inflexible, the more perceptive citizens would have sworn he was smiling. His wife, Alison, benefitted from two consecutive nights of rough sex, one of them with her husband. At tea-time one evening he told Lucy, with a wonderful smirk on his face, that if Paddy wanted a lift to Morriston Hospital he'd be happy to oblige.

"Why are you telling me?" asked Lucy, "he ain't my boyfriend. Hardly see him. Only when he comes into the library with some boring story."

"Lucy!" cried Alison. "If I remember correctly, we couldn't separate you two at one time."

"Thank God those days are over," declared the father, "nothing but trouble, that boy."

"Why d'you want to give him a lift, then?" demanded Lucy, sharply.

"Just to see that his friend's all right," gloated Jack Harries, trying his best not to choke on his boiled potato.

The following evening, with an excellent day of investigating potential felons behind him, Jack Harries repeated his offer to Lucy. His wife raised her eyebrows, wondering if another dangerous, but pleasurable night was on the cards, Lucy looking at him as if he was a half-shat turd. Then the phone rang in the hallway and Alison left the table dutifully.

"It's for you, Lucy," she called out. Lucy ran to take the receiver, anxious to see where Gwilym planned to take her that evening. Her mother blew her lips and shook her head in an effort to convey the voice was new to her.

"Hello!"

"Is that Lucy?"

"Ye-s."

"Oh, hi, my name's Gwanwyn. Gwanwyn Pierce. Sorry to

164

bother you, love. Found your dad's number in the phone book, I did. I'm a neighbour of Eddie Spring, live in the upstairs flat, I do. I've been trying to get hold of Paddy, but I'm in work 'til ten this evening and I need to get a message to him."

"I'm not his girlfriend, now. I'm going out with Gwilym James."

"I know that, love, and I wouldn't have phoned if it wasn't urgent. Me and Paddy went up to see Eddie in hospital last week. I had a call from the sister on the ward 'bout an hour ago to say that he's passed away. Paddy's his best friend, he needs to know."

Lucy dropped the receiver, stunned by this bolt out of the blue; Eddie Spring was a larger-than-life character, he couldn't just die.

"Lucy? Are you there? Lucy?" Gwanwyn's voice hung in the air and Alison Harries, who'd been listening in, sensed that something was wrong.

"Lucy….."", but Lucy reached up for her coat hanging on her special peg and made for the front door. She turned back to look at her mother.

"If Paddy isn't at home, he must be in the pub. I'm going up the Globe to see him. Oh, and tell dad, no, I *don't* want a lift."

41

When Paddy caught up with Gwanwyn, she told him that on the day they'd visited Eddie the staff nurse had warned her he might not survive the weekend. Lying in that ditch full of water for over three days had led to 'trench foot,' giving him painful blisters. Although gangrene hadn't set in, which would have meant amputating his lower legs, he had since picked up an infection, triggering a condition called 'sepsis'. Considering his age, he hadn't been able to fight it.

"But he was fit as hell, Eddie was, Gwan."

"I know that, Paddy, but even a young, healthy person might not have survived three days and nights unconscious in a ditch like that."

"He told me it wasn't an accident, Gwan. Said Bastard's scrap lorry came up behind him and forced him off the road."

Gwanwyn was aware that bereaved relatives often needed something to blame. She didn't want to burst his bubble, but Eddie Spring had hardly said a word, and if he *had* talked to Paddy, could well have been confused. She liked Paddy, but had her own life to lead and knew she couldn't replace Mr Spring as a close buddy. Neither was it her job to arrange the funeral and she hoped that the hospital authorities had contacted Social Services, as promised.

Paddy wasn't stupid. If good people like Dai Grease and Gwanwyn didn't believe his story, then no-one would. He wouldn't be getting any sympathy cards through the post, even though he was grieving and his life had stopped. He wondered what his good friend had meant by not wanting to die 'like Eleanor Rigby.' Who the hell was Eleanor Rigby? And who would listen when he told people he thought Mr Spring wanted to be buried in

Twpsant churchyard, alongside his father? No-one! Worse than that, Paddy was in shock and couldn't think properly. Mr and Mrs Watkins would have helped, but they were visiting their daughter, Angharad, in London.

Paddy looked at a photograph Gwanwyn had taken of him and Mr Spring about to set out for work one sunny morning, without a care in the world. Instead of feeling comforted by the image, Paddy felt an anger well up inside of him, directed at his old friend. He had been managing well enough, thank you, before Eddie had come into his life, forcing friendship and happiness upon him. And then he'd died on him without saying goodbye; there one minute, gone the next. He'd wanted to see the body, but the hospital had dismissed his request because he wasn't a relative. Paddy was on his own, unable to fulfil Eddie's last wishes. He felt bad and he felt tired.

42

PC. Prys Paddler wasn't easily shocked. He had, after all, been patrolling the streets of Downhill since he'd started, but when Paddy Trahern told him in unequivocable language to 'fuck off,' he took a step backward, an embarrassing situation for a servant of the peace who had vowed to never take a backward step. Whatever had come over the boy? Well, no, he was a man, wasn't he? All he'd asked him to do was move the trike off the road, where it was causing an obstruction, despite the absence of double-yellow lines. He'd never heard Paddy use such language and his mam and dad would be turning in their graves.

Before Prys could straighten his helmet or adjust his truncheon, Paddy had stormed off in an excellent direction for washing windows. The houses in Dust Street always needed a good scrub, which is why the residents were entitled to a communal discount. Some took advantage by throwing eggs at their own bathroom windows, but in general people were hard-boiled and played it by the book.

Paddy was fizzing like a Roman candle, angry that his friend had died and that nobody cared. He'd wash those windows so clean the birds wouldn't dare shit on them, and today he couldn't give a fig about the cash. Mrs Adams at the top of the street always let them use her outside tap, and Paddy trundled purposefully back and fore with his bucket, refusing to cry over the odd spilt gallon. If it took all day to do Dust Street, so be it. As Paddy was telling Mrs A about Eddie he caught sight of Miss Chatterley sneaking out of her house and driving away in her car.

"See that," said Mrs A, "one minute she's on the pavement, next thing she's in the driver's seat. Did you see her open the car door?" Paddy certainly hadn't. "She've got supernatural powers, that one. I'm sure she dabbles in black magic. Back on her broomstick after dark. 'Be careful she don't put a curse on us all."

Paddy didn't want to start a bonfire by confirming that Miss Chatterley was not just a witch, but one whose speciality was frying innocent children. The last thing you'd want was a dust-up in Dust Street, but as the morning slipped away he harked back to the cruelty he'd suffered at her hands all those years ago. The nearer he got to her house, the more preoccupied he became with that physics 'experiment,' and could almost feel the electric wire in his hand.

It was no coincidence that her house was painted black or that the name she'd designated to her abode, *Y Crochan* – 'The Cauldron', also served as a warning. The name, in slate, had been there for a spell now. Mr Conicky next door offered to replenish his bucket, but Paddy could see Mrs A hovering at the top of the street. It was *she* who filled his bucket; if Mr Connicky wanted to be water boy, he could find another bucket to top up. Mr Connicky thought better of it and retreated without dignity, catching his trousers on a rusty nail.

Paddy liked the small terraced houses in Dust Street, where he could plonk the ladder fair and square on the sill of the upper window. Even for a man of his height, there was no dangerous stretching involved. Miss Chatterley's bedroom curtains were open, and when he started de-griming the glass he noticed that the bottom sash of the old wooden window had been raised a little inch. Paddy decided to celebrate Devil May Care Day by using both hands to give it a good tug. To his surprise it sprung open like a well-oiled dumb waiter and he was lucky to keep his balance, let alone his fingers. He looked up and down the street, then dived inside, doing a roly-poly onto the carpet.

Paddy had dreamt about getting even with Miss Chatterley, but could never envisage a credible scenario. Now the opportunity had fallen into his lap, and he wasn't about to waste it. Neither would he waste time. He recollected his dad rewiring the house, when he'd watched his every move. On one occasion he'd forgotten to replace the cover of the switch in the *cwtsh dan staer*, and when Paddy had gone looking for Rusty's lead, he'd received a nasty shock fumbling for the light. Well, now it was his old teacher's turn to complete the circuit.

He had a screwdriver in his back pocket for just such an occasion, but didn't need it – the dome-like bakelite switches were identical to his dad's and all Paddy had to do was unscrew one of them with due diligence. He chose the socket in the back bedroom, smiling at the thought of her scrawny fingers being burnt as she groped for the light switch. It was a junk room, filled with books on the occult, toy dolls, black moon crystal balls and children's prams, nothing out of the ordinary. It might be some time before she needed that particular switch, but it would be worth the wait. Paddy was elated as he slid back down his ladder, amazed at how easy it had been to trick-or-treat a witch.

On his way home it was impossible to miss the blaze of red wrapped round Jenkins and Son as they made their way toward the Globe in sheepskin coat and flat cap, carrying overnight bags. Pricks! Off to Twickenham with other beer-bellies for the weekend, show the world how servile the Welsh were, impress the women with their acid wit and finest smut. One of the two must have popped back to retrieve a toothbrush, for the keys were still in the door. Paddy called after them, but they were already round the bend and beyond help. He pocketed the keys and made a mental note to return them when father and son stumbled back home. Or he could keep them, of course. He'd think about it; for now, he wanted to have a bath, then practise his darts.

43

They stumbled noisily out of the *tacsi* on Monday evening, letting the street know that the heroes had returned from the fray.

"Uggy, uggy, uggy!" resounded among the chimney pots, the only song they could sing in tune. Paddy completed the chorus with a "Twats, twats, twats!" Wales had narrowly lost by 30 points, the supporters narrowly pissed on 30 pints. Jenkins Senior couldn't find his keys, so Junior fished out his set. Paddy would have offered them the ones in his kitchen drawer, but couldn't be bothered.

Griffith Jenkins may still have been under the influence the next morning, but that was no excuse. Paddy had been listening to the dawn chorus for the past hour, most of the songsters having congregated high up in the elm tree, whose leaves had started to appear over the last fortnight. He spotted a female blackbird and assuming it was the January widow, willed her to stay where she was, but to no avail. She swooped down into Jenkins's row of broad beans, little knowing it was her last act on earth. Bang! The little brown bird had been summarily executed by the brave PE master.

Paddy was incensed, rushing downstairs with every intention of avenging the widow's death. He plucked a dart from the bullseye on the kitchen door and charged into the garden.

"You bastard, Jenkins, you bastard!" Paddy hurled his missile as high as he could. It cleared the wall easily and sought some sort of target. Paddy heard Jenkins scream, followed by the sound of breaking glass, a faint gurgling noise, then an eery silence. The birds knew when to shut their beaks, they could talk about it later. Back in the bedroom Paddy cowered beneath the sill and snuck a look. Griffiths Senior was hovering above his prostrate son, who appeared to have something sticking in his neck.

Paddy was happy to move his trike for the ambulance, which arrived a minute after the policeman. A crowd of nosy well-wishers had taken up every square inch and PC. Paddler gave instructions to stand back through his imaginary loudspeaker. He would surely receive a commendation this time. Once the ambulance had left the scene, the PC was inundated with questions, but he stuck to his guns and wouldn't be drawn. Not, that is, until he was sitting down in Mrs Probert's parlour, which had a seating capacity of sixty-five when required. It appeared that the rear garden of Number 12 had been the scene of a tragic accident. Ex-PE teacher and popular rugby supporter, Griffith Jenkins, had slipped and fallen unto his greenhouse, shattering the glass, a shard of which had pierced his neck. Blood had been spilt, but it was unknown at this time whether anyone had died in the incident. More information would be available after the second mug of tea.

*

No-one was to know that Griffith Jenkins had stumbled, avoiding the dart headed his way. The man was in no condition to give an accurate account of the incident and Paddy prayed that *his* contribution had been instrumental in the wounding. He couldn't see that he'd done anything wrong, and as the hours passed, was inclined to tell the world of his part in the mischief. His main concern was still Eddie Spring.

On Thursday morning Paddy thought he'd kill two birds with one stone – call in the Co-op for a tin of beans and pick up his monthly payslip at the same time. There was an air of excitement on the streets, huddles of chinwaggers in threes and fours, repeating what the usual suspects had told them. Paddy called in to Willy Phawsgin's shop, where he would at least get the bones of any story.

"Two accidental murders in less than four and twenty hours, the wife told him. Deeds of dreadful note."

"Who's dead?"

"Both of those, Paddy, both of those. One with my throat cut, nasty business, the other electrocuted with wet hands."

"Any names?"

"By heaven, don't stand idly by. There could be more of them!"

He had to wait for the news at six o'clock to make head or tail of it. Griffith Jenkins had died shortly after arriving in hospital, while Miss Chatterley had been discovered by her sister, electrocuted, it would seem, after having a bath. The double tragedy involved two teachers who had retired from Llan Comprehensive five years ago, but the incidents weren't believed to be related. Paddy felt no remorse listening to the reporter; rather, it had given him a sense of self-belief. Onwards and upwards!

44

Lucy was first out the door that Monday morning and this time the message was in red. She couldn't be bothered to read Chalksy's latest witticism, but was intrigued it had been left on the pavement outside the house, and called over her shoulder to her mam. Alison Harries was none the wiser, even after reading it from all points of the compass, but she had more important fish to fry. Looking heavenward, she could see that the elements were extremely favourable. Washing clothes was her favourite pastime and the warmth of the sun and the crispness of the westerly breeze meant she would be a happy bunny come three o'clock. If she had time, she'd erase the artwork with a pail of soapy water.

Jack Harries seemed satisfied with what he saw in the hall mirror, though if the looking-glass could talk, it would have told him his appearance was just as creepy as when he'd come home Friday evening. He was infuriated by the meaningless graffiti scratched by some shiftless arse with the IQ of the piece of chalk he'd used. Why the hell had it been deposited outside his house like an unwelcome turd? He could make no sense of it, no matter how long he stared, and he was damned if he was going to be late for work.

He have scotch'd the snake <u>AND</u> killed it

What the hell? Some junky, off his head, or a group of reprehensibles, sniffing that hippy crack his clientele had told him about. "Alison, get rid of this graffiti at once!"

"Good as done," said Alison, the dutiful wife who heated his pies, before quietly telling him to go fuck himself with his own choice of implement, the rustier the better. She had other tasks to fulfil and unaware of any irony, was enjoying her favourite Richard

174

Clayderman song, *How Deep Is Your Love?* The Prince of Romance did it for her every time, unlike her husband, Jack Harries, who sounded as if he was blowing up leather balloons when he made love.

That afternoon the Trading Standards Officer stopped at a hole-in-the-wall in Llan, wrapped the blood money in a thick purple rubber band and cleverly concealed it in a padded envelope of some quality. He drove erratically, but arrived at the yard at the agreed time. It was eerily quiet; not only had Bastard sent his men on metallic errands, it seemed he'd right-hooked the Rottweiller. Jack Harries found the scrappy in his office, examining a piece of snot he'd extracted not half-a-minute previously.

"Dusty work, see, Mr Harries," he said by way of explanation, then tucked in, moistening the hard lump by sliding it behind his front teeth with his tongue. The salty treat always put him in a better mood, and when he saw the envelope he cleared his throat by swallowing the rest of the nugget. "Ah, I see you have the readies."

"Our agreement was to get him out of the way."

"Which I saw to."

"Didn't tell you to kill him."

"Did my job. Run him off the road. Not my fault if he snuffed it."

"And you're happy about that?"

"Listen, Mr Harries. 'Far as I can see you're quids in. Everyone knows what a madman he was on them roads. No-one's going to question what happened, least of all the *moch*. Not exactly a great loss to this town, is he?"

Lucy's father couldn't disagree with the sentiment. Edwin Spring's contribution to society was risible and decent folk had to stick together. Anyway, the man had apparently died from an infection, *not* from any injuries due to his accident. Jeff Bastard leafed through the wad of notes with his sticky thumb, then proffered his hand to his client.

"Just give us a call if you need me again, Mr Harries. Always willing to oblige."

On his way to the car, Jack Harries took out his pocket handkerchief, spat into it and wiped his hands thoroughly. His heart felt lighter, any regret carried away in the crisp westerly breeze, and he never heard the cock crowing in Farmer Cack's barnyard. Neither did Farmer Cack, who was humping Marlene Wynn-Jones, not the voluptuous barmaid who worked at the *Wheatsheaf*, but his favourite piggy, a sassy sow of ill-repute who happened to have the same name.

Jack Harries continued eating pies; there was no reason not to. It was as he was tucking into a crusty delight his wife had lovingly prepared the following Friday, that he heard the letterbox clank. If he hadn't been in the middle of his grub, he would have left the table in anger and shred the leaflet or whatever other rubbish had been posted. He seethed that so many people were illiterate – there was a sticker on the front door warning all-comers to stay away. The proscribed list for these nuisance callers clearly included the word 'leaflets.' What was there not to understand? Did they think their leaflets more important than everyone else's?

The apple crumble arrived with a jug of fresh cream, Alison no longer expecting any appreciation of her efforts. Lucy was dieting for her new boyfriend and wouldn't eat the pud. On the way upstairs she caught sight of the flyer by the door, picking it up on her return. Beneath it was a folded piece of A4 paper, addressed to her father. Jack Harries confirmed that it was, indeed, for him, unless there was another 'Jack Harries' living in the house. He laughed at his own joke, but those living under the same roof were less enthusiastic, gnawing lower lips and yawning loudly before fleeing the room. Jack unfolded the letter to find a communication of sorts in bold ink.

He have had his cake AND ate it

The choir treasurer was baffled, but for now had to prepare for the Friday night practice. A shit, shower and shave later, he was in a better mood, ready to *basso profondo* with the best of them. If his wife really wanted to know how low he could get, she only had to sit next to him in the second row. When Jack Harries and Albert Snout let go together, you'd swear you were in the bowels of an old sailing ship during a mid-Atlantic storm. Conductor Huw Prys knew how lucky he was to have such an abundance of basses, men for whom other conductors would give their third tonsil.

For Jack Harries, the choir was essential therapy at the end of a stressful week, but as the evening wore on he felt something tugging at his guts, and during the interval was unable to absorb the scraps of gossip Philip Main was offering him on a plate. He had laughed off the scrawl – in fact, it had been written rather neatly – that had appeared on the pavement that morning, but wished, now, that he'd made a note of it. All he could remember was the word 'snake,' but the boys would pull the piss if he started asking about locals who kept reptiles. He'd heard talk of Downhill's own graffiti artist, the clever bastard they called 'Chalksy,' but a message pushed through someone's door was a step too far. It was personal. Was the handwriting the same? Why had Alison been so rash as to wash it away, what was she thinking?

He felt in his jacket pocket for the offending note, which he had at first crumpled up, before straightening it out again. He studied it hard, as if examining it for the humpty-dumpteenth time would shed light on its penmanship. There was nothing cryptic in it, everyone knew what the idiom meant, but why on earth had it been addressed to him? Was it a threat? If so, it was illegal and the malfeasant could be prosecuted, but imagine taking such innocuous 'evidence' to the police. They'd laugh their boots off! His deliberations were interrupted by Albert's stentorian tones booming into his ear.

"Ransom note, is it, Jack? Here you are." Albert's humour held no bounds. He slapped two ten-pence coins into his partner's hand. Jack tittered nervously, Albert refusing to take the money back, insisting he put it towards his next steak pie.

45

Since his friend's death, Paddy had been unable to get his head down properly, unaware the grief was taking a heavy emotional toll on him. For the first time since being given his new clock, Paddy was late for work, ignoring the alarm and pulling the blanket over his head. Maurice Spackman called him into his office and told him that such neglect of duty would not be tolerated in Swindon. Even if he'd been listening, he wouldn't have had a *clem* what the bloke was on about.

Paddy struggled through his shift, incorrectly stacking beans on the shelf reserved for tinned prunes, and directing old Mrs Zimmer-Jones to the digestives, when she'd clearly asked for dog biscuits. Spackman sent Phil scooting up the aisle to deal with the foul-up, with an offer of *'buy one get one free'* on any cat food.

Paddy felt better when the grey afternoon clouds lifted, and was almost ecstatic when a full, pink-coloured moon presented itself at eight o'clock that evening.

"So shine on, shine on April moon," he crooned, leaving the curtains open for his old lunar mate, just the tonic he needed. Anyone in the medical fraternity would have described what happened next as a series of hallucinations, caused by sleep deprivation. The light projected onto the wardrobe mirror produced the most fantastic show Paddy had seen. First up was a troupe of sexy Moulin-Rose pigs doing the cancan, followed by the Devil Incarnat himself, signing copies of his latest book, *Turpitude for Beginners*, at Swansea's Waterstones bookshop, but it didn't unnerve Paddy at all, why would he be frightened by his childhood friend? The celestial cabaret finally moved on to the top of the bill – Eddie Spring himself, in a magician's suit, about to pull something out of his hat.

"Watch this carefully, now Paddy!" Paddy didn't need to be told a second time. He was transfixed as his old mate rubbed his white-gloved hands together and produced not a rabbit, not a bouquet of pink carnations, but a smiling red-nosed clown! And not any old clown, either – this was his old school chum, Mathew Griffiths, the class joker. Despite his bandy legs, Eddie held Mathew up like a toddler, then squished the top hat on to the boy's head, laughing like a fool. After taking a bow, he disappeared in a puff of purple smoke. Dream or hallucination, it didn't matter, the moon had sorted it. Paddy slept like the dead.

*

As he slurped down his hot choc the next morning, Paddy started to feel better and things became clearer. Eddie's plan to take revenge on Bastard had to take a back seat for now. The priority was to give him the burial he wanted – in Twpsant churchyard, alongside his father. Quite where Mathew Griffiths fitted into the new plan, he had no idea; he hadn't seen his old school chum for years, but the message was crystal clear, it was *he* that would help Paddy.

And Paddy needed help. Gwanwyn had recalled the sister in Ward A saying the Social Services would be involved, and suggested Paddy contact the blokey who'd called on Mr Spring a few weeks ago. The other obvious point of contact was the funeral home in Llan, where, no doubt, Eddie was holed up. This would be his first port-of-call, and making his way to the back lane, he couldn't get over how smart the trike looked, a true tribute to his deceased friend. Wait a minute - might as well buy some mints in the shop before setting off.

"Ah, Paddy Trahern, haven't seen him for many a month."

"Morning, Mr Phawsgin. I was in here last week, mind."

"Come for the cat food, was he, girl?"

"No, ain't got a cat. Used to have a dog. You might remember him – *Rusty*, golden Labrador."

"Aye, he was in here tomorrow evening. Lovely nature. How old are they?"

"He died 'bout ten years ago, now, Mr Phawsgin."

"Not enough oil, prob'ly. How shall we help him?"

"Quarter of mints, please." The Love Hearts were redundant now that he and Lucy were no longer an item. It still hurt, but he had more important things to attend to.

"Lucky bastard, mind," said Willie Phawsgin, tapping the front page of the *Llan and District Clecs*. "Millionaire three times over, we wouldn't be surprised."

Paddy glanced at the headline – *Llan Boy Makes Good* – but it was the photograph that took his breath away. Grinning at him, wearing safety helmet, cowboy shirt and hi-viz waistcoat was the unmistakable figure of Mathew Griffiths. Bloody hell, what a coincidence!

"Just returned from Australia, truck driver in world's biggest gold mine, 'pparently. We went out twenty years ago, earns more in one year than the wife made in his lifetime."

"Does it say where he's living? Has he come back to Llan?" Paddy couldn't hide his excitement.

"Start at the beginning, he would, Paddy, start at the beginning. Not worth a punch-up."

Paddy trembled as he climbed on to the trike, then threw the metal stepladder into the cart. Soon his arms were catapulting the artic in the direction of Llan, where he was hoping to kill two birds with one stone. He couldn't hope to reach the heady heights of Mr Spring, but if he *was* stopped by the police, knew that his breath was fresh. And the practice of undoing their fly before they asked you to blow into their 'breathalyser' had been declared illegal and eventually banned in the area.

One or two impatient drivers screamed past him with unkind jibes scorching the air, but there were those comforted by seeing the familiar wagon wobbling gracefully along.

Paddy veered left into Llan's Tesco store and parked in one of the disabled bays provided for people like him. Gethin Gittins, chief trolley boy, was cock-a-rollick when he saw the gleaming trike and sprinted over to help the driver alight from his saddle, letting out a string of silent farts to match each enthusiastic stride. He was sad to hear about Eddie Spring's demise, but reassured Paddy he was there to help on every occasion. As if to prove his point, Gethin deftly trapped a passing paper bag under his right foot and drew Paddy a map showing the shortest route to the undertaker's. He offered to wheel Paddy there in his best trolley, but had to be content with keeping an eye on the machine while Paddy set forth on his important mission.

46

"How can I help you, boy?" Mr Pidding had been an undertaker for as long as he could remember, which in his case meant since Tuesday last. Apparently, a bottle a day kept death at bay, and he was living proof. A hundred per cent proof, as he jokingly told mourning families, sometimes, ironically, after mid-day.

"Is Edwin Spring here?"

"No-one of that name here, boy, 'far as I know." He turned and shouted up the stairs, "Spud, 'ave we got a Hedwin working 'ere?"

"Not as far as I know, Dick. We got a corpse of that name, though. Spring, did you say? Yeah, bounced in yesterday."

"Can I see him, please?"

"Who are you, exactly, boy?"

"I'm his friend. Eddie and me was business partners. He ain't got no family."

Once Paddy had related the history, something flickered in Dick Pidding's brain. Eddie Spring was a familiar figure on the roads, having overtaken the hearse on many a sad occasion. He had great sympathy for any driver, like Paddy's friend Eddie Spring, who suffered abuse from impatient motorists. He'd had to put up with it for years, twats who thought the area permanently played host to the Welsh Grand Prix. He took Paddy into the chapel of rest and told him to take his pick, giving him a few minutes on his own. It was a shock to the system, but Paddy was glad to see his friend was at peace and being well cared for.

Mr Pidding came back in and tapped a folder he was carrying with his index finger.

"He's being cremated next Thursday, ten o'clock, up in St Sizzle's."

"No, no! He wants to be buried next to his dad in Twpsant."

"Not what it says here, boy."

"But…."

The funeral director could see Paddy was upset and motioned him into his office. Only once had he had to deal with a case with no family involvement, what some of the old folk called a 'pauper's funeral.' He showed Paddy the paperwork confirming the council had arranged the cremation and assured him that if his friend had left instructions for a burial, the authorities would have respected his wishes. He could only suggest Paddy phone the council and speak to someone.

Yeah, and who was that 'someone' who would help? Life was a mess in the pants, with no light at the end of the tunnel. Paddy left the funeral home a dejected man. He'd call in *Gwiff's* for a steaming cuppa, but even that wouldn't be the same without his old chum.

Gwiff was one of Llan's curiosities, well over seven foot in height, but with small, compressed ears, which necessitated securing his glasses with Elastoplast on the mornings he hadn't worn them to bed. As early as six-thirty on occasions.

He'd only met Paddy once, but greeted him like a long-lost friend.

"How are you, Dai?" A fervent Welshman, he knew he'd be right fifty per cent of the time. Gwiff insisted Paddy pay for the mug of chocolate himself and told him to take a seat, he'd bring it over in a minute. Paddy explained why he was in town, but Gwiff, like most people, was not a good listener. The fact he had compressed ears didn't help. Statistics proved that only one in a hundred people with compressed ears showed any interest in what others were saying, though as many as three in ten used it as an excuse.

Paddy knew that gin made you cry and chocolate made you feel good, but halfway through his mug of brown stuff, he may as well have been drinking the blue. Where were his friends? He didn't normally indulge in self-pity, but why had Mr and Mrs Watkins chosen that very week to go on holiday? Until recently, Lucy was someone he could rely on, but was now acting like a stuck-up bitch. The boys up the pub would sympathise, but were as much use as Old Mr Fffff, and to be fair to Gwanwyn, she had done her bit. She worked long hours and the funeral wasn't her problem.

"Well, Paddy Trahern, how the devil are you?" Paddy looked up to see the sun-tanned figure of Mathew Griffiths grinning at him. "And what the devil's brought you all the way to the metropolis?"

Paddy couldn't hide his delight. "Mathew, mun, how are you? Heard you been in Oz."

"Yeah. Long story, boy, but I went out on spec 'bout fifteen years ago an' ended up driving trucks in the gold mines. Back for a month or so, I am."

"Saw the story in the Clecs. Old Phawsgin showed it to me in his shop."

"Willy Phawsgin! Still flapping around, is he? Bloody hell, he must be getting on. Hey, can I sit down? What you having, mun?"

For the next hour or so, the two former youngsters clinked their mugs and overdosed on huge slabs of nostalgia, the laughter punctuating the stories putting everyone in a good mood. Gwiff couldn't believe it – his customers were buying a second and third cup, even ordering slices of his home-made carrot cake, the staler the better. Paddy was heartened to see that Mathew hadn't changed, still very much the clown, though he wouldn't have dared mess with the enormous Caterpillar trucks he drove. The photo Mathew fished out of his wallet showed a yellow monster, bigger than most houses in Downhill. The cab was only accessible by climbing a small stairway and though Mathew was tall, the tyres towered above him, at least twice his height. Eddie would have loved a go on one of those if he wasn't dead!

The conversation inevitably turned to the good old schooldays, what the girls and boys in their year had ended up doing. Who had moved away to pastures new? Which girls they had fancied, now in boring jobs with boring husbands, and a plague of kids to look after. Although the two friends hadn't met for the best part of twenty years, it was like picking up a story they'd shared in the pub the night before and Paddy felt no embarrassment spilling his troubled love life to Mathew.

On to the teachers, then; the good, the bad and the sadistic. The screams of the red-faced Griffith Jenkins competing with the tempest blowing across the rugby pitch, the freezing rain bending young fingers into shapes even beyond God's creative abilities. Remember the day the witch had tried to electrocute them? The packed café turned their heads as the two school mates doubled up, recalling the cold-blooded sorceress expounding the benefits of electricity. Mathew asked if she was still amongst the living, adding that the general view was that she never had been. Paddy had news – Miss Chatterley had moved to Downhill, living in a house in Dust Street and no, she was no longer alive. Electrocuted in her own home. Mathew was in tears, so delighted at the irony that Paddy was unable to elaborate on the part he'd played in disposing of the old cow.

One of Mathew's great virtues was that he was genuinely interested in people, a great listener. He wanted to know what shape Paddy was in after all this time and noticed how much his motor skills had improved. God, he'd been the butt of some awful mental bullying in school, expertly administered by teachers and pupils alike. It could have destroyed him. When Paddy got around to his good friend Eddie Spring, the spirit of comradeship between them was palpable, and Mathew understood the deep hole his death had left in his friend's life.

As Mathew waded through the crowd to order a third refill, Paddy remembered the moonlit Mr Spring holding Mathew aloft, and decided that it was now or never. Mathew listened intently as the story unfolded, unsure if he could help in any practical way, but determined to provide emotional support.

"Eddie said he didn't want to die like Eleanor Rigby. No idea what he was on about."

"Eleanor Rigby? Beatles song, Paddy." Mathew started to sing the lyrics and the chilling significance hit him.

Eleanor Rigby - died in the church and was buried along with her name, Nobody came......

He didn't have to explain to Paddy. The man could work out what his friend Eddie had feared most; not death, but departing the world alone. The least Mathew could do was accompany Paddy to the funeral, but was 'the least' good enough? The mood in the café had darkened in an instant and outside *Morus y Gwynt* had invited the clouds to the party, smothering any sunlight and before long *Ifan y Glaw* would turn up unannounced.

Mathew walked back to the car park with Paddy, eager to see the artic Paddy had raved about. Not as big as his Caterpillar, maybe, but its bespoke nature making it a lot more impressive. He took Paddy's number and promised to be in touch before the funeral, then stuffed a tenner into the hand of the faithful Gethin, who was starting to leak. On his return journey Mathew called into Dick Pidding's funeral home which, coincidentally, was next door, but one to his own house in Lock Street. Receptionist Ffion Stevens was immediately charmed by the tall, bronzed bit of stonk who wanted to choose a coffin for his uncle. She even turned the pages of the catalogue for him and was more than willing to give him a tour of the chapel of rest.

47

What happened next happened very quickly, based on the principle that unless you moved your arse, nothing would get done. After all, there were only four days before Edwin Spring was due to be cremated. Mathew drove Paddy to Swansea, where he splashed the cash on a couple of stylish outfits and a slap-up meal in Kath's Kitchen. Kath wanted to know all about Oz and was impressed by Mathew's giant Caterpillar, even more by the tip she discovered hidden under the saucer.

The next day, Paddy had a bath, plastered himself in aftershave, then put on his new suit. He still hadn't mastered the art of crossing the wide end of his tie over the narrow part and looping it into a knot. He'd always relied on his mam or dad in the past – or Lucy. Lucy! Why not? Paddy's batteries had been fully recharged by the chance meeting with Mathew and he was on a high.

He ignored the wolf-whistles some of the tarts on the corner of High Street aimed in his direction and arrived at the library out of breath. Lucy wanted to ignore him, but was deputising for Mair Watkins and had to behave with a bit of decorum. Besides, she had to admit that Paddy looked stonking in his navy suit, white shirt and tan Oxford brogues. The Co-op must be paying well – either that or he'd washed every window between here and Llanelli. With a gaggle of admiring Catherine Cookson fans looking on, Lucy planted her hands on Paddy's shoulders and told him to stand straight. The Burgundy silk must have cost a bob or two as well, but Lucy held her tongue and sealed the knot to a round of applause.

Mr Spring had chosen wisely. Mathew Griffiths had cash, a sense of fun and a working knowledge of construction vehicles.

On Monday morning he spent time staking out Llan Job Centre, carefully signing up half-a-dozen skint men and true in a sort of arse-backwards press gang operation. He approached them individually and after checking they could read and had access to a phone, gave them a note with strict instructions for the morrow. Twenty quid in their hand and another hundred once the job was done. His copy of *Yellow Pages* furnished him with a couple of firms hiring mechanical diggers, but he wanted to sort this face-to-face. Neither boss was willing to rent one out without their own driver, but Mathew was able to slip Ieuan Jones a bob or three at his second port-of-call. The driver would deliver the mini-digger and it was up to Mathew to settle up with him. No paper work was needed, of course, but Mr Jones gave a cast-iron guarantee he would castrate Mathew if there was so much as a scratch on the digger. Mr Griffiths had enough money in his wallet at that moment to buy the digger outright, but thought it wiser to say nothing.

Paddy arrived at Mathew's house on Tuesday midnight, parking the trike at the back. They were up at seven, feasting on a sumptuous breakfast by quarter past and peering out the front window twenty minutes later. Mathew, in black suit, glanced at his watch nervously, then patted the back pocket for his wallet, in case he had to move to Plan B.

The sleepy, secluded Lock Street suddenly woke up. Dick Pidding could be seen flying in and out of his premises, adjusting his coat and shouting instructions into his mobile phone. He made for the 'first call' vehicle and fired it up, heading for the junction that would take him to the far side of town.

"Right, Paddy, out in the lane with you, get on that trike and wait for us. Have the tarp ready." Paddy was on his way, the thick drizzle saturating his thick hair. Mathew had counted on Pidding panicking, and sure enough, the door was unlocked. He located Edwin Spring's coffin in the chapel of rest, then checked to see if the three boys had turned up. Damn! He wiped the rain out of his eyes, but the street was empty. Surely they wouldn't turn down a hundred quid – on top of the togs he'd bought them. He retreated into the funeral home, aware that he was leaving wet footprints on the carpet and that the receptionist may arrive any minute. In the chapel he wheeled the bier alongside Mr Spring's coffin, saving no time, but giving him something to do. He heard the front door clatter and dived behind the coffin, knowing the game was up, and trying to think of a way to extricate himself.

There was only one thing for it – bluff his way out. He pushed the chapel door, wearing his best smile and ready to bid Ffion a very good morning. No-one there, perhaps she'd gone upstairs. As he made for the main entrance, his three recruits appeared, passably dressed. He motioned for them to keep still while he crept upstairs to see what was appertaining.

"Hello? Ffion?" He held his breath, but one of the boys farted a stinker, loud enough to wake the dead and setting off the smoke alarm. But with no show from the receptionist and none of the dead apparently awoken, Mathew regained some of his composure. In the end, the operation went smoothly, and he hoped the old lady and her dog would see nothing odd in a body disappearing into the back lane, rather than the hearse out front. Mr Spring was deposited carefully into the cart and the tarpaulin secured over the coffin. Mathew reminded Paddy to move off slowly and obey the traffic laws, and as the seven-wheeled hearse disappeared into the murk, he reached into his back pocket and paid off the boys.

48

When Mair and Talfryn Watkins embarked on their journey to London, they had left a sleepy old town stuck in a mire of parochial complacency. They returned from the bright lights to find that nothing had changed apart from two accidental murders and a missing corpse.

Mathew's plan had worked to perfection. He'd chosen his recruits well, unconcerned about the high risk involved, confident that Dick Pidding would be open to a fat wadge of banknotes if things went tits-up. At a quarter to eight that Tuesday morning the undertaker had been woken from his stupor by three consecutive phone calls, family members reporting a death in the night. The addresses given would take his first-call vehicles to the far side of town, north and south, and to the village of Nantyffos, five miles down the road. The hoax had kept Mr Pidding and his staff busy for two hours, leading to the director's angry rant being mistaken for a localised thunderstorm. With no sign of him calming down, Ffion tried to advise him of Mrs Crawly's burial at one o'clock; relatives appreciated it when you turned up with the coffin of loved ones, especially if you were the man who'd agreed to arrange the funeral.

The mini-digger had been booked for the following day, the driver leaving it in a layby near the crumbling church of Twpsant. Mathew took over the controls, squeezed it through the rusty iron gates and found Paddy waiting at the side of Andy Spring's headstone. It soon became obvious that Eddie would have to be buried in the same grave as his father, and within half an hour, Mathew and his bucket had skilfully scooped enough earth to get the job done. They used a plank to slide the coffin out the back of the cart and grunted and groaned Mr Spring to his last resting place. Paddy thought Eddie'd be fine with him dancing on his grave in order to pack the earth in solid. Paddy had wanted to invite Gethin and Gwanwyn to a party in the disused church, but Mathew persuaded him that a shindig in the pub was the better option – on the day of the *official* funeral.

Both Gwan and Geth were working on the Thursday, but were looking forward to the sesh in the Globe at seven o' clock. That morning, Mathew picked Paddy up in good time for the short journey to St Sizzle's crem, helping him fix his Burgundy silk, which completed his stylish comportment. The trees were being bent by the April gales and a tardy fox was making his way home at the top of the hill, but there was very little human activity. The two mourners stood expectantly at the side of the chapel entrance as though they were posing for a quirky photograph. Five minutes later the manager appeared, standing on the steps, glancing at his watch. He looked at the be-suited Burke and Hare as if they were to blame, then retreated into his lair. After more wringing of hands, there was a ringing of phones, then an oath of disbelief.

A red car screamed into the car park to their right, followed by a black Mustang. Two men came running over and were met by a seething manager of reddish hue. Paddy recognised the first to arrive as Jack Harries, Lucy's father, who announced he was representing the local authority. The body snatchers sidled towards the conversation and were as surprised as anyone to find that Edwin Spring and his coffin had disappeared off the face of the earth. Social worker Steve Charmer added that the funeral would be postponed, the manager ushering everyone out of the way while mourners arrived for the next scheduled funeral.

"Hope this time the hearse arrives with a body," muttered Mr Crem, still of reddish hue.

Mathew was keen to catch up with the councillor and his minion chatting furtively by the bonnet of the red car. The social worker was on the receiving end of Jack Harries's famous tongue.

"Postponed indefinitely?"

"Yes – pending police investigations."

191

"You called the police?"

"Yes, this could be a criminal act."

"Did you approve your call with anyone? Someone, perhaps, in a senior position? Someone who could have dealt with it competently?" He sighed deeply as Paddy drew up. "Looks like your friend's up to his old tricks, Paddy, doesn't want you to bury him."

"Mr Spring said that he wanted……"

Mathew interrupted Paddy before he dumped them in it. "Have you any idea what happened, sir? How can a coffin go missing?"

"Don't know," snapped Harries, "but when they find it I'll supply the nails. Come to think about it, Paddy, I'll find some lag bolts. That should do it."

"Come to think about it, Mr Harries, why don't you fuck off. That should do it." Mathew dragged his mate away before Jack Harries had time to process Paddy's light-hearted banter. It was time to get ready for tonight.

*

The boys would rather have watched *Pobol y Cwm* and *Corry*, but Mathew had put a thousand quid behind the bar and they reluctantly struggled through the warm spring air, lining up politely to be served. Landlord Freddie Sauce, as the *maître d'hôtel*, wore a red polka-dot dicky bow and his wife of forty years, Maureen, barely anything. Freddie had been too mean to employ extra staff, so in the end, the boys jumped over the bar and helped themselves.

From the television screen above the bar the beaming image of Eddie Spring lorded it over the clutter of serial boozers, while Richard Clayderman boomed out over the speakers, supported by Pink Floyd. No-one realised Mr Spring had such an eclectic taste, assuming it was confined to beans and sausages. Dai Tote opened a book on who would be the next to snuff it, and a fight broke out when old Humphrey Price was declared odds-on favourite at 3/5. Billy Walters thought *he* should be favourite because of his long-standing heart condition, while Teddy Buck put in a strong claim, citing his lumbago and suggesting odds of 4/7.

Mathew told Gwanwyn the funeral had been postponed, but didn't go into detail, and with two days off work she was keen to get stuck into the vodka. It wouldn't take long for the story to become public knowledge, but Mathew was confident Paddy would stay *schtum* about the burial. He'd drummed into him the consequences of spilling the beans. They'd made sure Eddie Spring *hadn't* died like Eleanor Rigby and now he must rest in peace. As a *persona non grata*, Mathew didn't think the authorities would be keen to investigate thoroughly and there'd be no family or friends to rock the boat.

49

Paddy knew the importance of keeping quiet about the grave-robbing expedition, but was on pins to tell the truth regarding the 'unexplained' deaths of the two teachers. It wasn't his conscience bothering him, he was happy they'd croaked as they did, but he felt the public should know why both deserved to die.

Paddy and Tal were now working two nights on the scenery, because as the backcloth was being painted and *Sir Timothy's* garden furniture put in place, they didn't want to obstruct Mair's rehearsals. Paddy turned up Wednesday evening to find Tal and Dai Grease playing with a chassis the mechanic had made from an antique pram. Having lugged it onto the stage, the two men retrieved an old tank, which they positioned upside-down on the chassis.

"Where'd you find that, Dai?"

"Been up in the loft 'long as I can remember, Tal. Never bothered to get rid of it when the new boiler went in. It's a galvanised cold water tank."

"Well, it's just the job for our fire-engine." Then, turning to their small friend who'd joined them, he added, "your job to paint it, Paddy." He pointed to the tin of gloss at the front of the stage. "Nearest thing I could get to post-office red. It'll look a treat when it's finished."

Dai retrieved the thick cardboard carpet tubes that would run alongside the tank and a flat length of cream-brown fire hose that had 'fell off the back of a lorry.' Paddy reckoned there were a lot of those type of lorries in Downhill. As Tal asked Paddy to unroll the hose towards the front door of the *Bellboys* house, Dai Grease was keen to know how his work of art fitted in to the scheme of things.

Tal laughed. "Basically, it's a comedy, Dai. It's set in Dorset in 1804, everyone's in a panic because they think Napoleon is about to invade. *Sir Timothy* has a plan to fight the French single-handed, but his brother, *Lamprett Bellboys* is more concerned with his fire brigade. Ends up putting out all the signal fires the Local Defence Volunteers have lit warning people about the invasion."

"Sounds good. I'll have two tickets for me and the wife."

"Oh, you definitely got complimentaries after all the work you put in."

"My pleasure. Once you've painted everything, Paddy, I'll be back to help you fix the tank. And we'll need some strong glue for the tubes."

"It's going to look amazing. Next Wednesday suit you, Dai?"

"*Dim problem.* Ta-ra!"

Paddy was studious in his work, slow but meticulous, careful not to spill a drop on to the dust sheet, be it emulsion or gloss. The red was an exciting new colour and Dai Grease had primed the tank's surface to ensure the paint stuck. He'd offered to spray-paint it, but appreciated that this was Paddy's job. Paddy noticed a drip that was running down the edge of the tank and moved in to smooth it with a few expert brush strokes. A few small specks had spattered on to the dust sheet, reigniting the image of Griffith Jenkins bleeding in the garden. He looked up to see Mr Watkins at the top of his step-ladder, fixing a curved fanlight above the main entrance door of *Sir Timothy's* house. Whoever had made it had done a good job. Probably Mrs Watkins. Paddy rested his brush in his jar of turps, wiped his hands on his rag, heaved himself up off his knees and made his way over to bend Tal Watkins's ear.

"Done a good job, there, Tal."

Tal Watkins reached for the screw he was holding in his lips. "Thanks, Paddy. Is it straight?"

"Yep. Straight as a dart."

Tal smiled to himself. "Heard you're quite the darts player these days, Paddy. Regular member of the team, according to Freddie Sauce."

Paddy was proud of the dart he'd thrown into Jenkins's garden, straight into his neck, probably. "What exactly makes a serial killer, Mr Watkins?"

"Serial killer? Well, it's someone kills a few people."

"Would two be enough?"

"No, think it'd have to be more than that, Paddy. Why do you ask?"

"I've killed two people, see," said Paddy earnestly. "One with a dart, as it happens."

It took a lot to floor Tal Watkins, and unable to read Paddy's facial expression, he played along. "Two? You've been busy, Paddy boy." He tightened the last screw, backed down the ladder and made for the tin of *Evostik* to make sure nobody'd been sniffing it.

"Tell you what, Paddy, I think it's time for a cuppa. Stick the kettle on, will you, while I go for a wee."

Tal hoped Paddy would have forgotten about his new career in bloodshed, but he was raring to go once he'd plonked the mugs on the table. By the time Paddy had given an exhaustive account of his part in the unusual demise of the two teachers, Tal had doubts. How did Paddy know that Miss Chatterley's switches were made of bakelite, or how to ensure she got a shock? He knew Jenkins was a bully and that the animal community lived in fear of him, and could see why Paddy was angry about the blackbirds, but there was a difference between saying 'I'll kill the bastard' and actually killing the bastard, whether by electrocution or a dart through the jugular.

Tal was puzzled at Paddy's insistence, unsettled that the forensic evidence he offered seemed to add up. The fact that Ken Trahern, Paddy's father, was a sparky could be used on both sides of the argument; Paddy may have seen his father at work and learnt how to 'talk the talk,' but conversely may well have known how to fry a witch on a switch. No, surely it wasn't possible. And the police report confirmed that Jenkins had fallen through his greenhouse, a definite accident. No mention of poisoned arrows.

"Right, back to work, is it? That fire engine's going to be the star of the show, Paddy."

But Paddy's gleaming art work could wait, this discussion was far from over. "See, Mr Watkins, that wasn't no accident, neither."

"What's that Paddy?"

"My good friend, Mr Spring. He was forced into that ditch by Jeff Bastard."

"How do you mean?"

"He told me. In hospital when we went to visit him. Recognised the truck – run off the road, he was. I'll get him for it, though, mark my words, Mr Watkins."

Tal Watkins was of the same opinion as Gwanwyn. If Eddie Spring *had* said that, it was because he was off his head on morphine. The police had concluded Mr Spring had been speeding and referred to his vehicle as a 'vicious cycle.' Still, three accidental deaths in the space of two weeks was fodder for any conspiracy theorist.

He unburdened himself on his lovely wife that evening, then told her about Paddy's strange confession and his comical threat to liquidate the scrap merchant. It still came as a surprise the next day to find Paddy at the library desk, eager to learn about serial killers. Before long he was settled at a table reading the exploits of Dr Harold Shipman, who fortunately worked in Manchester, about 200 miles away. His own GP, Dr Lake, had once prescribed him a screwdriver, but had never used one on a patient as far as he knew. Mair found another book for him in the *True Crime* format, and this gave him what he wanted. To become a serial killer, he needed to increase his tally to three. That was well within his grasp.

50

It took the Clecs a few weeks to sniff out possible rascality at Dick
Pidding's funeral home. Dick should never have downed that extra
pint and mentioned it to his wife, a seasoned clecker of fifty years.
It wasn't every day that a corpse went missing, but those in the
firing line had weighed up the risks and agreed to keep quiet. Their
biggest fear was that Paddy and his new friend would demand to
know where the body was, but they seemed to be satisfied with
the riotous party they'd organised in Eddie Spring's memory. And
there were no interfering relatives on the horizon.

When Dick was approached by Clecs reporter, Clive Lewis, he
got on the phone to Jack Harries, who arranged a meeting for all
fearful personnel. As chair, he didn't bugger about, using hand
gestures suspiciously similar to those of *Der Führer*, masterfully
bawling at the bewildered gathering. After some veiled threats, the
agreed script was that Steve Charmers, representing the local
authority, had arranged the funeral, attended by a handful of
people. The ashes were being kept at the chapel of rest if anyone
was interested. Pidding's staff knew that should the truth be
revealed, the funeral home would become a laughing stock and be
forced to close. No more urnings.

The newspaper had to be careful what it printed, even though
it was servicing a population that specialised in cock and bullshit.
Editor Robert Hill decided to play it safe and consult his legal
team, Miss Mary Plum. Clive was a seasoned reporter, certain he
was on to something, but there was no proof that the body of one
Edwin Spring had gone walkies.

"He's a thorough reporter, Miss Mary. All the officials he
interviewed seemed nervous. No smoke without fire."

Miss Mary wasn't impressed. Clive Lewis's hunch was

immaterial; after all, as she understood it, Robert had employed Alan Allcock as delivery driver, and he only had one eye. "You can't prove a thing, Robert. If we're going to use idioms, I'm telling you to let sleeping dogs lie. The fire's only likely to burn your fingers and may even burn your house down." He always took Miss Mary's advice; she was the wisest owl in town. Pun or not, they would bury the news.

One of those nervous fellows was Jack Harries, normally confident and overbearing, who was now staggering from one jittery day to the next. He became the Clecs's most punctual subscriber, scanning the columns each evening with his heart in his mouth. Night sweats saturated the bedsheets, replacing the secretions generated by rough sex with Alison. His wife was woken by his mumbling in blue-striped pyjamas, making out the word 'spring' and wondering if it was the mattress bothering him. Lucy knocked on their bedroom door one night, afeared that some sort of violence was being administered. Her mother switched on the bedside lamp and put a finger to her lips, reassuring her daughter that the man writhing in the bed beside her was not wielding an axe. Lucy noticed her mother smiling and started to laugh, retreating to her room in a fit of giggling. Alison joined her and accepted her invitation to *cwtsh* up and get a good night's sleep.

Jack Harries could hardly eat a morsel at breakfast the next day, sipping his tea, but sliding the same bit of toast around his mouth like a cow chewing the cud. When his wife asked him what was ailing him, he mooed angrily at her, then at his daughter when she made her appearance. The women of the house looked at each other knowingly, Lucy shrugging her shoulders and raising her eyebrows.

Twenty minutes later she set off for the library, her father heading in the opposite direction. Why had he got involved with the thug up at the scrapyard? He should have stuck with what he knew – acceptable corruption within the local authority, not messing around with dangerous cowboys. If he thought a word with Bastard would alleviate his growing paranoia, he was wrong.

199

"Top of the morning to you, Mr Harries. Didn't think I'd see you again so soon. What have you got for me?"

"What have I got for you? What have I got for you? Ha, ha, what are you expecting, Mr Bastard, another five hundred pound?" Even Jeff Bastard, not a sensitive man by most people's standards, could see that the man was on edge, and decided 'say nothing' was the best tactic.

"No, I ain't got nothing for you."

Bastard thought it was time to bring the conversation to an end. "Well, you can fuck off then, stop wasting my time," he said delicately.

"All I wanted you to do was frighten the man, not…."

"Not this again. Jesus, can't you leave it alone!"

"He's risen from the dead."

"Didn't take you for a religious man, Mr Harries."

"His body's missing."

"You don't believe all that tittle-tattle, do you?"

"He's coming after me. You, as well, probably."

Jeff Bastard laughed heartily and had to sit down, overcome by an uncontrollable coughing fit. "Well, if he comes in here on his trike, ha, ha, ha, I'll be sure to let you know. It might be some time, mind. Oh, dear me! Pass me those that bog roll, will you? Ha, ha, ha! Perhaps we've been invaded by body snatchers."

Jack Harries could happily have killed Bastard at that moment. He left the scrapyard feeling desolate, more lonesome than he'd ever felt in his life. Every time he saw PC. Prys Paddler calling in on his radio or a police car in his rear-view mirror, he panicked. A knock on the front door made him spill his tea, and he was glued to all news reports on TV and radio. Dick Pidding started to lose patience after his third visit to the funeral home in a week and realised his reassurances were in vain. The man was delusional. Yes, the body had somehow disappeared, but Edwin Spring had been certified dead and as far as he knew, there were no 'resurrection men' listed in the *Yellow Pages*. He was puzzled why Jack Harries was so concerned; perhaps as a conscientious Trading

Standards Officer he couldn't let the matter go, might even end up prosecuting himself. Hopefully, he'd have something more serious to occupy him before long.

Things would get worse for Jack Harries before they got even worser, as the locals would say. At night he was plagued by Edwin Spring, appearing as guest soloist in the Christmas concert, or wining and dining his wife, Alison, at *Zits Ristorante*, but in daylight hours caught sight of him weaving manically through the traffic. He returned to his car one morning, after picking up the Clecs from a newsagent in Llan, to be greeted by Eddie Spring in the passenger seat, sucking a Polo mint. The apparition only wanted ten seconds of his time, but was enough to spook him for the rest of the day. Alison and Lucy could see that he was miserable, but every attempt to talk was rebuffed. He was losing weight, unable to find solace in the pies his wife lovingly placed in front of him. She was mortified when he declared his intention of giving choir practice a miss; that was like Ethel Jones refusing a bargain in Pet's Rescue. She eventually persuaded him the choir couldn't do without him, but had to re-assemble his tie before he stumbled out the front door.

Alison hadn't been driven purely by altruistic motives, for she wanted to put her feet up on the sofa with a glass of *Piña Colada* in her left hand, her right making sure George Clooney was earning his corn. She watched *Out of Sight* at least once a month, the fifth glass confirming her view that Jennifer Lopez was a shit actress. Lucy had gone to the cinema with Gwilym James and no doubt they'd be fucking in his flat later. He was tidy enough, not as dishy as George, but at least he had a discernible neck.

The singing of sweet songs and some decent male company was the palliative Jack Harries needed. Following the conductor's every movement, he felt a lot more composed, agreeing to a drink in the *Drovers* with Norman Rock and Alun Thomas, even insisting they buy him a pint. Jack asked Norman to drop him off at the library, intimating the fresh air would do him good. The choir treasurer jingled the coins in his pocket and hummed the bass part of *Myfanwy*, causing the town mongrel to poke his head out of the alleyway. When it ran down the road, Harries noticed that it had only three legs, one more than when he'd seen it on the roundabout. Perhaps he'd had one pint too many.

The air was almost balmy, with the hint of summer in the night sky. He could forget the spring. Ha! He laughed at his little joke – he could forget Mr Spring. He stopped under a lamp-post and sang his own version of the Duke Ellington song he'd learnt in school:

> *That ole' Mr Spring*
> *He don't mean a thing,*
> *That ole' Mr Spring,*
> *He ain't got no swing.*

He repeated his ditty several times for any dog that might be listening, his voice like a seagull with a sore throat, then turned into his street a happy man. He might even make a cheese and pickle sandwich and, if lucky, dip his lucky wick.

And then, like something out of *Friday the 13th*, his equilibrium was shattered by a clutch of ghost-white figures swaying malignantly at his feet. Another missive had been delivered on the pavement outside the Harries house by the light of the silvery moon. He knelt down, moistened his finger, and rubbed the writing to check this was no mirage.

Is this a dagger I see before me?

Dagger? Yes, he could see the dagger before him, how could he bloody miss it? Very artistic, he had to admit, in bottle-green, with bright red splashes dripping from the blade. If he'd been a detective he'd be looking for the proud owner of a box of coloured chalk sticking out of his arse pocket. Heaven help him when Jack Harries got hold of him, he'd skewer the bugger!

With not one marble to his name, he strode insanely into the house, eager to elicit his wife's sympathy. Ah, good, there was a light on in the living room, his beloved was still up.

"Alison!" he shouted. Even if he'd split the sofa asunder with a giant chainsaw, he couldn't have woken her. Alison Harries had had her fill of firewater, but the whooping it up had been short-lived, and she was dead to the world. The fact that his wife was in no position to help fed into his paranoia. He knew what was happening, he wasn't stupid. The 'deceased' Mr Spring was very much alive and with the connivance of the rest of the population, was striking terror into the choir treasurer. He no longer had any appetite for his sandwich and kicked out at the stool in the kitchen. He missed, and as he fell, he head-butted the metal bucket his wife had illegally parked behind the door. Never mind, the bucket had jogged his memory. *Every cloud*, he winced to himself, filling it at the sink and fetching the mop from the *cwtsh-dan-staer*. Lucy and Gwilym drew up in a taxi as he was trying to erase the dagger.

"What the hell are you doing, dad?"

"'Is this a dagger…' That's William Shakespeare, isn't it? said Gwilym James impressively.

"William 'Chalkspeare,' more like," giggled Lucy. "Mind you don't catch your death of cold out here, dad."

51

That weekend, life was chaotic in the Harries household. Alison woke at ten o'clock with a raging thirst, to be confronted by her husband with spiteful accusations of 'conspiracy to put the wind up him.' She was in no mood to argue, seeking relief in the kitchen, where she cupped her hands under the cold tap to receive the blessed water. She splashed her face, then lapped greedily, as skilful as any dog. She couldn't work out why the bucket was full of water in the middle of the floor or why the mop was propped against the fridge, but that was the least of her worries. She swallowed a couple of fat aspirin tablets and made her way to the comfort of her bed, ignoring the peculiar whingeing of him indoors.

Lucy kept out of her father's way, sharing her mother's concern when they discussed the situation on Sunday afternoon.

"If he goes on like this, Lucy, I'm going to speak to Dr Lake."

"I'll come with you."

"No, you won't. I know you, you're finding all of this very amusing."

Lucy's face reddened. "No, I'm not, I feel sorry for him," she replied defensively. "Anyway, you were laughing the other night."

"That was different. Talking in his sleep, a lot of people do that. It's as if he's cracking up. Something to do with the messages he's been receiving. I can't remember the first one he got, can you? You saw it first. He deals with a lot of dodgy characters in his work, takes some to court. Perhaps he's being threatened."

"Or blackmailed."

"What do you mean?"

"Well, if he's taken a back-hander off someone?"

"No, your dad would never do that. Straight as a die, he is."

Lucy wasn't convinced. If her father was being threatened, why wouldn't he report it to the police? In work the next day she buttonholed her boss, Mair aware of Paddy's wish to be a serial killer and wondering if he'd given her a blow-by-blow account of the two 'murders' he'd committed. She was relieved to hear it was the strange behaviour of her father that was bothering her. This was a matter for the family, not her concern.

But then the conversation took a twist. Lucy told Mair she'd caught snippets of a conversation her father had had on his mobile phone one evening at the bottom of the garden. Lucy had been in her bedroom with the window open. Her father was speaking to a man called Alan and they'd discussed a 'price' for doing something. Most of the exchange had been *sotto voce* (a musical term her father brandished about to show everyone he was a twat), but he'd raised his voice at one point.

"He definitely said 'arson' and 'a particular person' and 'put the frighteners on him.' I reckon he was up to something dodgy and it's come back to bite him on the bum. Why would he go right up the garden? He didn't want me and mam to hear, that's why!"

"Have you spoken to your mam?"

"She thinks, with his job, he'd never do anything naughty, but the way he's behaving, Mrs Watkins, well.....!" Lucy put her hands on her hips in a dramatic pose, making Mair laugh. There never seemed to be a dull moment when she was about. The plot was definitely thickening, especially in the light of Paddy's resolute belief that Mr Spring had been targeted. Yet 'arson' didn't make any sense and who the hell was 'Alan'? And messages in chalk? She mentioned it to Tal that evening, both concluding it was like trying to fit the pieces of three different jigsaws together and that Lucy's father needed psychological help. Perhaps he had a drink problem.

Jack Harries's problem was that he couldn't get enough drink, but when he did imbibe, it merely fed his paranoia. He was still recovering from the fiasco of Friday night, picking at his evening meal, when Alison found another missive, and despite her best efforts could not hide it from her husband.

Out, out, brief candle!

It wasn't the content, which could have been a cryptic clue from the *Times* crossword as far as he was concerned, more about the fact that there was a message *at all*, clearly addressed to 'Mr Jack Harries' and delivered by hand.

"Right," said Alison, "we're going to the police."

"No, no, no! They're not going to be interested in some stupid notes pushed through someone's letter-box." He doubted whether the resurrected Mr Spring's fingerprints would be of use. He left the table, his glare leaving his wife and daughter in no doubt that no further action would be taken.

An incident the following supper time brought matters to a head, narrowing Alison's options. Jack had got into the habit of returning early from work, eager to scrutinize every word in the local rag. That day was no different, Jack moping around the house until the arrival of the paper at four o'clock struck terror into him. He snatched it out of Alison's hand and spent the next half-hour poring over it uneasily. His wife kept an eye on him from the hallway, but could never have guessed he was looking for a letter to the editor from someone brought back from the dead. What on earth was troubling the man?

Jack Harries put down the paper with a huge sigh of relief and closed his eyes. After three days without food, the smell of cooking wafting in from the kitchen aroused his senses and his spirits improved. Life wasn't so bad, after all. Although he didn't need a shit, he decided to shower and shave, look tidy when he came to eat his good-looking pie.

Lucy was already seated, having plonked the bowl of new Pembrokeshire potatoes in the middle of the table. Alison called up meekly to her husband, who was adjusting his tie and admiring his neck in the mirror. She then returned to the kitchen and the juicy steak pies, transferring them in orderly fashion from the oven to the pre-warmed dinner plates, just as Jack required. As he made his way downstairs, a feast was awaiting.

Lucy was spooning some spuds on to her plate when her father appeared.

"Hi dad, have you had a good day?" She netted a baby 'tato, unaware that her father had frozen to the spot. Alison wouldn't start until Jack had cut his first slice of pie and wondered if he was playing some sort of game.

"Are you going to.........?"

"Aaaah!" he shrieked, "what's *he* doing here?" He pointed in terror at his chair, then bolted out of the house, leaving his wife and daughter totally bewildered.

"Right, that's it. He's seeing Dr Lake in the morning."

"Good luck, there, mam, we'll probably have to tie him down. These spuds are delicious, by the way. And the pie, of course. And the veg." Alison tried to smile.

She need not have worried, for in the morning Jack Harries followed her to the surgery like an obedient dog. His face was vacant, his mouth unable to return the sing-song chorus of '*bore dâ*'s that flew his way. Alison smiled weakly, acutely aware that her husband had no neck and that in the bright sunshine he looked like a hard-boiled egg wedged into its cup. Dr Lake's receptionist, Elsbeth Morris, believed that patient confidentiality was something best channelled through her and her hair appointments and she did her utmost to squeeze the story out of Jack's wife. She gave up after an hour and reluctantly conceded that the surgery was the right place to come if you wanted to see a doctor. Although they had been swamped that morning with dozens suffering from seasonal Chimney Flu, the receptionist would try and fit them in. And true to her word, before the clock could strike mid-day, Alison was seated alongside Jack in front of the good doctor, who was putting his name to a prescription.

"Tall, curved spine, size thirty-six waist. That's another one done," he beamed. "Now then, Alison, how can I help you?"

But before Alison could open her mouth Elsbeth Morris burst

through the door with good news for the hippocratic oaf sitting at his table.

"Myles Better is in reception, Dr Lake."

"No, can't say I can place him, Elsbeth."

"Yes, you know, thinner than them whippets he do keep." Dr Lake's canine knowledge was second to none, but he still appeared mystified.

"The little *gay* man."

"Is he? Well, what's his problem?"

"You promised him an asthma pump, doctor."

"Did I? Good Lord!" Dr Lake heaved himself up and made for the medicine cupboard, rooting around commendably on the second shelf.

"Here you are, Elsbeth, he can have this one. Tommy Jones has finished with it now that he's dead."

"Thank you, doctor." The receptionist triumphantly made for the door.

"Oh, and Elsbeth. You say he's gay?"

"Yes, doctor."

"Gay. You mean he plays the tin whistle?"

"No, he's an homosexual, doctor."

"Ah, I see. An homosexual? Mm…" Dr Eurig Lake took the pump back for a minute and turned it over in his hand. "Here, tell him not to overdo it. No more than two puffs a day."

Alison was almost tearing her hair out by the time Dr Lake eventually turned his attention to her.

"It's Jack, doctor."

"Yes, I know Jack. He's your husband."

"He's not well."

"Who's not well?"

"Jack. My husband." Not wanting to embarrass her husband, she tried to catch the good doctor's attention and mouth the words, *He's started to masticate in front of me and Lucy at breakfast*, but the medic was fiddling with his hearing aid. Alison changed tack, upping the volume.

"No appetite, keeps seeing things. And he's been getting these messages through...."

"I want to speak to Dr Lake by myself. You can go," Jack snapped at his wife. She looked at their GP, her eyes imploring him to help. He escorted her to the door, squeezing her hand in reassurance, telling her to make herself a cuppa and return in half an hour.

"Now then, Jack," he shouted into his stethoscope, "let's have a listen, shall we? Roll up your shirt. Still got no neck, I see," he joked, hoping to lighten the atmosphere.

"He was there, last night, saw him clear as day."

"Who's that, Jack?"

"Edwin Spring. Sitting in my chair dinnertime, tucking into my steak pie."

"Eddie Spring? Jiw, jiw, he was in here not that long ago with his mate Paddy."

Jack Harries grimaced on hearing the names of the two reprobates. "Alison and Lucy said they couldn't see him, but he was there all right."

"Um..." Dr Lake was making notes. "Was it just the pie he ate, Jack? If I remember rightly, Eddie Spring loved his veg and 'tatoes."

"Didn't stay around to find out, doctor. Put the wind up me."

"Yes, pie sometimes has that effect. You know he's dead, Jack, don't you?"

"Might have been once, doctor, but he's very much resurrected."

"Um..... how do you spell that, Jack?" He shuffled over to his cupboard and poked around behind some medicine bottles that had gathered cobwebs. "Ah, here they are!" He stood at Jack's right shoulder. "Now then, is it a flat-head or a Phillips?"

"Eh?"

"The screw that's loose. Need to know which screwdriver to use. It shouldn't hurt."

When Alison Harries returned, it was suggested her husband

be referred to the Social Services, with a view to admitting him to residential care. Jack Harries agreed, on condition that it was a temporary measure, for a maximum of six months. First hurdle over! Alison whooped quietly and hoped that the sentence would be extended.

Steve Charmer visited the family home on the Thursday, efficient as ever, three forms of different colours in his briefcase. 'Planned convalescence' he called it. Alison and Lucy plied him with tea and biscuits and would have added their savings if it would guarantee taking Jack Harries away for a while. Charmer knew that nothing was as easy as it appeared, but as a skilled social worker, had one or two tricks up his sleeve, as well as some birdshit running down the back of his jacket. Mother and daughter earwigged at the door as Jack Harries 'ummed and 'awed on hearing the first proposition.

"Well in that case, Mr Harries, you'll have to go to Neath."

Jack's face turned a desperate hue that rather suited him at times. "Neath?" he exhaled in barely a whisper.

Charmer knew he had won.

"Yes, Jack – Neath. Katherine Jenkins has set up a home for retired mercenaries." Charmer knew the cost would be prohibitive, but his bluff was working anyway.

"No, anywhere but Neath." The Trading Standards officer had been humiliated on more than one occasion by the market traders of that town selling their *spinning snowmen* at three times the going rate. He had attempted to take them to court, but had faced mass protests and jostling from citizens willing to pay the price.

Once things were agreed, the social worker offered to transport Mr Harries himself, but his family wanted to pack his toothbrush and help him settle in. They would see Steve Charmer there. And so, on Sunday afternoon, two cars pulled up at an impressive old building outside Twpsant and Jack Harries could look forward to some peace of mind in his room on the upper floor of the Home for the Ridiculous. He kept very much to himself, his only companion Rhodri Bellows, who'd been found ridiculous after he'd been found wanking over pictures of right-wing populist politician, Ann Widdecombe. If it had stopped there he might only have received a caution but things became stickier when he started stalking her.

52

"*You say he's from Downhill?*"

"*Yes, guv,*" *replied PC. Ian Davies.*

DI. Cudgel coughed a nervous laugh and exchanged a knowing glance with his partner, DI. Hammerhead. Several months previously, they'd been requisitioned to that very town, where a bloke called Spring had made a monkey out of them. For the sophisticates who worked in Swansea Central Police Station, the rule was to steer clear of the community nestled in the beautiful rolling countryside some miles west of the city. It had, in fact, become an official directive written in bold red ink on the noticeboard, to which some wag had added the words, 'OBEY or REGRET FOR THE REST OF YOUR DAYS.'

"*And he says he's murdered two of his ex-teachers?*" *DI. Hammerhead this time.*

"*Yes, guv. And he's going to murder the local scrap merchant says killed his friend. Reckons three will make him a serial killer.*"

"*Well, he's got more ambition than most of them live in that backward hole,*" *sniggered Cudgel. "It'll certainly put our little country on the map. Anything the Yanks can do......*"

"*Really should refer it back to Dyfed-Powys, but they won't be interested. Bloke sounds like a nutter,*" *reasoned DI. Hammerhead.*

"*He's bright enough,*" *said Davies, "but there's something a bit off-beam about him.*"

"*No! Off-beam? Lives in Downhill? Wants to be a serial killer? Can't believe that,*" *chortled the larger of the two detectives.*

"*Even showed me the murder weapon.*"

"*What the hell!*"

PC. Ian Davies opened his hand to reveal a lightweight dart with a red plastic flight. "Not this little beauty, but one in the same set. Reckons he stabbed his old PE teacher with it." The detectives took turns to feel its weight and assess its killing capability. Messrs Cudgel and Hammerhead were not noted for their sensitivity and could see a clear opportunity for a bit of sport. Ian Davies was a keen, intelligent police officer, too honest for his own good. He was wasted on the beat and his superiors had him lined up for promotion to sergeant, then DI.

"Why don't you take it on unofficially, Ian? Do a bit of snooping around. It'll all be grist to the mill when it comes to your exam." DI. Cudgel was famous for his generosity in dispensing sage advice to other souls living on the same planet.

*

Paddy was becoming a seasoned train traveller and had gone straight to Mike Scabs on arrival at Swansea station. Mike's smile was wider than a boxful of nine-year old Urdd competitors. Although the cop-shop was within walking distance, Mike told Paddy to get in.

"Police station, Paddy. Turning yourself in, are you?"

"Yeah." Paddy brought Mike up to date with the carnage that had visited his hometown, impatient to flag up his own contribution.

"I've murdered two already, see, Mike."

"Good for you, Paddy."

"And Jeff Bastard's next."

"Jeff Bastard – that's a good name, Paddy."

"Yeah, and he *is* a bastard, Mike. He killed Mr Spring."

"Eddie. He's dead?"

"Yeah, he's dead, Mike." Paddy described the extra bit of carnage. "Once I've topped Bastard, that'll be three. I'll be a serial killer then, see, Mike. No-one can take that away from me."

"Wouldn't mind killing a few people myself, Paddy. Don't think I'd stop at three, though," he laughed. "Well, here we are Paddy, sock it to 'em, boy!"

PC. Ian Davies was called to the front counter by his mate, Janet Mahoney. She found Paddy charming and was sorry to hear

213

about the trouble he'd had with his two teachers. As soon as the door to the interview room closed shut, Paddy hit the straps and PC. Davies was conversant with the 'facts' within five minutes. He excused himself, asked Janet to arrange a cup of tea for the prospective serial killer, then legged it upstairs to apprise DIs Cudgel and Hammerhead of the facts.

Ian Davies returned to the interview suite, aware he could send Paddy Trahern away, write up a short report and file it. Job done. But there was something that intrigued him both about the man and his story. He wouldn't allow the two suited dinosaurs upstairs to push him around, but *would* check the Downhill obituary columns and have a quick chat with Paddy's workmate, Mr Tal Watkins. Perhaps he'd shine some light on the unusual events that had somehow bypassed the civilised world.

53

On the hottest day of the year, PC. Ian Davies sweated his way west towards the alleged scene of three appalling homicides, the vandalised 'Welcome' sign blinding him as he negotiated the U-bend into Downhill. His homework had unearthed three obituaries that correlated with the deaths Mr Trahern had laid out. According to the articles in the Clecs, each one had been attributed to a tragic accident. Edwin Spring was described as 'an eccentric', often to be seen manically pedalling along the country roads, plaguing the traffic and outwitting the local police. Miss April Chatterley, a 'much-loved' physics teacher, had served the pupils of Llan Secondary diligently for over forty years. Mr Griffith Jenkins, a colleague of Miss Chatterley, had been at the heart of the rugby community, playing hooker for Downhill RFC and feared by every team he went up against.

It was Ian's day off and he'd dressed in his civvies, not wishing to draw attention to himself. He needed to break his thirst, but not wanting to bump into Paddy in the Co-op, called into a newsagent's shop, where a thin, bespectacled man was spooning a load of chocolate peanuts into a bottle of mint humbugs.

"Morning," Ian said brightly.

"Probably. Don't stand idly by, girl, the sweets won't mix ourselves. He can have a candle for a shilling. Or a French duck."

"French duck?"

"*Je ne sais quack.*"

"I'll have a bottle of water, please. Warm morning."

"A coke'll do him," insisted Mr Phawsgin, "best shaken if possible."

"No, no, don't shake it up. It's water I want – please." Mr Phawsgin reached into his fridge, took out a can of coke and pulled the ring back hard, laughing at the hissing sound it always made. He took a quick slurp before handing it to a startled Ian Davies, who assumed it was on the house.

"Right as rain. Last can he had, cost us more."

"Oh, could I have a bottle of water as well? I noticed you had a few bottles there, next to the coke."

"All done then, shall he call it a tenner?" Davies hesitated. "Or we can throw in a quarter of chocolate peanuts for another fiver. Thirty-five quid if he's not mistaken. Quite a bargain, *yr hen gont*."

Ian Davies didn't really want to part with the money, but reasoned that getting out of the shop in one piece *was*, indeed, quite a bargain.

The library was the next stop. He'd rung Talfryn Watkins, who referred him to his wife, Mair. She had known Paddy for years and was up to speed with all the gossip. They'd arranged to meet at eleven o'clock and Davies arrived in good time, browsing the crime fiction and sport sections. He was an aphid reader, but couldn't find anything specifically on insects. However, under 'crawlers,' he found Nicholas Witchell's *The Loch Ness Story*, the author's sickly smile adorning the title page, a squished bluebottle making the snivelling sycophant look like a snivelling sycophant with a black patch over his eye. Lucy clocked the handsome newcomer looking at the information board and sidled up smartly, asking if he was interested in any of the night classes on offer. No, he had a meeting with Mrs Watkins. Well, the least she could do was show him to her office and make him a cup of tea. No, she didn't have a bottle of water, but he was welcome to the can of coke she'd brought in.

He found Mair Watkins very personable and intelligent, but understandably wary of being drawn into unsubstantiated tittle-tattle. Three accidental deaths in a small town within such a short space of time was unusual, but her understanding was that the police had investigated thoroughly and were not looking for the 'Downhill Ripper.'

Ian Davies laughed. "So you don't think Paddy Trahern is

capable of murder? I mean, he described to me how he roly-polied into Miss Chatterley's bedroom and unscrewed one of her switches."

"Were Paddy's fingerprints on it?"

"Not according to the report. It seems our physics teacher enjoyed playing with electricity. Little experiments around the house."

"Is that the current theory?" Mair guffawed at her own joke, but Ian Davies's face was deadpan.

"And Paddy says he threw a dart at Jenkins next door."

"Is there such a thing as 'accidental murder,' Sergeant Davies? I know Paddy was angry when Eddie Spring died."

"And he's convinced the scrappy ran his friend off the road."

"But I don't think he'd kill anyone. He sometimes gets over-excited about things, tries his best to help everyone, but there's no side to Paddy."

"Honest, you mean?"

"Totally. He dobs himself in it when he tries to tell a lie."

"That's what worries me, Mrs Watkins. He's now threatening to kill Jeff Bastard."

"Call me 'Mair,' please! Yes, Tal told me."

"But you don't think he'd do it?"

"Not unless he did it accidentally, Sergeant," Mair chuckled.

Ian Davies then broached the subject he'd avoided. "Is Paddy disabled in any way, Mair?"

"I'd say he does have a slight learning disability. I'm not blaming schoolteachers, they haven't got time to spit, but once you're labelled as 'slow', you're left behind. I think he was bullied in school, more confidence is what he needs. He's been helping Tal with the set for our little drama and my husband reckons he can use any tool in the box by now. He just gets on with life, knows everyone in the community. And he's a member of the pub darts team – oh, perhaps I shouldn't have mentioned that!"

"Seems he knows how to hit the bulls-eye," joked Ian.

"Yeah, taken him a while, but when he has his mind set on

217

something… Believe it or not, that young lady out there was assessed as having a low IQ, but when she came to adult lit. classes we found she was slightly dyslexic, that's all."

"Lucy?"

"Yeah. She stuck at it night and day and now she can read and write as well as anyone."

"She's a stonker as we say in Swansea."

"Ha! She's spoken for. As it happens she went out with Paddy for a while, but she and her new boyfriend have got leading parts in the play we're performing. Learnt her lines before anyone else had opened their scripts."

"What play are you doing?" Mair sat back in her chair, clearly relaxed, and gave the earnest policeman a run-down on her 'baby.' She had adapted a play called *A Penny For A Song*, a comedy set in England during the Napoleonic Wars, and there would be a musical number in each of the two scenes. This was for the benefit of their American visitors, who this year were from the Milwaukee area and would be arriving in Britain next week. After fawning over the residents of Buckingham Palace and Windsor Castle, they would savour the delights of Llanelli and district during the second week. The long-established cultural exchange programme would see them being wined and dined at a reception in the town hall, followed by the big performance in Downhill, two days later.

"What date is it?"

"Friday the 13th."

"August? Can I buy a ticket?"

"Really? You can have a complimentary, on me."

"No, no, I'll pay for it. Thinking about it, have you got three? I'd like to bring two of my colleagues."

54

The Rinaldis were amongst the thirty Americans on the bus, mostly hypochondriacs, who had at last landed at the holy site of Downhill. Brenda-lee's fondness for 'drug stores' had taken them off the beaten track and they'd become separated from the others with whom they were supposed to meet for lunch. Having failed to make themselves understood by a group of chavvy youngsters, they decided to find the local police office. Bradley was perceptibly shorter than his wife, though she was the short-sighted one of the two, with thick spectacles and an unfortunate hairstyle, not dissimilar to that of her mother-in-law. Her husband guided her towards the desk, where she stretched her neck like an ugly swan.

"What's he doing, Bradley?"

"Not too sure, Brenda-lee. Don't look too good to me, boy's sweating awful." They were referring to PC. Prys Paddler, who was asleep in his chair.

"God help me! God help me!"

"Is he praying, Bradley?"

"Sure is, Brenda-lee, sure is! Praying in Welsh."

"Could tell he was a good Christian boy 'soon as I set eyes on him. Let's pray with him, Bradley. Boy needs our help."

And so it came to pass that the Rinaldis stood either side of the praying policeman, linking hands in a holy trinity. As one of the pillars of Milwaukee Evangelical Church for the Intolerant, Brenda-lee Rinaldi sure knew how to beseech the Lord.

"You are awesome, God! We ask that you assist this police officer as he fights the evil doers. Do not let Satan rule this city or gloat over the suffering he has caused in our midst...... We forgive all those who have wronged us, except the Muslims.

Oh, Lord, You know that nothing pleases my daughter-in-law,

Martha, the conniving bitch! We entreat You to work in mysterious ways and find Your way to causing her a mishap, something to remind her of the sting of disappointment we felt when she married Bradley Junior.

We ask Your grace and blessing, Lord, in our financial dealings - I think you agreed a ten per cent minimum profit. Oh, yes, and straighten out my varicose veins....... Finally, O God Yahweh, we ask in Jesus' name that You will let this lieutenant direct us toward the bus. We are, Your humble servants, O God. Amen."

Brenda-lee poked her husband in the ribs, a good, forceful jab. "*AMEN*, I said, Bradley!"

"A-men!" repeated the shorter of the two dutifully, as Prys surfaced from his dream. Facing him when he opened his eyes, at a distance of six centimetres, was an enormous locust with a beehive hairdo, which under most circumstances would have made him shit his pants twice. Prys was totally disorientated, and when Bradley and Brenda-lee Rinaldi started to talk, it was like listening to a sauna full of Brummies.

"Our son Bradley Junior's a police officer, just like you, Lieutenant. Works for the MPD." PC. Paddler looked blankly at the towering locust.

"MPD – that's Milwaukee Police Department," explained Mr Rinaldi.

"He's a fine boy. Always thinking 'bout other people. For years he kept on to his father to buy a gun – got to protect yourselves, he told us. We stopped several times at the 'Shoot and Reload' Store in South 43rd Street, but could never make up our minds what to get us. Too much choice, I guess. Then, last Thanksgiving, he brings us a present and he could barely conceal his excitement, could he Bradley?"

"Sure couldn't, Brenda-lee, sure couldn't. Like a worm in a rainstorm!"

"Three boxes he's got us. Three! He rips the paper off the first like he was a three-year-old again. Hands me the prettiest revolver you ever did see. Smith and Wesson, Model 10, 38 caliber, 4-inch barrel!'"

"And he's got me a .357 Magnum, Model 60, five shot, 3-inch barrel, double action!'"

"And in the other box was two sets of cartridges. That's the most loving gift any parent could wish for. We held hands and praised Jesus.'"

"'Course, Bradley Junior uses a Glock 22. Swears by it. It'd sure be great if you could meet him, Lieutenant.'" 'Lieutenant' Paddler was still unsure what was happening and pinched himself to see if it hurt.

"Nobody gets the better of Bradley Junior. Last Christmas Eve some low-life holds up a drug store on North 23rd Street. Asshole's got a short-barrelled shotgun – that's an illegal firearm in the state of Wisconsin.'"

"Bradley Junior's first on the scene. Don't take him long to sum up the situation. Plugs the moron plumb between the eyes.'"

"Straight up Broadway! No-one gets a chance to mess with Bradley Junior a second time. Do you have a gun, Lieutenant? You know what we say back home? A gun's got but two enemies – rust, and them damn interfering politicians!'"

PC. Prys Paddler had been brought up on American cop shows and loved the *Dirty Harry* films. All kids played 'cops and robbers' or 'British and Germans,' and came to accept the world was divided into 'goodies' and 'baddies.' Hadn't he joined the police force because he was a good guy? He'd never been to the States, but on retiring that's the first thing he wanted to do. He'd never really thought about *real* guns, *real* bullets or *real* shootings, just that *good* guns loaded with *good* bullets shot by *good* men, rid the world of *bad* guys. So why was he uneasy when they'd asked him if he had a gun? Guns were good, weren't they? Yes, nothing wrong with guns. It was just that there was something vulgar about these people stood in front of him. He would gladly find their bus for them and with a bit of luck avoid Bradley Junior at the official reception that evening.

*

After an hour in their company, Mair Watkins felt she and Tal had drawn the short straw, though Paddy, on the same table, was enjoying the tales of the Wild West. The meal of mushy peas, fish and chips shut them up for a while as did the short speeches, but once Elwyn Jones started on his accordion, the conversation resumed. Mair glared at her husband every time he went to the bar and became increasingly annoyed that the Rinaldis had no intention of reciprocating. Even Paddy, drinking orange juice, bought a round.

Elwyn took each request in his stride, much to the delight of his American guests, though only those on Mair's table at the front were treated to the extra notes. Paddy noticed first and doubled up, telling Mair to listen carefully. Elwyn Accordion was farting an extra bass line courtesy of the mushy peas and before long the stink had modulated from a minor to a major key. The evening got even better when Paddy took Bradley Junior over to the bar to meet PC. Prys Paddler, giving Mr and Mrs Rinaldi more opportunity to bump their oversized gums.

After returning from the bar for the fourth time, Tal was greeted by a wound-up Bradley Rinaldi, who pulled a cigar box out of his pocket and laid it on the table.

"Look at this, Tal. Brenda-lee gives me a different one each birthday. Personalised Patriot Humidor. Get my full name engraved on the front of the box – Bradley *Littleboy* Rinaldi." The Rinaldis looked at Mr and Mrs Watkins expectantly, in anticipation of the question always asked at this juncture in the endlessly repeated drama, but it never came, taking the wind out of their sails for a moment. Tal knew the significance of the middle name, but was damned if he was going to indulge these asinine dim-wits, who probably assumed he and Mair yearned for the right to bear arms.

"My husband was born on August 6, 1945," said Brenda-lee Rinaldi, by way of explanation. Still no whiff of interest from their hosts. The Bradleys looked at each other. Brenda-lee tried again. "Same day we zapped a hundred thousand Japs. Fried 'em good and proper!"

Mair looked at her husband as if to say, *What the fuck are they on about?* Tal simply delivered the word 'Hiroshima' as softly as he could, but the Rinaldis had picked up on it and proposed a toast to Littleboy. Tal could stomach it no longer and excused himself, making for the door and some fresh air. Mair, none the wiser, half-raised her glass and cursed her husband under her breath.

Over by the bar PC. Prys Paddler was rapidly getting up to speed on the benefits of American society. Bradley Junior had assumed his small-town compatriot was conversant with handguns and blasting projectiles at the shooting range. For his part, Prys enjoyed being the most respected person in town, but was happy enough helping Mrs Zimmer-Jones and her new poodle, Morris, cross the road. He was finding the American cop overbearing and wondered if it was true what he'd heard - that it was easier to get a gun than a doctor in the States. When Bradley Junior went to the restroom, the PC. legged it, much to the surprise of Paddy, who was lapping up the lecture on legalised brutality.

Disappointed with the British policeman's lack of enthusiasm or handguns, Bradley Junior honed in on his new audience, asking Paddy if he owned a firearm.

"No, Bradley Junior, I don't. Wish I did, though."

"Pity, I could give you a few pointers, Paddy. Teach you a solid stance, how to grip the gun, how to aim. Even your breathing is important if you want to plug the felon. I don't understand you English folks. What if someone breaks into your house? Everyone needs a gun."

Bradley Junior had given Paddy an idea. "I could get hold of a gun, Bradley. Air rifle."

"Air rifle? *Gamo*, is it, Paddy?"

"No, 's a air rifle."

"Well, let's have a bit of target shooting tomorrow, shall we? I'll skip the boring old tour."

"What tour's that, Bradley Junior?"

"Some local poet's going to show us the historical sights of your town." Paddy didn't think that would take very long, but fair play to Sid Freeman, he found something 'historical' to add every time the Yanks visited. This year he'd commissioned Sadiq Rhys Huws, owner of the local kiln, to dump a pile of bricks behind the rugby posts at the canal end of the pitch. The residents of Downhill were on pins to see what Sid had up his sleeve.

Paddy and his new mate returned to the table, where the Rinaldis were responding to Tal's toast to the *Hibakusha*, assuming it was a traditional Welsh joke. Their boundless stock of stupidity had taken its toll on Mair. She was glad to see Willy Phawsgin mount the stage and grab hold of the microphone, in an effort to announce the last act of the evening.

"If she could have their attention, please, ladies and gentlemen, while Elsie gets ready. May he introduce to us all, a man taller than Napoleon, his very own magician, Eric Vile." The visitors rose to their feet as one, clapping, whistling and a-whooping it up, a hooley of hollering hillbillies. The locals glanced at their watches. Five minutes went by, ten, fifteen. The Americans gasped when the lights went out and someone shone a powerful torch on to the centre of the stage. Then Mr Phawsgin appeared again, tripping over the top step.

"It's his unfortunate pleasure to proclaim that their local magician, Mr Eric Vile, she 'ave disappeared." Thunderous applause greeted the announcement.

*

Paddy made for the rugby field at eleven o'clock the next day, where he found Bradley Junior and his fellow-countrymen huddled around Sid Freeman. Sid was dressed in his best bedsheets, with a towel around his head, claiming to be the Archdruid, the bricks now a circle of *gorsedd* stones commemorating the first National Eisteddfod of Wales, held at Downhill in 1066. Out came the cameras, more digital bullshit with which to impress their friends.

Earlier that morning Paddy had let himself into the house next door, the keys still illegally in his possession. Mr Jenkins was spending the week with his sister, living it up in her caravan at Trecco Bay. He took a quick glance through the back window and fancied he saw his dart embedded in a tomato plant in the greenhouse, red liquid oozing down the stem.

Paddy enjoyed having a good nose, upstairs and down, and if there'd been any fresh milk in the fridge, would have made himself a mug of chocolate. He eventually found the weapon – he'd been looking for a rifle, not a box – under Mr Jenkins's bed. He was excited to find a scope inside, but where were the bullets? He rifled through the cupboards, fingered any books for metal lumps, then made for the kitchen. Next to the baked beans was a large silver tin which rattled when he shook it. Bingo! There must have been a hundred bullets, all in mint condition. He carefully replaced the lid, then scooped the tins of beans into the solid Co-op bag. They would make good targets and thankfully, were well within their use-by date. Everything was going to plan - Bradley Junior would be pleased with his English scout.

Bradley Junior hurdled into the trailer clutching the aluminium box and Paddy set off for Farmer Cack's barn five miles up the road. The lieutenant was blown away by the quaint old machine and insisted on giving 'high-fives' to lucky front-seat passengers in overtaking cars. Farmer Cack and his girlfriend, Marlene Pig, were hard at it when they arrived, and happy to carry on while the two trespassers set up their target. Paddy went to the far end of the barn, where he found a grumpy-looking mechanical cyclops guarding his corner. He was wary at first, but needn't have worried; the old, grey 1950s Massey Ferguson was glad of a bit of attention after years of neglect, and a broad smile spread across its tin face. Paddy gave the tractor's vertical exhaust a quick tug by way of greeting, then unpacked the beans and carefully checked the use-by date again. They were fine, not obsolete for another eighteen months. Grumpy Ferguson told him the tins would be quite safe on his bonnet.

Paddy made his way back to BJ, who had assessed the rifle and ammunition, and was now mounting the scope. He thought the distance to the targets was about forty feet.

"*Daystate Huntsman Regal*, Paddy. Excellent condition. Where'd you get this beauty?"

"I think it was Electrical's Accepted," Paddy lied. "Best shop in town."

"And the *Diabolo* pellets?" Bradley Junior was impressed that Downhill had its own gun shop. "Right, let's get this show on the road." Ignoring the grunting of the lovers in the hay bales, BJ took aim and plinked each tin in turn. Paddy could only gape in wonder as his American friend spent the next fifteen minutes repeatedly discharging the bullets, forcing the beans into the open with their hands up.

Paddy's first few shots hit the sagging beams of the barn, causing Marlene, riding sow-girl fashion, to lose her rhythm for a moment. Bradley shepherded Paddy to within five yards of the tractor, and once he'd perfected his stance, was rewarded with success. Paddy would have stayed all night, but Bradley was hungry, reminding his friend that tomorrow was the big day. He was looking forward to the musical.

55

Talfryn Watkins loved his wife dearly, and tonight Mair looked ravishing in her sleek, green dress, which matched her sexy copper-coloured hair. She was understandably nervous, but had complete faith in her gorgeous husband and his backstage crew, and the dress rehearsal earlier in the week had gone with a bang. The choir and band were at last working in harmony, though any more than two musical items would have been pushing it.

Tal and Mair were first to arrive at the school, followed closely by Lucy, who was keen to bag her seat in front of the dressing-room mirror. She knew she was pretty, knew how to apply her make-up and would wow the American visitors in her fashionable scarlet gown. Her mother was proud of what she'd achieved since leaving school, where she'd been regarded as lazy, and was grateful that Mair Watkins had taken her under her wing. Tonight, Jack would be sitting next to her in the audience, Steve Charmer kind enough to taxi him back and fore, alleviating the stress somewhat. Since he'd entered the institution at Twpsant, his humour had improved as his hallucinations receded.

Returning from the toilet, Mair was accosted by Charlotte Adams, organiser of the Wauwatosa (Milwaukee) Mob, who assumed Mrs Watkins wanted an alphabetic, if not chronological, account of her life. Tal and Paddy checked the pulley and scaffold, and in the absence of Mrs Watkins, Lucy supervised her fellow-actors, helping to adjust costumes and dab on face-paint. Gwilym James looked stonking in his military uniform.

Getting rid of Charlotte Adams was like trying to remove chewing gum from your trousers. Mair tried to catch Ian Davies's eye as he waved his three tickets at Mrs Probert on the door, but he didn't see her. DIs Cudgel and Hammerhead followed him to

227

the fourth row, where they took their seats beside Jack, Alison and Steve Charmer. The social worker coughed nervously and tried to hide from his interrogators, but his long trendy hair and thick sideburns gave him away. There was only one Steve Charmer and the detectives made a point of enquiring about his health, before chuckling into their sleeves.

The front three rows were taken up by the small-town Americans and important local officials. By this time Downhill's mayor, Reggie Hopkins, had celebrated his ninety-fourth birthday and had come in his pyjamas, ready to go to bed if necessary. Idris Nyfe, mayor of Llan, had always been about forty years younger than Reggie, but was a difficult man to age. Some put him at fifty, others forty-eight. His wife, Betty, estimated his age at forty-nine, though she'd failed all her maths exams at school, barely able to do the 'one-times' table.

Jeff Bastard wasn't into drama, but his curiosity got the better of him; after all, he'd erected the scaffold and given Tal Watkins his expert advice on the pulley system. He was looking forward to seeing the moving parts in action and slipped into the back of the hall to witness the fun. Paddy peeped out from the stage curtains, gratified to spot Mathew Griffiths, for whom he'd bought a ticket. The old school clown would be packing his bags for Oz in a few days and they'd arranged to go for a quick drink after the performance. Paddy relayed the news that the hall was filling up quickly, heightening the nervous tension backstage.

Mair used the mellow, stately sound of the brass instruments to excuse herself from Mrs Adams's grip.

"Better take your seat, Charlotte. Boys and girls of the band are tuning up!" She blew out a huge sigh of relief, then legged it to the dressing room, where everyone was on edge. She noticed one or two of them taking a sly sip of vodka, but no-one appeared drunk, and she slipped out to have a quick word with Tal. He and Paddy were looking relaxed, ready to rock, confident that everything was in order. Over their laughter they heard the clatter of footsteps and Lucy appeared, clearly worried about something.

"Don't shoot the messenger!" she cried.

Mair's heart sank. "What's up, Lucy?"

"Dai Scratch is missing."

"What do you mean?"

"He hasn't turned up." Mair followed Lucy back to the dressing room, where the costume of fencible *Rufus Piggott* hung on its hangar, unclaimed. Nobody had seen Dai, and Mair cursed herself for not paying full attention to her checklist.

"I know!" cried Lucy, "Paddy can play him. He's only got one line."

Lucy had been exaggerating; *Piggott*'s speaking part consisted of the word 'What.' All he'd have to do was march in with Huwcyn and Bob, playing the other two fencibles, *Joseph Brotherhood* and *James Giddy*. A monkey could do it. Lucy dragged Paddy down to the dressing room and helped him into his costume, then handed him a wooden stick.

"What's this for?"

"It's your gun. You're part of the home defence."

"Oh!"

Mair called Huwcyn, Bob and Roger, playing the part of *Selincourt*, commander of the Local Defence Volunteers, over to the corner, and introduced them to the newest member of the cast.

"Dai Scratch isn't here, so Paddy's playing *Piggott*. Paddy, all you've got to do is follow Huwcyn and Bob onto the stage and stand around like an idiot. Wherever they go, you go. Nothing to do in the first scene. In the second, you've only got one word to say and we'll practice that now. Just say 'what'."

"What," said Paddy.

"Sorry, say it as if it's a question."

"What?"

"Good – right, now Roger is going to say his line, the one before you say 'what.' Okay?" Paddy took it in his stride.

"*Piggott!*" shouted Roger.

"*What?*"

"*You will mount guard on some object over there.*"

"When Roger says that, Paddy, move over to the well. You'll be guarding the well." Paddy did as he was told.

"Brilliant! Let's run through it one more time." Once again, Paddy responded instinctively to his Captain Mannering, beginning to feel he'd missed his vocation in life. A relieved Mair went in search of a reassuring *cwtsh* from her husband before the curtain went up. "Sorry we've taken your right-hand man away, Tal. Good old Paddy, you can always rely on him."

Bandmaster Tony Needle thought he'd use Arthur Sullivan as a curtain raiser, something the Yanks would appreciate. One verse of *Onward Christian Soldiers* and repeat the chorus. He wasn't prepared for the fact that they knew every single word, and every time he tried to conclude the piece by slowing the tempo, they enthusiastically belted out the first line of the next verse. There must have been at least six verses and the only way he could get them to stop the resulting 'hallelujahs' was by decking the bespectacled Rinaldi woman in the front row.

There was no way to dampen their enthusiasm, however, the scenery earning a thumping ovation when the curtains opened. Mair was no longer worried about minor mistakes; even if somebody dropped dead on stage they'd think it was part of the plot. Light laughter greeted *Humpage*, the look-out in the tree who keeps falling asleep, turning raucous when he accidentally bumps the brass bell he is holding with his telescope. When *Sir Timothy Bellboys* hit the bell with his pistol, the Rinaldis pointed their fingers and imitated shooting each other, inciting the others to do likewise, their favourite game.

Whether the visitors understood the play was unclear, but they burst into applause as each new character made their entrance and were blown away by Lucy's portrayal of *Dorcas*, as was everyone else. The philosophical debate between radical soldier *Edward Sterne* and conservative sceptic *Hallam Mattews* certainly went over their heads and they cheered *Dorcas* when she rebuked *Edward* on his attitude to patriotism:

230

EDWARD : *Don't stand under a flag, stay far away from anybody in a fine bright uniform, take a look at the sun so that you'll always know which way you're running, if there's a loaf of bread about put it in your pocket, and if there's a hole in the ground sit in it. Ignore all cries for help, stay deaf to all exhortations, and keep your trousers tied tight about your waist. In any difficulty, look stupid, and at the first opportunity go to sleep.*

DORCAS : but *that's the philosophy of a coward!*

MILWAUKEE MOB : (Loud boos, jeering, hollering, cat-calls etc.) *Coward! Son-of-a-bitch! Moron!*

BRENDA-LEE RINALDI : *Motherfucker!*

BRADLEY Sr. : *Asshole!*

BRADLEY Jr. : *Ya' yellow-bellied deadbeat! Git the hell out of here, ya' bum! Ya' lily-livered loser!*

Fair play to Gwilym James, soldier *Edward Sterne*, who kept playing his part with magnificent equipoise, having read a history of the war in Viet-Nam. The band struck up and he and Lucy performed their duet with the choir sweeping in on the chorus. Jack Harries joined in instinctively, and caused the chairs around him to rumble, leading to rumours of another earthquake at Bridgend college.

At the end of the first scene the audience were treated to the sight of a hot-air balloon overhead as *Sir Timothy Bellboys*, off to fight the French single-handedly, descended the well, to the accompaniment of an explosion loud enough to keep the Americans happy.

During the interval Peter 'Turd,' aka *Sir Timothy*, was on pins to grab Tal Watkins's attention, and bolted as fast as his tight *culotte de casimir* would allow, from the bottom of the well underneath the stage up the stairs to the backdrop curtain.

"Mr Watkins, there's something wrong with the rope. I felt a lot of tension as I was going down the well."

"Probably the pulley, Peter. Stay there a minute while I go up and check." In the second scene *Sir Timothy* would appear in the gondola of the balloon, before descending the well involuntarily. When the balloon rises again, the gondola would be empty. The pulley was crucial to the finale of the story. Tal mounted the ladder and asked Paddy, who had been ear-wigging, to operate the winch. Why had the system decided to misbehave tonight? The rope was slipping, not every time, but he couldn't risk it. He slid down the ladder and turned to Paddy and Peter.

"It's slipping, boys. Not every time, but Sod's Law, it'll malfunction second half. We need someone up there to ease the rope over the block."

"I'll do it," cried Paddy.

"No, no, Mrs Watkins is relying on you to play your part."

"I know who can do it – Mr Bastard."

"Lives too far away." The band was still playing *The British Grenadiers* and *Heart Of Oak*, but Downhill folk could only take so much, needing to be tucked up in bed by ten o'clock. Paddy the fencible ran across the hall and returned with Jeff Bastard in tow. Tal explained the problem and though most people would have felt uncomfortable perched precariously over the scaffold, the scrappy took it in his stride.

In the dressing-room, Mair was giving her faithful cast a final pep talk.

"Where's Paddy?" asked Huwcyn.

"Helping Mr Watkins, a minute, he is," said Peter.

"Right, *pob lwc* boys and girls, they're all enjoying it."

At that moment, Paddy was, in fact, hurtling homewards on the trike, unworried by any traffic on either side of the road. He found what he was looking for, flung it into the trailer and pedalled back furiously to complete the last part of the drama. This was the fencibles' chance for fame, on and off stage three times in the second scene. Paddy arrived just in time.

"Where the fuck 'ave you been, Paddy?" asked Huwcyn, graciously, "we're on in a minute, you muppet."

"Be with you now," said Paddy. "Just going to the dressing room to pick up my gun."

"Fuck's sake, hurry up."

The audience continued to lap it up, mesmerised by the shiny fire-engine spouting steam and the quirky cannonballs thundering across the garden. Mair was unaware of any technical problems, but her cool husband had complete faith in the muscle of Jeff Bastard.

Paddy played his part like a pro, remembering his lines and retreating to the well. He looked up at the scaffold to see Mr Bastard peering over the edge, while *Sir Timothy* sat hunched on the flyover, awaiting his big entrance in the gondola. Five minutes later the Local Defence Volunteers, 'a ragged band of scruffy, drunken, ill-disciplined louts' and the sole defence against Napoleon Bonaparte, were on again. Commander *George Selincourt* claimed they had blown the Frenchman from the mouth of the tunnel, causing him to fly over their heads.

Tal Watkins held his breath as Peter descended in the gondola and disappeared down the well. The gondola rose again, this time without its occupant, much to the mirth of Downhill and the USA. Bastard had been up to the job; Tal could relax.

Paddy's final appearance came towards the end of the play, when *Selincourt* realises that *Sir Timothy* is not Bonaparte, even though he is dressed as such, and they find they have a common interest in cricket. On the scaffolding, Jeff Bastard had a bird's eye view of the farce and was becoming more cultured by the minute. No-one seemed to notice that this time, *Rufus Piggott* was carrying a different type of gun.

The curtain call seemed to last forever, followed by the presentation of a bouquet of flowers to Mair Watkins and a flagon of Farmer Cack's cider to the two conductors. Paddy chose a rare moment of silence to do the deed, aiming at the target above him. Crack! Jeff Bastard tumbled from the scaffold down the well and the audience waited for him to reappear. Dr Lake was summoned from his seat in the second row and let carefully down in the gondola. In the hall you could hear a pin drop, which made it very easy to hear a huge fart emanating from Elwyn Jones's hairy arse, much to his wife's amusement. After a couple of minutes, the doctor's voice could be heard clearly as he shouted out from below ground.

"He's as dead as Hitler's dog. Don't think it was a cyanide tablet, though. Looks as if he's broken his neck. Prescription won't help. Now can you get me out of this shit-hole, please? Paddy pushed his way to the front of the stage.

"Now do you believe me?" he entreated his audience.

DI. Hammerhead turned to his colleagues and in a mocking tone, said "Looks like we've got our first handicapped serial killer!" His words were drowned by the howls of delight coming from the visitors, who thought this was the third act of the play. Mair Watkins ushered her cast into the dressing room while Tal closed the curtains. Tony Needle brought band and choir in on 'Downtown' to end a perfect evening.

56

"Lucy, can I have a word with you, please?"

"What now, mam?" It was Friday afternoon and Lucy had finished work for the week, looking forward to dancing the night away with Gwilym down at the club. Why was her mother upstairs, anyway?

Lucy was willing for Alison to run the hoover over her carpet occasionally and dust the furniture, but wasn't aware that her mother regularly sneaked into her bedroom. It was reassuring to find the condoms in the bedside drawer every month; she liked Gwilym, but didn't want any screaming grandchildren just yet. She didn't normally do a full search, but something during the concert had rung an alarming bell. Lucy's performance had left the audience spellbound and while her daughter took everything in her stride, celebrating with the other actors at the reception, Alison and Jack had been surrounded by adoring admirers. Her husband had heard the whisper that Jeff Bastard was dead and the stiff grin on his face seemed to indicate he was not heart-broken by the news. When Steve Charmer told him it was time to return to Twpsant, he skipped his way to the car, laughing like a drain.

"Bastard's dead," he informed each bemused bystander, "can't harm me no more, bastard's dead!" Skip, skip, skip.

Alison was thankful when Mair sat down with her at a table in the corner, well away from the fastest gunslingers in town. She complimented the librarian on the performance, adding that Mair was probably the only person with enough patience to bring such a diverse crew together. Mair laughed, telling Alison how her daughter had bossed everyone around, making sure they learnt their lines and turned up on time.

"There was a time, see, Mair, when Jack and I had given up any

235

hope she'd be able to read. You worked miracles with her."

"Tell you the truth, Alison, once she'd mastered the basics, all I did was find some subjects that interested her. We even read an excerpt or two from *Macbeth*, 'cause she'd done it in school and couldn't make head or tail of it."

"She's always liked drawing. When she was a *twt* she'd spend hours doodling with pencil and paper. That's all she wanted to do."

"Yeah, she enjoys doing posters for us. And once she started reading books, she'd show me and Jan pages of what she'd written. Every day, almost. Her handwriting was beautiful, Alison, and she enjoyed using different coloured pens."

Alison could visualise those notebooks her daughter was so proud of, visualise the bold colours and the crafted letters which gave her that unique style. And then, for some reason, it slapped her in the face. She could see that same script transposed in chalk on the pavement outside the house and in the notes pushed through the letterbox, addressed to Jack. It couldn't be, could it?

Her daughter was still on a high after the concert and her mother was reluctant to challenge her, but on the Friday she pushed open Lucy's bedroom door and made straight for the pine chest. The drawers were stiff and she had to shiggle them back and fore, setting them squealing like little piggies.

It was the neat stack of photocopies at the back of the bottom drawer that aroused her suspicions. Lucy must have copied a whole book, weird drawings of monkeys, one triggering a detonator, the other dressed as Her Majesty, the Queen. It was called *Banging Your Head Against A Brick Wall* and didn't make any sense. Looking at them was like banging your head….. Fumbling beneath them, Alison pulled out a tin of coloured chalks, which put the lid on it.

Lucy climbed the stairs warily, placing her right hand on top of the landing banister rail.

"Where are you, mam?"

"Here."

"What?" Lucy scuttled into her room, where her mother was sitting on the end of the bed, the evidence laid out in culpable order.

"I don't suppose you're this *Chalksy* fellow that goes round town vandalising walls and lamp-posts?"

"Hang on, you've missed something." Lucy rummaged in her knicker drawer and emerged clutching a folder labelled 'Macbeth,' a three-page play written very quickly by William Shakespeare. Lucy showed her mother the phrases she had highlighted in luminous orange. A game of snakes and daggers.

"You know you frightened shit out of your father, don't you?"

Lucy thought about it a minute. "Yeah," she said, at last. Mother and daughter burst into laughter, *cwtshing* one another on the bed.

Paddy was sad to see Mathew go, meeting him for a cuppa before he boarded the 9.15 express to Swansea. The old class clown told Paddy he'd work in Oz for another five years, by which time he'd have accumulated enough to retire.

"You will come and see me, though, when you get back?"

"'Course I will, Paddy, mun, 'course I will. We're mates, aren't we? What are your plans, anyway?" Paddy showed him the leaves he'd torn out of his *Yellow Pages*.

"Got to find a good solicitor, see, Matt."

"Right. The killings?"

"Yeah, the killings."

Despite all his efforts, Paddy was unable to find a law firm that would initiate proceedings against himself. Ian Davies and DIs Hammerhead and Cudgel admitted that four accidental deaths in as many weeks in the same town was irregular, but there was a rational explanation for each one. Mr Trahern was adamant he'd committed murder, but no further investigation was warranted. His talent as a serial killer would go unrecognised. Unless.....

*

Talk about two buses arriving at the same time. Or rather, two of Downhill's literary giants. The following week, Paddy called into the Globe for a pint and noticed Clecs reporter, Clive Lewis, hunched over the bar, studying form. Minutes later the local poet turned up, bought a pint of Cack's, and sat down beside Paddy. A few of the boys gathered round, registering their interest in any witty stories likely to surface when Sid Freeman held court.

"Unusual to see you in here, Sid."

"On the lookout for more stories, I am. Updating Dan the Lanwad's book."

"Read it twice, Sid. I got two copies, see, so I read them both. Now he's gone, you're the only historian we got. Everyone in Downhill's relying on you."

"Time don't stand still, see, Paddy. History's being made as we speak. Got anything for me?"

"Yeah, I'm Downhill's first serial killer." Those within earshot smirked evilly and moved in closer, eager to see where this conversation would lead. Clive Lewis sensed the vibes and moved towards the assembly. Being a tall man, lately measured at six foot five, he commanded a good view of proceedings and refused the seat offered by Wally Spit. Besides, Wally only had one leg.

"These deaths need to be recorded in the town's annals, Paddy, but the police seem to think they were accidental." Some of the regulars laughed knowingly, their eyes mocking the diminutive supermarket worker who could hardly reach the shelves he had to stock, but there were some among the crowd, long in their teeth, who understood that in Downhill not everything was as it seemed, and would await the words of wisdom from their local bard.

"Did for Miss April Chatterley when I was cleaning her windows. Electrocuted the witch! She done an experiment on me, in school."

"Aye, I saw Paddy doing a roly-poly through her window," asserted Edna Prune, who lived opposite the teacher's house in Dust Street.

"Well, that makes sense," said Sid, "What about Griffith

Jenkins?"

"He was shooting the birds. Threw a dart over the wall at him. Got him in the jugular."

"But the police reckon it was a shard of glass from his greenhouse."

"How many of you trust the *moch*?" asked Brian Hook, no relation to Billy Hook, his brother. "Hear of evidence being buried all the time."

"Brian's right," said Benny Hook, related to neither of them, but vice-captain of the darts team. "You only throw two darts these days, Paddy, where's the other one?"

"In Griffith Jenkins's neck!" shouted the people's assembly, realising the significant direction all this was taking them.

"That makes you a double-murderer, Paddy," declared Sid, "and we're all grateful to you, but you need at least three to qualify as a serial killer."

"I know that, Sid, that's why I dispatched Bastard. Bastard ran my good friend Mr Spring off the road."

"But he fell off the scaffolding."

"Yeah, 'cause I shot him with my air-gun."

"I heard the shot," cried Wes Davies, dispelling any further doubt, despite not being a ballistics expert. Sid Freeman asked for a vote and a delighted Paddy was unanimously found to be a serial killer, amongst much vilification of the police for not doing what they were paid to do.

Barely had everyone patted Paddy on the back, than the door of the pub crashed open, and PC. Prys Paddler proceeded to the bar, enquiring of landlord Freddie Sauce if a certain 'Paddy Trahern' had been seen in his pub. Freddie Sauce nodded in the direction of the boys and girls in the corner. The officer pushed his way through the crowd, where he towered above Paddy.

"Am I correct in assuming that I'm speaking to Mr Paddy Trahern?"

"Fuck's sake, cut out the bullshit, Prys. You know who he is, mun."

"Paddy Trahern, I am harresting you on suspicion of killing Miss April Chatterley, Mr Griffith Jenkins and Mr Jeff Bastard of this town, sometime between ...."

"Yes, yes! At last...."

"You do not have to say anything, but it may harm your defence if you do not mention, when questioned, ..." Paddy wasn't listening, and neither were his supporters, who applauded him as he was escorted out of the pub. The night was young, but Freddie Sauce announced a lock-in anyway, in case anyone thought they had to leave.

Down at the police 'office' PC. Prys Paddler offered Paddy a cup of tea and asked him if he'd mind staying overnight. He was released in the morning without interrogation, but formally warned that the spate of killings had to stop. Paddy neither worried about being brought to court or going to prison. In the eyes of his own people he was a recognised serial killer, a fact confirmed by a front-page spread in the Clecs and a chapter in the new edition of the Concise History of Downhill. All courtesy of Mathew Griffiths, who had stuffed the pockets of the local policeman, the local reporter, the local photographer and the local poet.

Over in Twpsant, Jack Harries was making good progress, even enjoying life in the Home For The Ridiculous. With Jeff Bastard extinct, there was no-one who could testify to the sordid little deal that had ignited the paranoia. As summer receded, the leaves of the trees overlooking the old church disappeared, giving Jack Harries a cracking view of the graveyard. He slept well at night, so never saw the ghost of Mr Spring effortlessly pedalling along the country roads. But when the time was right, the night of the Harvest Moon, perhaps, Eddie would tap on the window and wake Jack Harries from his slumber.

And then the fun would start.

Milton Keynes UK
Ingram Content Group UK Ltd.
UKHW020616250124
436675UK00010B/264